# War Bug

# War Bug

*A Novel*

HENRY G. BRINTON

RESOURCE *Publications* · Eugene, Oregon

WAR BUG
A Novel

Wipf & Stock
An Imprint of Wipf and Stock Publishers
199 W. 8th Ave., Suite 3
Eugene, OR 97401

www.wipfandstock.com

PAPERBACK ISBN: 979-8-3852-1016-9
HARDCOVER ISBN: 979-8-3852-1017-6
EBOOK ISBN: 979-8-3852-1018-3

07/29/24

To the Residents of Occoquan, Virginia
Past, Present, and Future

# Contents

# 1

## First Month 1862

HEAVY SNOW WAS FALLING as the sun rose on First Day, the fifth day of First Month, 1862. Powder swirled through the air and stuck to the branches of the trees across the Occoquan River, making the wooded hillside look like it was covered by an enormous lace tablecloth. The small timber house was dark and freezing until Ann Bagley added wood to the embers in the fireplace, causing the logs to ignite and begin to radiate heat throughout the main room. In the light of the dancing flames, Ann entered the kitchen and used a dish towel to wipe condensation off the window and peer into the early morning light. A foot of fresh powder was on the ground, and a glowing white blanket stretched across the frozen Occoquan River. "Come see," she called to her sons. "The world has changed."

Samuel, the eldest at twenty-two, was the first to emerge from the small bedroom he shared with his brother. Wrapped in a wool blanket, with only his face and thick brown hair showing, he walked to the window, put his arm around his mother, and asked, "How?"

"Look at the river. Gone. It is now a white valley."

"So flat," said Samuel. "Like a sheet."

"A shroud," said William, who had crept up behind them. "A pall. A burial cloth."

"Thou art morbid," said Ann, who turned and tousled her twenty-year-old's blond hair. "*Death is but crossing the world.*"

"What?" said William.

"*Death is but crossing the world, as friends do the seas; they live in one another still.*"

"Didst thou just invent that, Mother?" asked Samuel.

"Not at all," said Ann. "Wise words from a Friend, William Penn."

"Thou speakest of him as if he were still alive," said William.

"He is," said Ann. "*Death cannot kill what never dies.*"

"More Penn?" asked Samuel.

"Indeed."

William turned toward the fireplace, warmed his hands, and said, "That is a bit too much of the spirit before breakfast."

"I agree," said his mother, pulling an iron pot off a shelf. "I will make porridge. Samuel, cut some bread and slice some cheese. William, set the table."

Samuel glanced out the window again and realized that William was right: The river was a shroud. It reminded him of the white burial cloth that was put over his father's wooden casket before he was laid to rest in the Quaker burial ground up the hill. That particular pall was community property, and it was used frequently to cover the caskets of the deceased before they were put in the ground. Whether the person was buried in a simple pine box or in an ornate oak casket, they were equal in the eyes of God. Every coffin looked the same, as long as it was under the white pall.

"There is no dark night in her soul, is there?" whispered William to his older brother.

"Never has been," said Samuel, glancing at their mother. He loved that about her. He had been only fifteen when his father died, so neither he nor William were old enough to work. But his mother never gave any hint of despair. She made clothes for her ever-growing boys, grew vegetables in the garden, did laundry for other families, and even joined the men of the community on deer hunts. The family was never without food or shelter or clothing, since Ann never gave up. This impressed Samuel deeply, so when he turned eighteen, he went to work in the gristmill. And then, two years later, William followed him. Any financial difficulties that followed their father's death were now a thing of the past.

"Table is set," said William to his mother. Then, looking toward the fireplace, he noticed that there was only one log remaining in the firewood rack. He knew that the temperature in the room would drop quickly once the fire burned down, so he said to the other two, "I will dress and get some more firewood." William considered himself to be the practical one, as his father had been. His mother and brother were hard workers, he knew, but they were easily distracted. Put a book in their hands, and they would sit in a house with a dying fire until there was frost on the inside of the windows.

"I can help," said Samuel, delivering the sliced bread and cheese to his mother.

"Farewell," said Ann. "But come back soon." As a member of the Society of Friends, Ann would never say "Good-bye." That was an expression that non-Quakers used, meaning "God be with you." Since Ann believed that God *was always* with you, it was unfaithful to express a wish that God *would be* with you.

Friends believed in plainness of speech. They spoke truth, not wishes.

"Where is the split wood?" asked William, trudging through the snow to the backyard. The wind was pushing the snow into large drifts against the side of the house.

"I did not do it," said Samuel.

"What?" said William, frustrated. "That was thy chore for yesterday."

"I know," Samuel admitted, his cheeks beginning to flush. "Let us do it now."

"Will not be easy in this snow."

"I will get the axe," said the older brother.

William used a gloved hand to brush the snow off the logs piled near the house. They had been sawed in two-foot lengths and left to cure, but they still needed to be split for the fireplace. He felt a rising anger toward his brother, who should have split enough wood yesterday to get them through several days. With heavy snow falling, it would be difficult to swing the axe accurately. Dangerous as well.

He put a log on the stump they used for splitting just as Samuel came back with the axe. "Careful," said William. "Thou wilt have a difficult time finding thy mark with all of this snow."

William stepped back and Samuel put the blade at the center of the log. The eldest son was tall and wiry, while the younger was short and compact, with well-developed shoulders and arms. Samuel reared back and swung the axe in a long arc, splitting the log down the middle. But as the axe head cleaved the log, he lost his footing and came close to falling.

"Spread thy feet," said William. Then he picked up half the log and placed it on the stump. Samuel widened his stance, swung the axe again, and split the log into quarters.

3

"I should have done this yesterday," Samuel admitted, wiping snow off the axe handle.

"Verily," said the younger brother, placing the other half of the log on the chopping block.

"I had a dream last night," Samuel said, after swinging the axe again. This time he missed his mark to the left, splitting the log into two unequal pieces. "I was a delegate to the Virginia Convention."

"Thou thinkest highly of thyself!"

"It was a dream. A fantasy."

"Which convention?" asked William, moving pieces of wood around. "The one last February? Down in Richmond?"

"I suppose," said Samuel, lining up his axe to split another log. "I was there to argue for the Union, to speak against secession."

"I should hope so," said the younger brother, setting up one of the halves.

"I was in a large room, packed with men. Angry words were spoken." Samuel swung the axe hard and the quarter pieces flew left and right into the snow. "One man shouted 'Secede!' and many others cried out, 'No!' Other voices called for secession, but then others cried out 'Union!'"

"Who was winning?" asked William, picking up the pieces.

"I was heartened," said Samuel, "because the Unionist voices seemed to be drowning out the secessionist voices. I even saw Jubal Early across the room, smiling under his big beard."

"The 'Terrapin from Franklin,'" William said. "He moved slowly, not wanting to secede."

"His people were making money," said Samuel.

"Selling tobacco to the North."

"Very profitable," said Samuel, wiping the snow off his face and preparing to swing again. "In my dream, I thought we were winning. 'Secession is short-sighted,' thundered Early, 'and likely to lead to war!'"

"Strange words for a military man."

"Indeed," said Samuel, splitting another log. "I wanted to speak about us, Southerners who do *not* own slaves. Secessionists speak about *their* rights, but how about *our* rights?"

"This damned collision of arms," said William, "all for the benefit of slave-owners."

"I tried to speak, but I could say nothing. I was mute, and my frustration was rising; I knew that my argument would carry the day. But then the secessionist delegates grew louder and louder, cursing Lincoln. They said that he would force Southern states back into the Union, using the military. The tide began to turn, and with horror I saw that Virginia was going to secede."

"And that is what happened," said William. "Thy dream was hardly prophetic."

"But why was I there?" Samuel asked. "Why was I in a room with Early and all of those delegates?"

William shrugged his shoulders, and put another log on the stump. "I think this log will be the last."

"Could I have prevented the division?" asked Samuel, swinging the axe again.

"Not likely," said his brother. "Lincoln himself tried to prevent division by allowing slavery to continue."

"Truly?"

"Indeed. He supported an amendment, one that would have preserved slavery. Majorities in both the House and Senate favored it."

Samuel wondered how he missed this news. "So, Lincoln would have tolerated slavery?"

"Yes, in states like ours," said William, "but he would not have allowed it to spread."

"I have heard that many Northerners want mainly to preserve the Union. They care little about slavery."

"That is true," said William. "And here in the South, there are many who want only to fight the tyranny of the North. They have little concern for the tyranny of slave-masters."

Samuel pondered his brother's words, sensing that secession was more complicated than he had realized. Then, returning to Lincoln's politics, he asked, "What happened to the amendment?"

"Southern states would not support it. They could not trust Lincoln or Congress. They did not believe that the North would abide by it."

"Should they have done so?"

"We will never know," said William. "Once Confederates fired on Fort Sumter, the amendment was moot."

"The rebellion had begun," said Samuel, picking up the axe again. He wanted to split at least one more log.

"Less than a week later, our convention voted to secede."

"In my dream, the vote was close," said Samuel. "What was it, really? Eighty-eight to fifty-five?"

"That sounds right," agreed William, brushing snow from his face. "I do not recall the exact numbers. But it was sufficient."

"By May, we were in the Confederacy."

"There was no changing course," said William.

"Damn those secessionists," said Samuel, swinging the axe wildly and just nicking the edge of the log, sending it tumbling into the snow.

"Splitting is ugly work," said William.

"Indeed."

"I think we have enough," William said. "Thy frustration is putting us both in danger."

A voice from the house came through the snow, "Boys, porridge is ready."

"Let us just gather the wood we have," William said.

The fire had died down while the boys were splitting logs, but it came roaring back once they added several pieces of wood. In moments, the room was so warm that they stripped down to one layer of clothing. They were dripping wet, both from their perspiration and from the snow that had fallen on their heads.

"I saw Abigail Washington yesterday," said William as he spooned porridge into his mouth. "She said good morrow."

"Thou knowest we do not say 'good morrow,'" said Ann, always the teacher. She was small in stature and physically strong, much like her younger son, while the height of her late husband was reflected in her eldest son. She was also a bit contrary, as William often was. The physical trait she shared with Samuel was her dark brown hair, while her husband's blond hair had been passed on to William.

"She's not a Friend," William said, "so she can say anything she desires."

"True," admitted his mother, "but she should know better. All days are equally good, so there is no reason to say 'good morrow.'"

"She was trying to be polite," interjected Samuel, the peacemaker.

"Yes, I know," said Ann. "What didst thou say to her, William?"

"I said, 'How art thou?'"

"That is a good one," Ann said, nodding. "Or, 'How dost thou do?' We have a number of polite greetings among Friends."

"Yes, we do," said Samuel, "as thou hast taught us."

"I am a mother, always," Ann said, picking up pieces of bread and cheese. "But be careful when talking with any of the Washingtons."

"Why?" asked William.

"Their family owns slaves."

"But not here in Occoquan," noted Samuel.

"No," said Ann. "But Abigail's uncle has many in the southern part of the county."

"No matter," said William. "I do not believe in slaves."

"Believe in slaves?" asked Samuel, putting bread in his mouth. "What dost thou mean by that?"

"If a slave hunter asked me if I were hiding an escaped slave, I would say no," explained William. "In my mind, there is no such thing as a slave. Only a free man."

"That may be true," said Samuel. "But as Friends we should not break the law or disrupt the peace."

William nodded, ate a chunk of cheese, and then asked, "But what if the law does not support the peace?"

"Then we break the law," said Ann.

Both boys stopped eating and looked at her.

"Yes, that is right," said Ann. "When a human law defies God's truth, we must break the human law."

Samuel was surprised. He had never seen his mother do anything to disturb the peace of Occoquan. She valued the serenity of their town, especially since they were in a religious minority and could easily be demonized. He asked, "What dost thou mean by that?"

"Read thy Bible," said Ann. "God delivered the Israelites from slavery in Egypt. God told Moses to go in unto Pharaoh and say, 'Let my people go, that they may serve me.'"

"Moses cared not about Egyptian law," added William.

"No, he did not," said Ann. "Nor do we. My cousin Thomas Garrett had an Underground Railroad stop at his house in Delaware. He was put on trial and found guilty of helping a family of seven to escape."

"What happened to him?" asked William.

"He received a fine. One thousand, five hundred dollars," said Ann. "The penalty left him ruined, financially. But he stood up in court and made a statement."

"Really?" said Samuel. He had never heard this story.

"Yes," said Ann. "His statement impressed me. It was published widely in the newspapers, so I cut it out and saved it. Dost thou want to hear it?"

"Of course," said William. Ann got up from the table, walked to a bookshelf, took down the family Bible, and removed a folded piece of newsprint.

Returning to her seat, she unfolded the paper and read aloud, "*Judge, thou hast left me not a dollar, but I wish to say to thee and to all in this courtroom that if anyone knows a fugitive who wants a shelter and a friend, send him to Thomas Garrett and he will befriend him.*"

"Our relative?" asked William, clearly impressed.

"Yes, my cousin," said Ann, folding the paper and tucking it back in the Bible. "People say that he has helped more than two thousand slaves escape."

"Why did we not know this?" asked Samuel.

"We try not to be proud," said Ann.

"But we *should* be proud," said William. "Thomas has done God's work."

Ann nodded, and then said, "He has broken the peace, but for a godly cause."

William said, "Thou knowest the words of Jesus: 'Think not that I am come to send peace on earth: I came not to send peace, but a sword.'"

Ann drew back, startled and concerned. Samuel tried to ease the tension by saying, "Not a literal sword. Jesus had no use for weapons."

William sat back in his chair, unwilling to offer a response. He looked out the window for a moment, and then got up and put on his coat, his hat, and his gloves. He told his brother and mother that he would be going for a walk.

He did not return.

# 2

## New Year's Day 2022

A STEADY RAIN FELL through the morning on the first day of 2022, soaking the streets of the Town of Occoquan and filling the drainage ditches along the sides of the roads. A heavy mist blanketed the river, making the trees on the opposite bank look like hovering ghosts. It was a Saturday, and most residents of the little town were moving slowly as they nursed hangovers from New Year's Eve celebrations or began the melancholy process of taking down holiday decorations.

Pastor Harley Camden spent the morning working at his desk, listening to the water rattle through the downspouts. He sat in the turret of his Victorian townhouse and tapped on his notebook computer, composing a sermon for the first Sunday of the new year at Riverside Methodist Church, sipping coffee and periodically looking out the window at the river to the north. Occasionally, he would run a hand through his thinning grey hair or stroke his goatee. The rain was heavy at times, but nowhere near the downpour that had flooded the town in 2018, causing extensive damage to businesses and homes.

*"Worst I've seen since seventy-two."* Harley remembered the words of Tim Underwood, the town maintenance man, on the morning after the deluge. *"Hurricane Agnes. A steel bridge was swept away and downtown Occoquan was completely flooded. People saw empty caskets flowing down the street."*

The precipitation was a gentler rain on that New Year's Day, and Harley hoped for a break in the showers so that he could get out and go for a run.

*Tap. Tap. Tap.* Fingers on the keyboard, echoing the rain on the windows. The house was as quiet as an ancient catacomb, as it had been through much of the pandemic. *Tap. Tap. Tap.* Then silence, as he pondered his next line.

Harley leaned back and ran a hand across his growing belly. While he could not do much about his thinning hair or his failing eyesight, he had discovered in his sixties that running was the key to weight control and physical health. *Mental health as well.* The pandemic was killing his congregation, and making him feel like a failure. If he did not get out for a run, he knew that the rainy day would drag him even farther down.

*Tap. Tap. Tap. Tap.* The Occoquan flood of 2018 had knocked the cross off his steeple and filled the church basement with water, but it had not damaged the spirit of his congregation. If anything, it inspired the members to get off their couches and come together to restore their church building. But the pandemic? The lockdown had prevented them from gathering for an entire year, and then their return to gathered worship had been painfully slow. Harley feared that some members would never return, and he had no idea of how to inspire them.

*I know I'm failing. The church is going to die, and the blame will be put on me.*

Then his cell phone buzzed. The Caller ID flashed "Leah Silverman" and he pressed the answer button. "Harley," she said. "How are those shoes?" A pair of running shoes had been her Christmas present to him.

"Great," he said, "hope to go out for a run." All of a sudden, he sensed that the room was filling with sunlight, but maybe he was imagining it.

"Not exactly a Sepphoris day," she said.

"Right about that," said Harley. *Brilliant sunshine, day after day. So bright. So beautiful.* In 1985, he had been a Duke Divinity School student and she an undergraduate religion major. He developed a crush on her when they worked side by side at an archaeological site in Sepphoris, a city in Israel not far from the hometown of Jesus. Although her hair had turned from brown to silver, she still had bright eyes and a radiant smile.

"You were so skinny that summer," she teased him. "You didn't need to run."

"Of course not," he said, smiling for the first time that day. "You made me do all the hard work." For weeks, they had dug together, flirting and trying to figure out who they were as they moved into adulthood.

"You were trying to impress me," she said. She had loved his kindness and sense of humor, and he had been attracted to her intelligence and playfulness.

"Yes, indeed," said Harley, nodding. After that summer, they had drifted apart. It was not until decades later, when Harley's bishop moved him to Riverside Methodist Church in Occoquan, that he discovered that Leah was working as the CEO of a community health clinic in nearby Woodbridge.

"Anyway, just calling to check in about dinner tonight." Since their reunion, they had met for a meal or a drink almost every week, and their meet-ups had been an antidote to his loneliness, especially during the lockdown. "You're coming, aren't you?"

"If I finish my sermon," he said.

"Finished or not, we're getting together. Don't let me down."

"I won't," said Harley, knowing he had no choice. "Thanks for calling." After hanging up, his mind went back to the fall of 2018, a time when he had been struggling after the flood. Leah had taken him into her home and cared for him. Feeling the warmth of her hands around his, he realized that he had not been touched so tenderly by a woman since his wife died. *I was beginning to see that Leah loved me. Not an erotic love, nor even a sisterly love, but a love that puts the other first.*

He needed her love, now more than ever.

A few minutes after noon, the sun poked through the clouds and Harley saw his opportunity. He flipped down the cover of his computer, got up from his desk, and walked toward the coat closet by his front door. There, he grabbed a couple of items that formed a timeline of the marathons he had run in his forties: A mesh cap that said "NYC 26.2" and a warmup jacket with the logo "Boston 2006." Climbing the stairs, he went to the dresser in his bedroom, where he pulled out socks from the Berlin Marathon in 2009, a long-sleeve running shirt from Tucson 2005, and pair of sweatpants that bore the Marine Corps logo from his first marathon in the year 2000. After putting on his running clothes, he caught sight of himself in a full-length mirror. *Who is that old man, and who is he trying to impress?*

His wife Karen and daughter Jessica had always cheered him on. Yes, they were in the shadow of the Washington Monument for his first Marine Corps Marathon, and next to Berlin's Brandenburg Gate for his final long race. *That had been a confusing one—kilometers instead of miles, and almost everyone cheering in German.* That had been their last trip to Europe before Karen and Jessica were killed in Brussels.

*Terrorist attack. Nail bombs in the airport.*

*Still hard to believe.*

Shaking off the memory, Harley headed for the door. The warmth of the day surprised him as he stepped on to the porch and descended a flight of wrought-iron stairs on the side of his townhouse. *January snow and ice—no way today.* Turning left, he began to run east along Mill Street, which quickly turned from a business street into a residential road. His route ran parallel to the southern shore of the Occoquan River, with the river to the left and a hillside to the right, and Harley did his best to avoid stepping in the deepest of the puddles along the way. Although the showers had slowed to a drizzle, rainwater continued to rush downhill through the snaking ditches that were cut into the hillside, and the stream made the sound of a waterfall as it poured over large round stones and then disappeared into a storm drain under the road. By the time he reached the sprawling Lake Ridge Marina, he was so warm that he slowed to a walk, peeled off his Boston Marathon jacket, and tied it around his waist.

*How can this be January?* he wondered as he began to run again. A large v-formation of honking geese crossed the grey sky heading east, probably confused about where to fly in the unseasonably warm weather. He thought of his occasional running partner Jim Black, the pastor of Sacred Heart Catholic Church in nearby Woodbridge, who had been an atmospheric researcher before entering seminary. When Occoquan flooded in 2018, Black told him that rising global temperatures were leading to heavier rainfall. "The warmer the air is," the priest said, "the more water it can hold." *The result: Downpours and destruction.*

Harley ran along the marina sidewalk next to sleek million-dollar yachts that never seemed to leave their slips. Looking across the river, he saw the enormous grassy mound that covered acres of land in southern Fairfax County, a sleeping giant of a landfill that had swallowed decades of garbage from hundreds of thousands of businesses and homes across the region. *What secrets did it contain,* wondered Harley, *what evidence was hidden forever under the lifeless winter grass? Weapons? Skeletons? Toxins?* The mound loomed over the river and dominated the northern horizon, an unbroken expanse of grassy earth except for the incinerator tower that jutted into the air and belched white smoke. *Will my church end up in such a place? When the doors finally close, will its pieces be carted off and burned or buried?*

*Dark thoughts.*

At that moment, Harley's toe caught a joint in the pavement and he flailed wildly in an attempt to stay on his feet. Stumbling forward, he made two awkward strides and managed to get upright before hitting the ground. *Focus forward,* he thought, *eyes on the path.* Regaining his balance, he passed through a gate and jogged into Halliburton's Marina, a small mom-and-pop operation that stored his twenty-three-foot powerboat through the winter months. *Nothing dark about this place.* Slowing down for a break, he walked into the storage yard where several dozen boats were sitting on their trailers, winterized and covered. Harley spotted his boat, a 2003 Chaparral that he had bought when he moved to Occoquan in 2017.

*Five years? Seems like yesterday.* Harley remembered attending a mandatory Coast Guard course, being taught to tie knots, learning about the law of the sea, and taking a test. He had scored a ninety-eight, missing only one question about the importance of running a blower to clear gas fumes before starting a powerboat. Harley had felt so proud when they issued him his captain's license, and he never forgot to run his blower.

*Also . . . an eternity.* Harley's church had begun to grow in his first couple of years, but then the pandemic hit and quickly reversed any gains. At least he had his boat. She had been his vessel for countless trips up and down the river, and her deck was a safe place to gather with church members, with the wind on the water providing protection from the coronavirus. He loved the boat—a bowrider with seating in the front and back, and a powerful inboard-outboard engine—and he could not wait to get her back into the water. *My happy place,* he thought, a floating sanctuary during a stressful and unhappy time.

Reaching the sidewalk that bordered Route 123, Harley started back toward the Town of Occoquan. Rain from the trees dripped on his head, and he was glad that the bill of his New York City Marathon cap was keeping the water off his glasses. His run was beginning to lift his spirits, and Harley remembered how much he had enjoyed that particular marathon. It had begun with a worship service under a huge tent in an old military installation on Staten Island, including Communion for all the runners who wanted it. The marathon also had the longest outdoor urinal that he had ever seen, one that hundreds of men could use simultaneously. *Truly disgusting,* he thought, *and oddly awe-inspiring.*

After eating, hydrating, stretching, and relieving themselves, the runners crossed the Verrazzano-Narrows Bridge into Brooklyn, and then progressed through the remaining boroughs until they reached the finish line in Central Park. Harley had started the event behind tens of thousands of others, since his goal of running a four-hour marathon put him far behind the elites and the celebrities who hugged the starting line. One of the big names that day was the rapper P Diddy, who was running the marathon to raise money for the New York City Public Schools. As Harley trudged along, he saw signs along the route saying "Diddy Runs the City," and he sensed real excitement for this New-York-born celebrity running his home-town race.

"Harley, that you?" said a man, interrupting his New York remem-brances. Turning, Harley saw Father Jim Black, gaining on him. Black had salt-and-pepper hair, a beak-like face, and long legs.

"Hey, Jim," he said, as the priest came alongside him. "Looks like you're running strong."

"Looking good yourself. I like your hat: NYC 26.2."

"Yeah, ran it back in '03."

"That must have been great," said the priest, keeping pace with him along Route 123.

"Ran it with P Diddy."

"Who?"

"The rapper," said Harley. "Diddy. Caught up with him at Mile Sixteen."

"Way to go!" said the priest, giving him a punch on the shoulder.

"Was on a lonely stretch of bridge between Queens and Manhattan," said Harley, panting as he matched Black's strides. "There were no fans on the bridge, so I had no warning that he was there. I just looked left and saw him. He was breathing hard, feeling the miles, digging deep."

"Did you speak to him?" asked Black.

"No, wanted to give the man his privacy."

"Good thought," said priest. "A marathon is personal. Got to face it alone."

"He was hurting," said Harley. "His celebrity didn't help him. Neither did his money or musical talent. But he was finding a way to put one foot in front of another."

"I respect that," said the priest.

"Indeed," said Harley. "But I passed him!"

"Just like I'm going to pass you," said the priest, pulling ahead. "Have a good one, brother!"

Harley was jogging a figure-eight that day, and after completing the eastern loop he crossed the large concrete bridge that spanned the river from Prince William County into Fairfax County. This six-lane bridge with a wide pedestrian walkway was the very center of his two-and-one-half mile run, and it offered panoramic views of the Occoquan River to the east and the west, along with the chance to catch an occasional glimpse of a bald eagle in the trees by the shore. Glancing downward to his left, he took a long look at *el Castillo*, a whimsical home that had been built out of large grey stones in order to look like a medieval castle.

His pace was slowing as the bridge sloped upward into Fairfax County, and he was working hard on the incline. He dropped down to a walk and took a minute to gaze down at the empty house beneath the bridge. The structure had turrets in all four corners and a series of arrow slits in the walls, purely decorative. Its large wooden front door had forged iron hardware, and seemed to be strong enough to repel an attack. The second floor of the house was smaller than the first and set back from the stone walls, giving the impression that the upper level was rising like a castle tower out of the first floor. This sturdy structure sat at the end of a curving driveway that snaked downhill from the road that ran along the north side of the river, and the only deviation from the medieval motif was a series of large plate-glass windows that faced the river.

Harley remembered the thoughts that had gone through his mind when he first saw the house. *Who had lived there, and where did they go? Was it built by a couple, scrimping and saving to put a down payment on their dream house? Did they make love in that house, conceive a child, scream at each other, drink themselves to sleep? Why the castle motif—was that the husband's choice, or the wife's?* He had entered the home just once, to take a look around with the caretaker of the empty house. They had descended into its dark basement, one that was carved out of solid rock long before the construction of *el Castillo*.

"*It was the cellar of the ferryman's house, back in the 1700s.*" Jefferson Jones, an African American businessman who had owned the home as part of his real estate empire, had told Harley the story of the house. "*There was no bridge over the river in those days, so a ferry had to take people across. The ferryman lived in a house on that site, and his basement was used as a prison during the Revolutionary War. Terrible things happened in that basement.*"

Jefferson was a brilliant, shrewd, and intimidating man who knew a tremendous amount about Occoquan and its people. He had grown up in the town and spent his entire life as a member of Emanuel Baptist Church, the congregation that had built the structure that now housed Harley's church. Emanuel had been founded by a formerly enslaved man named Bailey in the late 1800s, and for generations African-American members had found strength in that church. In particular, they were inspired by the Jesus portrayed in the window behind the pulpit. He was a black Jesus, ahead of his time, installed in an era in which most stained-glass figures were as white as Scandinavians.

*Black Jesus*: The image was a perfect fit for twenty-first-century Occoquan, a dark-skinned savior who was eternally calming the waves of a stormy Sea of Galilee. Jesus watched over a community that was growing more racially and culturally diverse every day, a town that was filled with people from around the world but was being pulled apart by political polarization and community fragmentation. Harley loved to be able to look up at the black Jesus on Sunday mornings, as he gathered his people for worship in the days following the one-two punch of a flood and a pandemic. *Calm the storm, Lord Jesus. Give me your peace.*

Jefferson was now gone, and Harley missed him. Yes, he had been intimidated by the businessman at first, not knowing what to think of his rat-like face and his reputation for ruthlessness. But over time, Jefferson showed his heart through several acts of compassion and generosity, and Harley had come to admire him deeply. As he began to run again, he remembered when Jefferson's daughter Tawnya had called him with the news on a Sunday morning.

"*He died in his sleep*," *Tawnya had said, her voice cracking.* "*At least I told him I loved him.*"

Harley wished he had been able to say his good-bye as well. The last few years were feeling like an endless litany of losses.

Now, Jefferson's business was being run by his protégé Abdul Ali, an African American convert to Islam whom Jefferson had mentored when the younger man was in prison. *Haven't seen him in a while; wonder what the big man is up to.* Harley turned to the left at the top of the bridge, feeling relieved that the western loop of his run was now almost over. He jogged downhill along the road that ran along the northern bank of the river, and as he did so he looked down on the river that was running muddy, as brown as sewage, flowing slowly toward the east. Then he glanced to his right at the enormous rocks that had towered over the river for three hundred million years, as tall and strong as Easter Island heads. The rocks made him think of Abdul's massive arms and powerful legs, kept in peak condition by his obsessive weight-lifting and running. Harley reached the bottom of the hill moving as fast as he had all day, and as he took a sharp left on to the pedestrian bridge that crossed back into the Town of Occoquan, he almost crashed into him.

*Speak of the devil.*

Abdul Ali.

# 3

## January 1862

TALK IN MERCHANTS' MILL was all about the young white men of Virginia who were rushing to join the Confederate Army. By the sixth day of January 1862, Occoquan had lost several dozen men to the war effort, which took a toll on a town of one thousand.

"Emory and Henry College is almost empty," said Bushrod Washington, the brother of Abigail. Bushrod had bright red hair and a scar on his cheek from a childhood accident, and he was known to be a gadfly. Standing as tall as Samuel, the two made an effective team as they carried bags of grain from carts into the gristmill. There, the kernels of wheat would be ground into flour and returned to the carts. Most of the year, the grain would arrive by barges on the river, but in the winter months transport was limited to horse-drawn carts. Once, Samuel had seen grain carried across the frozen river in a sleigh, but such deliveries were unusual.

"Where are they going?" asked Samuel, after they poured the seeds into a hopper, which channeled grain to the mill.

"Some have gone to Richmond," said Bushrod, "to join the Richmond Howitzers. They will be part of the Army of Northern Virginia." Bushrod gave a nod to Josiah Farlow, the miller, who used his massive arms and shoulders to turn a wheel which activated a turbine under the mill. Power from the river spun the turbine, which then turned one of the two huge circular stones which ground the kernels into flour.

The Howitzer name sounded familiar to Samuel, so he asked, "They were involved in the trial of an abolitionist, were they not? John Brown?"

"That is right," said Bushrod. "Formed to provide security during Brown's trial and execution. The first captain was a grandson of Thomas Jefferson."

"Deep Virginia roots."

"Indeed," said Bushrod. "Almost as deep as Uncle George's." Bushrod was not a direct descendent of the first president, but he was proud to be part of the family.

Josiah carefully monitored the gap between the stones and the speed of the top stone's rotation, in order to make sure that the grain was being ground correctly. Merchants' Mill was the first automated gristmill in the region, developed by a Quaker named Nathaniel Ellicott, and it did a booming business, both in peacetime and in war. Josiah did not insert himself into the conversation of the young men, but glanced at Samuel when John Brown was mentioned. Josiah was a Quaker and an abolitionist, and Samuel guessed that he was sympathetic to Brown and to his raid on the Federal Arsenal at Harper's Ferry. Yes, Brown had acted violently, which Quakers abhorred, but he was attempting to free the slaves.

"Robert E. Lee had something to do with Brown, did he not?" asked Samuel, as he and Bushrod walked outside to get another bag of grain. The dry air was terribly cold, but they were so warm from their exertion that they did not need coats.

"Yes," said Bushrod. "He led the Marines who put down the raid."

"And now he is advising President Davis," said Samuel. He found it difficult to say the words "President Davis," since he and his family still supported Abraham Lincoln. But he lived in Occoquan, so people like him and Josiah Farlow had to be very quiet about their politics. Like it or not, Jefferson Davis was their president.

"Lee is a great man," said Bushrod. "Top graduate of West Point. Hero of the Mexican-American War. We are lucky to have him."

"He wanted our country to remain intact," Samuel said, taking a dig at Bushrod. "Thou knowest that."

"No matter," said his coworker, grabbing one end of a bag of grain. "He chose Virginia."

"Yes, he did," said Samuel, lifting the other end. He knew that family roots went deep in the state. Lee's father, "Light-Horse Harry" Lee, had owned the Occoquan Mill before the Ellicotts, and George Washington had been interested in using the Ellicotts' automated design in his own mill.

Choosing Virginia was a natural choice for many, even when it led to the division of the country.

"So, where is your brother?" asked Bushrod as they carried another heavy bag into the mill. "Off to join the Botetourt Artillery?"

"I doubt it," said Samuel. The Botetourt Artillery had been formed a few months earlier, out of a Virginia infantry regiment, after many of the men fought in the Battle of First Manassas, not far from Occoquan. Samuel knew that Bushrod was mocking him with his mention of the artillery, because service in the artillery was considered to be less demanding than service in the infantry. "No," he said, "William is not very good with a gun."

In actuality, William was an excellent shot. But Samuel doubted that he would take up arms for the Confederacy.

Aching from his day at the gristmill, Samuel sat down heavily on a wooden chair at the table while his mother served supper. He had eaten a big dinner in the middle of the day, so supper was a light meal of cold meat and cold potatoes. Fortunately, Ann had canned a great deal of fruit the year before, so supper also included some apples. Samuel appreciated having something sweet along with the meat and potatoes.

"How is Josiah?" asked Ann, as she put food on her son's plate. The deep darkness of a January evening had settled on the house, and only the cookfire gave light to the room.

"He seemed well today."

"I missed him at this week's meeting," she said.

"He might have been ill on First Day," said Samuel. "He spoke of spending time in bed."

"I will hold him in the light."

"Indeed," said Samuel.

Sitting down, his mother asked him to join her in prayer before the meal. She said no words, but led him in moment of silence. Their goal was always to enter into the presence of God, and to feel gratitude for all that God had given them. "*True silence*," said their fellow Quaker William Penn, "*is to the spirit what sleep is to the body, nourishment and refreshment.*"

The silence ended when Ann picked up her knife and fork and began to cut her meat. Opening his eyes and looking across the table, he saw lines in his mother's face that he had never noticed before. She looked neither nourished nor refreshed, despite the silent prayer. "How art thou?" he asked.

"Concerned," she said. "About William."

"Verily," said Samuel. More than twenty-four hours had passed since his disappearance, and they had heard nothing from him.

"To vanish is not like him," said Ann. The strain was taking its toll, and she was aging before his eyes.

"That is true," Samuel said, beginning to eat his supper. "He has always spoken plainly to us."

"But these are extraordinary times," said his mother. "Many young men are leaving their homes. The call to arms is strong."

Samuel swallowed and nodded. "Bushrod and I were talking about that. So many are joining the Confederate forces. Entire colleges are emptying." He could see the pained look in his mother's face. "But some are joining the Union."

His last comment did not seem to please her. She put down her cutlery and said, "Either way, it is the war bug."

Samuel knew what she was talking about. Quakers believed that war was always against God's will, and that conflict tended to create more problems that it solved. But with the recent division of the nation over slavery, some Quakers were leaving the faith to fight for the Union. "I know that the war is causing much discussion after First Day meeting," he said.

"Indeed," said Ann. "We are feeling tension not just between Friends and neighbors here in Occoquan. Stress is high in the meeting itself, between those who feel moved to free the slaves and those who want to avoid the conflict."

"If one were to fight for anything," said Samuel, "it would be the fight for freedom."

"But beware," said Ann. "Thou canst gain the whole world and lose thy soul."

Samuel sat back and pondered her words. He was naturally a peacemaker, and he felt a deep connection to his Quaker roots. But he wondered if it was selfish to hold to one's religious principals while oppressed people suffered. *What was worse: To refuse to fight while the nation divided itself? Or to take up arms, preserve the Union, and free the slaves?* He took a drink of water, and then said, "Our relative, General George Brinton McClellan, is taking that chance."

"Thy father's relative," Ann said, by way of correction.

"Yes, of course," said Samuel. "But he is part of our family."

"I suppose. He is a Calvinist, not a Friend. But his mother Elizabeth is from Quaker stock."

"I heard a good story about her," said Samuel, trying to lighten the mood. "She was volunteering at an army hospital in Philadelphia. She caused some conflict by ordering oysters for the wounded soldiers. The surgeons and nurses intercepted the oysters and feasted on them."

"How selfish," said Ann.

"The next day, Elizabeth asked about the oysters, and was told by the sick soldiers what had happened. The surgeons accused her of interfering with the treatment of their patients. They asked her who she was. 'I have a son in the army,' she said. 'Plenty of women have sons in the army,' one of them said, 'but still they have no right to interfere with the hospitals.' Then another asked her, 'What is the name of your boy, mother?' She said, 'George B. McClellan.'"

Ann had to smile at that.

"The reaction in the hospital was like a bombshell," said Samuel. "The surgeons and nurses rushed to make apologies, and the wounded soldiers cheered from their beds."

"I am glad," said Ann, "that she is humble. Her prominence in Philadelphia society did not prevent her from helping those needy soldiers."

"She was a hero," Samuel said. "The hero that many want her son to be."

"We shall see," said Ann, returning to her supper. The two of them ate in silence for a few moments.

"McClellan is determined to save the Union," said Samuel, wanting to continue the conversation. "During the summer and fall, he was able to organize the troops and improve their morale. People say that his men love him!"

"Still," said Ann, "he is leading them into battle. To kill, and perhaps be killed."

"True."

"May the peace prevail," Ann said to him, not wanting to talk about warfare. "What good can come of armed conflict?"

Samuel knew that her question was rhetorical, so he did not attempt to answer. "As of November," he continued, "McClellan became general-in-chief of all the Union armies. Now he plans to move an army to a point south of us. He wants to outflank the Rebel forces and capture Richmond."

"How dost thou know this?"

"People talk," said Samuel. "There is much tongue-wagging in the mill."

"But are not military plans confidential?"

"There are spies everywhere, from the North and from the South. Always listening, talking, spreading truths and spreading lies."

"How dost thou know thou heard the truth?" asked Ann.

"I do not," admitted Samuel. "But I heard about McClellan from a Fredericksburg merchant. I see no reason he would lie about a threat to his city."

Ann pondered this for a moment, and then asked, "And where is my son in all this?"

"Thy son? Dost thou mean me?"

"No, I am speaking of William."

Samuel was silent for a moment, and then said, "Mother, I do not know." He saw her eyes begin to well with tears.

"I do not want him to follow his neighbors into the Confederate Army," she said. "But I do not want him to fight for the Union, either. Neither path can be the will of God."

As the sun was rising the next morning, on a clear but freezing winter's day, a knock came on the door of the Bagley house. Both Ann and Samuel were out of bed and dressed for the day, the fire was burning brightly, and Ann was cooking a big breakfast of beefsteak, eggs, hotcakes, and fried potatoes. With a cup of coffee in hand, Samuel went to the door.

"How art thou?" asked Josiah Farlow, standing bundled up outside the house.

"Very well, Friend," said Samuel. "Do come in, out of the cold."

"I do not want to disturb thee, but I have some news to share."

"Please, come in," said Ann, who had appeared behind Samuel.

Josiah obliged and entered the warmth of the house. "Let me take thy coat," said Samuel.

"Have a seat," said Ann, pointing him to a chair at the table.

"Coffee?" asked Samuel, after hanging up his coat.

"No, thank thee," said Josiah.

Ann took the breakfast off the fire, and let it cool as they talked with their visitor. Eating would have to wait.

"Last night," said Josiah, "I was at the Occoquan Inn. I was meeting with a farmer who had arrived with several carts of grain. Samuel, we are scheduled to grind it today." Samuel nodded, and then sipped his coffee.

"The farmer is from Stafford, but he has relatives who live near Richmond. He told me a story that surprised and concerned me."

Ann and Samuel sat across the table from Josiah, mystified. "Go on, Friend," said Samuel.

"As the two of us were talking, the farmer said that he had been visiting with his relatives over the weekend. On his way home, traveling north to Stafford, he stopped at an inn for a meal. There, he met a young man, and the two began to talk. The young man said he was from Occoquan. When the farmer said that he was planning to take his grain to Merchants' Mill, the man said that he had worked there."

"William?" shouted Ann.

"Yes, I think so!" said Josiah. "I asked for description, and the farmer said that he was short and blond."

"Was he safe?" asked Samuel.

"Apparently," said Josiah. "The farmer did not indicate that he was under any duress. The young man simply seemed to be traveling."

"Which direction?" Ann asked.

"South," reported Josiah, "The farmer inquired about his destination, but he simply said 'south.' He gave no additional information."

"May I talk to the farmer?" asked Samuel.

Josiah paused, and then said, "That may not be wise."

"Why?"

"We are at war," said Josiah, "and not just war between the North and the South. Danger is everywhere."

"What kind of danger?" asked Ann, sounding alarmed.

"Danger from slave-owners who might harm him because he is a Quaker, an abolitionist. Danger from Confederates who might assume he is spying for the Union."

"Danger from supporters of the Union," added Samuel, "who might believe he is joining the Confederate forces."

"Supporters of the Union?" asked Ann, sounding incredulous.

"Yes," said Samuel. "Although thou mayst be surprised, there are Virginians who want to join the Union Army."

"Samuel is right," nodded Josiah. "If you go west of Harper's Ferry, most Virginians want to fight for the Union."

"We are a house divided," said Samuel.

"But why," asked Ann, "would William be traveling south?"

"I do not know," admitted Josiah. "But there is one more item of news that I must communicate. This is difficult to speak aloud, but I must. The farmer said that the young man was carrying a knapsack that said, '1$^{st}$ Regt Va Vol Howitzer.'"

"No!" said Samuel. "That cannot be."

"What?" asked Ann.

"The Richmond Howitzers."

# 4

## January 2022

"Good morning, pastor," said Abdul Ali as he arrived at Riverside Methodist Church under a brilliant blue sky. The clouds and rain from Saturday had been vanquished by a cold front that swept through during the night. The two men met outside the church on Sunday morning, as they had agreed to do on the pedestrian bridge. "Hope you have recovered from your run."

"Absolutely," said Harley. "It was a good one." Whenever Harley saw Abdul, he wished he had such a man in his congregation. Abdul radiated strength, from his powerful legs to his broad shoulders to his shaved head, which looked as though it had been carved out of a block of cappuccino granite. He had a sharp mind, and he seemed determined to be righteous—right with God, and right with the people around him.

"*Orandum est ut sit mens sana in corpore sano,*" said the big man.

"That sounds like Latin," Harley said, walking up the creaking wooden stairs on the side of the church building.

"It is," said Abdul. "A favorite phrase of one of my mentors."

"And what does it mean?"

"You should pray for a healthy mind in a healthy body."

"Yes, indeed," said Harley with a smile. "A worthy prayer. But I've got a way to go . . . in both areas."

"Most of us do," admitted Abdul, although Harley suspected that Abdul was closer to complete health than most people. He was probably the most disciplined person Harley had ever met—physically, financially, and spiritually. He worked out six days a week, skipping just one day to rest and recover. He drove hard bargains in real estate, as his mentor Jefferson had done, but he was scrupulously honest. As a devout Muslim, he prayed five times a day, without exception, and he donated two-and-one-half percent of his wealth to help the poor and needy, each and every year.

"So, who taught you that?" asked Harley. "Jefferson?" The two stood on the platform outside Harley's office, enjoying the crisp air and the brilliant sunshine.

"No, that line came from my cellmate in prison. His name was Arch; at least it was when I first met him. He was what you would call a 'polyglot,' a person able to speak multiple languages. While serving a life sentence, he spent as much time as he could in the library. He taught himself Greek and Latin, as well as Italian and French and Spanish."

"Amazing," said Harley. "I struggle with English."

Abdul smiled. "That particular line is from the Roman poet Juvenal. Arch used to drop it on me when we would lift weights together. He would spot me, and then I would spot him."

"So, how was he your mentor?" asked Harley.

"He introduced me to Islam," said Abdul. "Neither of us was getting much out of the Christian prison ministry, so we starting going to the Muslim prayer services. Arch began to pick up some Arabic—easier for him than for me."

"I bet," said Harley. "That's a tough language."

"Arch helped me to say and to understand the prayers. And then, eventually, to make sense of the Quran. In time, he converted to Islam and took the name Mehmet. I followed him and became Abdul."

"Good to have a spiritual guide," said Harley, beginning to feel a chill. He motioned toward the door to his office. "Please, come inside."

"I won't stay long. I know you have your worship service."

"Not for an hour," said Harley, opening the door. "No need to wear a mask, unless you want to." The pandemic had eased to the point that masks were optional in most places.

The two entered the pastor's office, which was no larger than a broom closet. There was not room for much furniture—just a solid oak desk, left to Harley by the previous pastor, and two wooden arm chairs that sat facing each other. Harley offered Abdul the chair closest to the door, and he sat in the other, their knees almost touching.

"I wanted to talk with you before your service today," said Abdul. "I would never want you to hear news from parishioners before you heard it from me."

"I appreciate that."

"First, I have made an offer to sell *el Castillo* to Fairfax County."

"Interesting," said Harley.

"They want to use it as a visitor's center," said Abdul. "The building has an excellent location at the very southern edge of the county, as you know. People can access it easily, after crossing the bridge from Prince William County."

"Makes sense," said Harley. He hoped that visitors would have a more positive experience of the house than he did, on his one and only visit. But given that terrible things had happened in the building's basement, he could not guarantee it.

"The building is also close to the Suffragist Memorial in the Occoquan Regional Park," said Abdul. "County leaders want to build on that history."

Harley recalled his introduction to suffragist history, offered to him by a witch named John Jonas, an outdoorsman with dark eyes, a bushy brown beard, and tattoos covering both arms. *"The prison by the river is where suffragists were imprisoned,"* John had told Harley when they ran into each other in the woods. *"This was after they protested for the right to vote."*

*"Right here? Didn't know that."*

*"Some were even beaten."*

*"Really?"*

*"Yes. When they were first taken to the workhouse, they were clubbed. One was thrown into a dark cell and knocked out. Her cellmate thought she was dead."*

*"Unbelievable."*

*"They called it the 'Night of Terror,' and it galvanized support for the cause."*

*"That makes sense."*

*"But the suffering continued. Rats ran in and out their cells. The women had no privacy. It was like they were being kept in a zoo, with Marines standing guard."*

*"All because they wanted the right to vote."*

*"Which they got, three years after the Night of Terror. It's amazing how people are imprisoned in one generation for something that seems so noble in another."*

Harley had first seen the witches of Occoquan performing a nighttime ceremony around a fire in a barrel. Before the pandemic, they gathered periodically in River Mill Park, near the Occoquan end of the pedestrian bridge, but now they seemed to be gone. John Jonas had disappeared at the beginning of 2019, literally dropping off the grid. Another Wiccan, Kelly Westbrook, had left town a year later to care for her ailing mother in North Carolina. It seemed that covens, like Christian congregations, had struggled to survive covid-19.

Abdul could tell that Harley was thinking, and he did not want to interrupt him. But after a minute, he asked, "Do you have any questions or concerns?"

"No," said Harley, returning to the conversation. "I was just thinking about the suffragists. Important history."

"Indeed," said Abdul. "So, that's my first piece of news. Second, I want to ask if my mosque could rent space in your social hall. For Friday prayers."

Surprised by the request, Harley was not sure how to respond. "Tell me more."

"We have been renting commercial space in a shopping center, but now the landlord has a store that wants to move into our space. We received a discount during the pandemic, but commercial enterprises can pay full rent. The landlord wants those sorts of tenants. It makes sense."

"Yes, it does," said Harley.

"So, we are looking for other options," said Abdul. "I thought of you and Riverside Methodist."

Usually, Harley was pleased when people thought of the church. But this request made him uneasy. Buying time, he asked, "When would you need it?"

"Fridays from noon to two o'clock," said Abdul. "That's our main service, like your Sunday morning service."

"And this would be our social hall," asked Harley, "not our Sanctuary?"

"Correct," said Abdul. "We pray on the floor."

Harley shifted uncomfortably in his chair. While he admired Abdul and wanted to help him, he knew that a mosque in his basement would be a controversial and possibly divisive arrangement.

"We are all Children of Abraham," Abdul continued. "Every one of us: Jews, Christians, Muslims."

Harley nodded, but remained silent. Political and cultural polarization had only increased during the pandemic, in both the Town of Occoquan and across the country. People were more divided than they had been since the Civil War—vaxxers versus anti-vaxxers, maskers versus anti-maskers—and sometimes it felt as though open warfare was going to break out. As Harley struggled to bring together the members of his tiny congregation, he did not want to do anything that would drive them apart.

"I hope you will look upon this request favorably," said Abdul.

Harley pictured church members screwing up their faces and yelling, "Muslims in the church basement? How could you?" A wave of anxiety rose up inside him. And yet, he knew that a stand for interfaith cooperation was exactly what his little town needed. Just like the suffragist movement, an effort that is controversial in one generation can be noble in the next.

"I'll have to run this by the leaders of Riverside," Harley said to Abdul. "I'll get back to you, as soon as I can."

Two weeks later, Martin Luther King Weekend arrived, along with more freezing temperatures. Harley wondered if the river were iced over as he walked under a cloudless sky, stepping gingerly and watching his steps on the frozen sidewalk. Temperatures were in the twenties, which felt bitter cold to him, and the dry air stung his face. *Steady, steady, don't want to go down.* He had fallen the winter before, shocked by how quickly he had hit the pavement. Pausing for a second, he looked north and saw that the Occoquan River was still flowing freely, which somehow reassured him. Harley suspected that a single cold snap would not return them to the Little Ice Age, the coldest period in the last thousand years. It had lasted several centuries, up to the time of the Civil War, and people had suffered terribly. Harley heard that New York Harbor actually froze one winter, allowing people to walk all the way from Manhattan to Staten Island. But he was not worried about that as he made his way to church; it would take weeks of freezing temperatures to turn the Occoquan into a block of ice.

Almost two years had passed since the start of the pandemic. Riverside Methodist Church had been emerging slowly, with people carefully and cautiously returning to the Sanctuary. Just last Sunday, Harley had made the covid-cautious decision to keep the doors to the Sanctuary open in order to improve ventilation, and several worshipers had complained. "What are you doing, pastor?" one frail senior citizen said to him. "Trying to freeze us to death?" The talk in coffee hour had been all about the freak snow storm that had knocked out power in Occoquan and caused traffic tie-ups on Interstate 95, leaving some people trapped in their cars without food or water for twenty-four hours.

*Yes, it's cold, but we'll survive,* Harley mused as he climbed the aging wooden steps on the side of the church. Then, as he put his key in the office door, he realized that he had not taken any action on Abdul's request to rent the church's social hall. Yes, it had been on his to-do list, but he had allowed himself to be distracted by a host of other concerns.

"Pastor, how is the archaeological dig coming along?" The question came from Andy Stackhouse, a retired Navy officer who was sitting in his office. Andy had the same buzz-cut that he had in the service, but his hair was now white and much thinner than it had been in his days of active duty.

"Andy, good morning," said Harley, not happy to see the man first thing in the morning.

"I've been very curious about what you have found in River Mill Park," said the military man.

Harley really did not want to talk about archaeology before church, but he knew that good volunteers were hard to find. "Give me a hand in the Sanctuary," he said, "and I'll bring you up to date."

The two men moved through the door that connected the pastor's office to the Sanctuary, and walked past the pulpit to the center aisle that divided two rows of well-worn oak pews. "Looks like we have some bulletins in the pews from last week," said Andy.

"Yes," said Harley, feeling guilty. "Let's gather them up before anyone arrives."

"Would be nice to have a church secretary to do this," said Andy.

"Yes, indeed," said the pastor, beginning to pick up the bulletins. The pandemic had been brutal on every aspect of the life of the church, and offerings were down. But in truth, the congregation's problems predated the arrival of the coronavirus, and their budget had not included a salary for a secretary for at least twenty years. When Harley arrived in 2017, he was the only employee of the church, and it fell to him to create and photocopy the worship bulletins for each Sunday service. Some weeks, he picked up the leftovers after worship, and other weeks he became distracted and did not get around to it. This was one of those weeks.

"I remember when Mary Ev took care of this," said Andy, walking along one row of pews.

"Yes, those were the days," said Harley, walking along the other row. They quickly snatched up the leftovers from each pew.

"So, how's the archaeology?" asked Andy.

"Pretty interesting," said Harley. "The William and Mary students got a lot done on their winter break. Excavated about a foot of the foundation of the Quaker house."

"Find anything?"

"Sure. Lots of pottery sherds. Some hardware from the windows and doors. Some charred pieces of wood, which indicate that the house burned down."

"Any idea when?"

"Still trying to figure that out," said Harley, as they reached the back of the church. "The pottery and hardware are being dated to the 1850s and '60s, so maybe around 1870?"

"An accidental fire?"

"Hope so," said Harley, picking up a stack of fresh bulletins for the morning service. "Now, if you can hand out the new bulletins, I'll throw these old ones in recycling. Service time is almost here."

"I took a walk one evening along the bank of the Occoquan." Harley started his sermon that morning with a personal story. "The sun had set, but there was still enough light to illuminate the charcoal grey outcroppings of rock that rose up from the edge of the river. These rocks are old, you know, formed about three hundred million years ago."

Harley saw nods among the members who had gathered for worship. Pre-pandemic, there would have been a hundred in the Sanctuary. Now, he was lucky to have fifty. "Putting my hands on a rock by the roadside, I began to make a connection with something much bigger than myself. Sitting down on the rock, I had the strange sensation that my center of gravity was moving down, down, down . . . past my shoulders and chest and waist, and deep into the stone beneath me."

He sensed that his story was hooking them. "*What, I wondered, had this massive rock witnessed as it looked over the Town of Occoquan? Native Americans and settlers, Revolutionary soldiers and Redcoats, slave-owners and abolitionists, blacks and whites, Jews and Christians and Muslims.* Even worse than the Red State Blue State divisions that we are seeing today! The rocks had seen it all, standing silently above the fading light on the Occoquan River."

Looking into the faces of his people, he could tell that they were engaged. Mary Ranger, the Occoquan postmistress, was right in front of him, a big woman with bleach-blonde hair. To her right, several rows back, was Bill Stanford, a tall, red-haired dentist who had played basketball at the University of Virginia in the early eighties. Gretchen Bennett was halfway to the back of the Sanctuary, a nurse with a kind, round face and brown eyes. Across the aisle from her was Juan Erazo, an immigrant from Honduras whose hair was dyed black but whose muscles were completely authentic. Together, these were Harley's people, and he wanted to inspire them.

"Pulling out my smartphone, I called up a psalm, the very same psalm that is our Scripture lesson for today: 'The Lord is my rock, my fortress, and my deliverer, my God, my rock in whom I take refuge.' *Get outside your head*, I thought to myself, *let yourself rest in the Lord of the rock*. This is what is really real, a fortress that can stand strong against any assault. Lean on this, rely on this—the rock in which you can take refuge. 'The Lord is my rock, my fortress, and my deliverer,' I repeated to myself, over and over again." Gretchen's large brown eyes were locked on him. Bill seemed to be looking past him toward the stained-glass window with the black Jesus. Juan's eyes were closed, but he was nodding in agreement. And a woman he had never seen before, a first-time visitor to the church, was smiling.

Harley knew that they all had a deep desire for stability, especially at this particular time. "The past few years have been chaotic for all of us," he continued. "First, we had the flood, with homes and businesses destroyed. Everything normal about our lives was washed away, and then—most shocking of all—the body of a young man was found in the debris. Two years later, the pandemic wreaked havoc on our schools, our workplaces, our churches, and our homes. Jobs were lost, educations disrupted, and marriages dissolved." Looking out on the small congregation, he could see examples of each of these traumas. "On top of this," he said, "our lives have been impacted by other challenges, ranging from political polarization to struggles for racial justice. On this particular Sunday, we remember the work of the Rev. Dr. Martin Luther King, Jr., and the work that still needs to be done in our community and our nation."

Harley paused to take a drink of water, and wondered if he should reflect more on the Scripture lesson or go straight to social justice. He decided to take the first path, and said, "When life feels like it is falling apart, God is a rock. God is as solid as the three-hundred-million-year-old rocks on the banks of the Occoquan River, unchanging in the face of upheaval in society and in individual lives. 'The LORD is my rock, my fortress, and my deliverer,' says the writer of Psalm 18, 'my God, my rock in whom I take refuge, my shield, and the horn of my salvation, my stronghold.' A popular praise song says that our God is an 'Awesome God,' and that is certainly true." He saw smiles on several faces when he mentioned this song, which they knew very well. "But the psalms make an even stronger case," he said, "that our God is a 'Rocky God.'"

*Yes, that will preach*, thought Harley. *Rocky God.*

He told the story of the Protestant Reformer Martin Luther, who experienced a period of conflict, illness, and intense depression, and then wrote the famous hymn "A Mighty Fortress Is Our God," basing it on Psalm 46. Harley said that for Luther, God was a Rocky God, "a bulwark never failing," a helper in the face of a "flood of mortal ills." Harley urged his members to remember the importance of community worship, an experience in which they can feel the solid support of God and the congregation. But then, knowing that every good sermon has to include both words of comfort and words of challenge, he shifted the focus. "When we gather for worship in community, we can certainly feel the support and help of God. But at the same time, we are challenged to become a community that is as solid as the God who supports us."

Focusing on the Rev. Dr. Martin Luther King, Harley said, "In his 'I Have a Dream' speech, King said, 'Now is the time to open the doors of opportunity to all of God's children. Now is the time to lift our nation from the quicksands of racial injustice to the solid rock of brotherhood.'" Harley scanned the congregation for reactions, and saw very few. "King knew that God was his rock," he continued. "But at the same time, he challenged each of us to *be* a rock—a solid rock of brotherhood, of sisterhood, of community. When we praise God in worship, we are aligning ourselves with the God who stands against deceit, injustice, ungodliness, and oppression. 'Now is the time to open the doors of opportunity to all of God's children'—that was true in 1963, and it is true today, almost sixty years later. Now is the time to lift our nation from the quicksands of racial injustice to the solid rock of community."

Harley saw Andy Stackhouse cross his arms, and he guessed that the Navy vet was thinking that the sermon was getting too political. *Come on, Andy, justice has been part of our faith for thousands of years.* "What will you do to take a stand for opportunity and justice?" said Harley to the congregation. He thought of suffragists being beaten and thrown in jail a hundred years ago, and Civil Rights workers suffering the same fate just fifty years later. *Sometimes,* he mused, *a great injustice can advance the cause of justice.* He asked them, "What will you do in this church, in this community, in this nation, in this world? You have a solid community around you, standing together on a rock-solid God." But then, realizing that it was time to wrap up his message, he said, "When life becomes chaotic, we can find stability in a Rocky God. Yes, life will surely distress us, but we can rest securely on the knowledge that God is our rock, and that we stand together—as a solid community—to do God's work in the world."

*Amen.*

Standing at the church door at the end of the service, at the border between the warmth of the sanctuary and the cold of the outside world, Harley shook hands and wished his church members well.

"Your Rocky God worked for me," said Andy Stackhouse on his way out the door, "but not the social justice message. A bit too woke."

Harley nodded, not sure what to say. *Should I bring up Abdul's request for the social hall?* But then Mary Ranger inserted herself, saying, "Give him a break, Andy! It's Martin Luther King weekend!"

Mary pushed Andy out the door, and then Harley found himself face to face with the first-time visitor to the church. She was petite, with a slender face and long blond hair. Harley guessed that she was in her fifties.

"Good morning, pastor," she said, smiling broadly and extending her hand. "I'm Nanette Glebesman."

# 5

## Second Month 1862

ONE MONTH HAD PASSED since William Bagley disappeared from Occoquan, and Ann was carrying a burden that surpassed any grief she had ever known. She had felt disoriented and adrift when her mother died, and then abandoned and isolated when her husband passed away. But the absence of William was a millstone that was grinding her down, slowly and relentlessly. Her clothes now hung awkwardly on her body, since food had lost its taste. Her chores were done mechanically, with none of the enthusiasm she previously brought to her work. And while she and Samuel still read in front of the fire after dinner, she stared at the same page all evening. Her mind was no longer on her book.

Fortunately, the Quaker community rallied around her. Hot meals were brought to the house, so that Ann and Samuel would not waste away. Josiah Farlow helped Samuel to chop firewood, so that the house would stay warm during the freezing nights of Second Month. And the women of the community drew Ann into their sewing groups, so that she would not slip into inactivity and isolation.

"Joseph is kind to let us meet in his home," Ann thought as she trudged up the hill to Rockledge, a large Georgian mansion standing by a cobblestone driveway. The snow was thick, so her progress was slow, but Ann did not mind the walk in the cold winter air. "He has compassion. He is a child of loss."

Joseph Janney was a businessman, thirty years old, who had been raised in a prominent Quaker family. His father John was an Alexandria merchant who lost his wife Margaret just a year after the birth of their son.

The loss haunted John, and it seemed to follow him everywhere, until he made the decision to seek a fresh start in Occoquan. He purchased Rockledge in 1834, when little Joseph was two years old, and then in 1837 he founded the Occoquan Manufacturing Company. The business boomed as the man and boy rattled around Rockledge together until John died in 1854. Now Joseph—tall and broad-shouldered, with jet-black hair—was the most eligible bachelor in Occoquan.

He was also a role model for Ann's sons. Joseph was a leader in the Society of Friends, always present in meetings and ready to help a brother or sister in need. He was generous to families in financial hardship, and opened his home for community meetings—as he was doing that day. He was politically active as well, often in ways that put him at odds with his non-Quaker neighbors.

*That's where the Liberty Pole stood,* thought Ann, looking eastward as she approached the house. The flagpole had been erected on the Rockledge lawn on Independence Day 1860, bearing a pennant with the name of Abraham Lincoln and his running mate Hannibal Hamlin. Being an abolitionist, Janney was a fan of Lincoln, the Republican candidate for president, but his stance was not popular among the Virginians who were preparing to secede from the Union. Several weeks later, the Prince William Militia arrived at Rockledge and chopped down the Liberty Pole, despite the objections of Janney and the shouts of other Union sympathizers who gathered around to protest. *Joseph is fortunate,* she thought, *that they did not destroy his house.*

"How art thou?" asked Ann, when Joseph opened the front door of the large stone house, which was covered in wood according to the fashion of the day.

"Very well," said the young man. "I welcome thee, Ann Bagley." Quakers tended to call each other by first and last names, with no titles.

"How goes the business of the gristmill?" she asked him, stepping into the warmth of the house. The Janneys had purchased the mill from the Ellicotts a number of years earlier.

"All is well," said Joseph, "thanks to the hard work of Samuel Bagley."

"Thou art kind," said Ann, taking off her coat. "I only wish that William were here to help him."

"I do as well," Joseph said, "I feel thy loss very keenly."

Ann wanted to say more, but a lump in her throat prevented her from speaking. She had no idea if Joseph had heard about William and the

Howitzer knapsack, but she suspected that Josiah has said something at the gristmill. *What questions of faithfulness and loyalty was he raising? What doubts were being sowed?* In the election of 1860, Lincoln only received fifty-five votes from Prince William County, and they all came from the Occoquan area. *My family had been so proud of our support for Lincoln! Now, what opinion does Joseph hold of us? Is William among the Howitzers?* The thought of William joining the Rebel forces filled her with shame, an emotion that rivaled her grief. Without saying any more, she handed her coat and scarf to Joseph.

"The women are in the parlor," he said, pointing with an open hand.

Walking through the snow to Merchants' Mill, Samuel was struggling. He kept his head down, appearing to be focused on his footing, but in fact he was trying to avoid eye contact with neighbors in the street. For most of his life, he had relished the security of knowing where he stood with his fellow Friends, and he appreciated the clarity that came from seeing himself as distinct from the non-Quakers around him. But William's disappearance was blurring the lines, making it difficult for him to guess what others would do or say. The ancient rocks of Occoquan were shifting under his feet, leaving him feeling off balance and insecure.

"So, William is now a Howitzer?" asked the red-haired Bushrod Washington, smiling, as he met Samuel at the heavy wooden door of the mill. "Good for him."

"We do not know," Samuel replied as he entered the storeroom. He did not want to have this conversation.

"They are a fine unit," said Bushrod. "Some of the best. We need them in this war of Northern aggression."

"Thou knowest that we are not fighters," said Samuel, turning to pick up a bag of grain, stacked near the entrance.

"Oh, I do know. You would not even join the welcome for Colonel Hampton when he came to town."

"We do not support the war."

"Obviously," said Bushrod, not moving to offer his assistance.

"We wish peace to all."

"Hampton's troops do not need peace. They need supplies."

"And we feed them," said Samuel. "Does not some of this grain go to them, to make their bread?"

"For a price," snapped Bushrod. "You Quakers do not miss a chance to turn a profit."

"The mill is a business," Samuel said. "There is no shame in commerce."

"Those Confederate boys are encamped around us right now, protecting us. They may lay down their lives for us, and all you care about is commerce."

"That is not all I care about," said Samuel, straining to lift a bag by himself.

"No," said Bushrod, "you care about protecting yourself. I saw you run when the *Stepping Stones* steamed up the river."

"Of course," he said. The sight had been terrifying. "It was a Union warship."

"Some of us were ready to fight, to protect our home."

Samuel pushed past Bushrod and carried the bag to the hopper. He poured out the contents, grateful for a break in the conversation.

"Why won't you defend yourself?" called out Bushrod from the storeroom.

"Defend myself from what?" asked Samuel, returning with the empty bag. "From the shell that the ship fired over the town? What could I have done, even if I wanted to fight?"

"You could stand up," said Bushrod, arms crossed. "Stand up like a man."

Samuel felt his face flushing and his anger beginning to rise. "Stand up? I hope thou standeth up . . . standeth up in front of the next shell that is fired . . ."

"Coward!" shouted Bushrod, clenching his fists and lunging at him.

Samuel dropped the bag and grabbed Bushrod's wrists, but the force of the attack pushed him against the rough wooden wall of the mill. The two men grappled against the wall, face to face, locked in what looked like a strange and violent dance. Bushrod struggled to free his fists so that he could throw a punch, but he was not strong enough to escape Samuel's grasp. Instead, he sputtered at him, "The Third Michigan is camping across the river. They want to kill us! Do you not know that? Why will you do nothing to defend yourself, defend your family, defend our town?"

At that moment, Josiah Farlow rushed into the room and used his superior strength to pry them apart and propel them to opposite sides of the storeroom. "In this mill," he barked, "there will be peace."

The fire in the Rockledge parlor was burning brightly, radiating heat throughout the room. Ann sat on an oak chair in a circle of six women, making work shirts for the men in their families, and most of them had removed their shawls because of the warmth of the fire and the bright winter sunshine coming in through the windows. They stitched slowly and carefully, with eyes on their work. Throughout the morning, they maintained an unbroken conversation about the war and its effects on their homes and community.

"*War's fierce tread upon our land / Severing once a kindred band,*" said Sarah Farlow, slowly and deliberately. She was the forty-year-old miller's wife, as tall as her husband and equally imposing, with long black hair and piercing green eyes. "*Child and father ranged for strife, / Brother seeking brother's life!*"

"What art thou saying?" asked Rebecca Cadwallader, a classmate of Samuel Bagley who was in her early twenties.

"I am reciting a requiem," said Sarah.

"And . . . what is that?" asked Rebecca. She was petite with curly blond hair, and was sometimes intimidated by the older women in the group.

"A remembrance of the dead," said the miller's wife. "*Requiem for 1861.* I read it in the newspaper, and it moved me."

Joseph Janney walked past the entrance to the parlor, and the women glanced up at him. Rebecca gave him a big smile, which he returned with a nod. She was ready to enter into marriage, and she had interest in both her classmate Samuel and the older man Joseph. *God's will be done,* she thought to herself.

"The words are very striking," said Patience Cadwallader, noticing her daughter's flirtation but not commenting on it. Looking downward, she finished a stitch and then turned over her garment. "Captures the war bug very well." Patience was blond, like her daughter, but was probably twice her size. Rebecca's small frame came from her father, the bookkeeper for the mill.

*War's fierce tread upon our land / Severing once a kindred band.* The words struck Ann Bagley to the quick, but she said nothing. She did not know if any of the women suspected William of defecting to the enemy and severing her family. She kept her eyes on her sewing.

"We are in the worst of times," said Elizabeth Milhous, a single woman in her forties who lived with her brother. "The hounds of hell have been released. Brothers fighting brothers, fathers killing sons. I never dreamed we would come to this."

"President Lincoln has issued an order that all of his armies will begin offensive operations this month," offered Emily Trueblood, who had been the town's schoolteacher until she married at thirty. Emily made a point of reading the newspaper every day, even though she no longer had a group of students to educate and inform. Her husband was a teller at the Bank of Occoquan, and the two of them enjoyed discussing the events of the day every evening at dinner. "They must commence by the twenty-second of Second Month, Washington's birthday."

"A significant deadline," said Sarah.

"Indeed," said raven-haired Emily, looking up for a moment. "I always told my students to honor the day, because of our first President. But now it has a darker meaning." Emily wondered if she would have been allowed to keep her teaching position, now that Virginia had seceded from the Union. The town council probably would not want a Quaker educating the children of Occoquan.

"President Lincoln also issued an order for the Army of the Potomac to move overland," said Elizabeth, who also tried to stay informed. "He wants them to attack the Confederates at Manassas Junction and Centreville."

"I cannot abide this war!" said Patience, sounding impatient. Her daughter looked at her with concern. "The aggression goes against everything I believe."

"Indeed, it does," said Elizabeth. "But we cannot ignore it."

Emily noticed that Ann had been quiet, so she reached out to her like the teacher she was. "Ann, what dost thou think?"

"I am aggrieved by it," she said. "It pains me deeply."

"But can anything be done?" asked Elizabeth.

"I heard that General McClellan objected to President Lincoln's plan," said Ann. Despite her Quaker convictions, she could not help but be interested in what her late husband's relative was doing.

"Thou art correct," said Emily. "He wants to move the army south."

"Would that bring an end to the hostilities?" asked Rebecca.

"We can hope," said Elizabeth. "I would support anything that brings this war to a quick conclusion."

"President Lincoln has agreed to support McClellan," said Emily. "Reluctantly." Ann began to worry that William would be caught in the fighting around Richmond. *What if he walked into the middle of a bloodbath?*

"Perhaps the war will be over by summer," said Patience, trying to sound hopeful.

At that moment, a shot echoed through the town. Then another. In seconds, volleys of gunfire filled the air. The women rushed to the window and saw Confederate troops, who had been training in the town's common area, trading fire with the soldiers of the Third Michigan across the river. Smoke from the gunfire formed a cloud which began to move toward them. Ann felt a rising sense of dread, realizing that the war had come to Occoquan.

Suddenly, a pane of glass exploded above their heads, and the women dropped to the floor, screaming. Errant Union shots were crossing the river and hitting Rockledge. Joseph appeared in the parlor doorway and called for them to crawl toward him, keeping low to avoid the fire. He then led them to a room in the back of the house.

"God, bring us peace," prayed Ann in silence, huddling with the other women. Shots continued to ring out, volley after volley, and the sound of windows breaking could be heard up and down the street. Confederate soldiers cried out to one another, calling for reinforcements to join the fight and for medics to evacuate the wounded. The smell of gunpowder wafted into Rockledge through the broken parlor window, stinging their noses.

But then, unexpectedly, a violent wind began to blow. The sky quickly became dark. Heavy snow fell from the sky, muffling the sound of the gunfire. In just a few minutes, the snowfall made it impossible for the troops on either side to see across the river. The shooting slowly stopped, and the Confederates withdrew from the wharf. The snow was so thick that no one could see more than a few feet in any direction. Nature had forced a cease-fire.

"Peace," said Sarah. The house was silent except for the wind blowing snow against the window panes.

"God's will has been done," added Ann. "On earth, as it is in heaven."

"Amen," said Emily.

*Now, God,* Ann said to herself, *if it be thy will, bring William home.*

# 6

## Presidents' Day Weekend 2022

NANETTE GLEBESMAN HAD MOVED to Occoquan in early January, taking up residence in a penthouse apartment in the newly constructed Gristmill building. She had grown up in South Carolina, and still spoke with a bit of a Lowcountry accent, but had spent the past twenty-five years in Seattle, working in human resources for a series of tech companies. For the last decade, she had been an executive at Amazon, and when her marriage went to pieces, she jumped at the chance to move to Northern Virginia and work at the new East Coast headquarters in Arlington.

"Good morning, Jessica," she said to the waitress at the American Legion Hall on Mill Street. Jessica Simpson was a woman in her thirties with highlights in her jet-black hair, arms covered with tattoos, and the face of a smoker.

"Mornin', hon," said Jessica to Nanette, dressed for church in a conservative Navy-blue jacket and skirt. The two had developed a bond in Nanette's first month in town, especially during Sunday morning breakfasts at the grille. Although there were twenty years between them—and Nanette's carefully coifed blond hair was a stark contrast to Jessica's streaky, black ponytail—the two enjoyed chatting as Jessica served members of the sparse Sunday breakfast crowd. Nanette had served for four years in the Navy after ROTC at Clemson, so she qualified for membership in the Legion and joined the post as soon as she arrived in Occoquan.

"What's good today?" asked the older woman.

"Depends," said the waitress, tapping her pencil on her order pad. "You want to be healthy?"

"Always a good idea," said Nanette, pondering the menu.

"Then I would avoid the biscuits and gravy," said Jessica. "Although they are delicious."

"I bet," agreed Nanette, remembering the food of her Southern childhood. "But I tell you want: I'll go for an egg-white omelet with spinach, and some whole wheat toast."

"Coffee?" asked Jessica.

"You know it." Within seconds, she had a steaming cup.

Nanette really like the American Legion, even though she did not have a lot in common with the Korean War vets who were already drinking beer at the bar on that Sunday morning. It reminded her of the various fraternal halls that dotted her home state, where she had gone to dances and parties as a teenager. After a quarter-century in Washington State, which was filled with people who wanted to get as far from the East Coast as possible, she was glad to be back home. She also enjoyed the easy camaraderie she found at the American Legion, where people came from all over the country and were looking to make friends in town.

The same was true for Riverside Methodist Church, which Nanette had begun to attend on the Sunday of Martin Luther King weekend. She had grown up in the denomination and had been a member of a Methodist church in Seattle, so she was pleasantly surprised to move to Occoquan and discover that the only church in town was . . . Methodist! In an era in which fewer and fewer people cared about denominational loyalty, and in metropolitan areas in which people were trending rapidly toward the secular, Nanette was an outlier. She was a woman who valued the ministry and mission of the Methodist Church.

"Going to church today?" asked Jessica, as she refilled Nanette's coffee cup.

"Absolutely," said Nanette.

"The pastor lives right across the street," said Jesssica, pointing out the window at a Victorian townhome, painted in a variety of sun-bleached colors and covered with whimsical ornamentation.

"Really?" said Nanette. "I figured he was local, but didn't know where he lived."

"Yeah," said the waitress. "Pretty luxurious digs for a pastor."

"Well, Methodists don't take a vow of poverty."

"Of course, he doesn't own it," said Jessica. "Story is, the developer was a Methodist, and when he finished the final townhouse, he had to dispose of the model home. He could have sold it, but his tax adviser suggested he donate it to the church. Some big write-off, I guess."

"Makes sense," said Nanette, sipping her coffee.

"So, Harley will live there as long as he is pastor of the church."

"Do you know him?" asked Nanette.

"Pretty well," she said, "I'm not religious, but we have talked. He came in here a lot when he first came to town, with a member of the Legion who is not around anymore." Nanette sensed that there was a story there, but she did not press. "Anyway," Jessica continued, "I still see him when I go outside for a smoke break, and he goes in or out of his house."

"What do you think of him?" asked Nanette.

Jessica paused for a second, and put the eraser of her pencil to her lips. "He's a good man, I think. He was really kind to a teenager who worked here. A Muslim dishwasher. The members of the Legion were pretty cruel to him, talking to him with a funny accent and making jokes about Muslims. Eventually he got fired."

"That's not right," said Nanette, thinking like an HR professional. *Bullying.*

"I agree," said Jessica. "I hated to see him go. But Harley became friends with him, and really helped both him and his family."

"I'm glad," said Nanette, knowing the hidden good deeds that so many pastors do. Ministry is more than Sunday morning sermons.

"Hey, your food is ready," said Jessica, seeing a hand signal from the cook. She scurried to the kitchen, came back with a plate, and put it down with a flourish. "Enjoy!"

As Nanette was eating, she thought of her recent Sundays at Riverside Methodist Church. She had loved the old Sanctuary from the moment she first walked in, with its oak pews and unusual black Jesus in the stained-glass window. Members of the church had been friendly to her, but not pushy. The choir was small but mighty, with several very good voices. The music was mostly traditional, accompanied by an electronic organ, with an occasional contemporary praise song thrown in. And the pastor? Not bad. Harley struck her as authentic. He spoke from the heart, with sermons that applied the Bible to modern life. He was open about the pain of his own life, and he seemed to be genuinely caring toward others. And he was attractive to her, in the way that men in their sixties could sometimes be attractive. He clearly tried to stay in shape, and he did not make the futile attempt to hide his grey hair with unnaturally dark dye. Riverside Methodist was a good find, so soon after moving to Occoquan.

Then, as she finished her last bite, she motioned to Jessica to bring her check. It came to twelve dollars, and Nanette put down a twenty-dollar bill.

"I'll bring your change," said Jessica.

"Keep it," said Nanette, getting up from the table. "It's yours."

"Thank you very much," said Jessica, smiling. "I'm going to call you No-Change Nanette."

While breakfast was being served at the American Legion, Harley was meeting with the finance committee of Riverside Methodist Church. He hated to have meetings before the eleven o'clock service, but it was a convenient time for most of the committee members.

"That was quite a wind last night, wasn't it?" said Navy vet Andy Stackhouse, taking off his coat in Harley's office.

"Thought we might lose power," said Mary Ranger, the postmistress. She was setting up a small circle of metal folding chairs.

Bill Stanford, the red-haired dentist, said, "We'd be shivering in the Sanctuary if the heating system couldn't operate today."

"Right about that," said Andy. "And speaking of the Sanctuary, I'm glad the American flag is in a prominent place."

"It is Presidents' Day weekend," said Harley, moving from behind his desk to the meeting circle. He despised the endless debates about when to display the American flag in church. *Anyone care about separation of church and state?* "We always display the flag on the weekends of federal holidays."

"Should be displayed every week," grunted Andy.

"Gentlemen, we are here to talk about the budget," said Mary, the chair of the committee. "Let's come to order."

Sitting in a circle, they each glanced through copies of the most recent financial report.

"Looks like giving is still down," said Bill.

"It has been since the beginning of the pandemic," said Harley.

"Many people switched to online giving," Mary said, "but others give only when they are in the pews."

"And unfortunately," Harley added, "there are many who have not yet returned."

"Do you think we'll get them back?" asked Andy, sounding skeptical.

"Hard to say," said Harley. "I'm glad we pivoted to online worship at the beginning. It was necessary during the lockdown. But there are some who still want to worship from home, even though we are back in the Sanctuary. People got out of the habit of coming to church, and I'm afraid we're creatures of habit."

"It is convenient," said Bill. "When I'm traveling, I like to be able to worship online."

"I don't like it," said Andy. "It's too easy for people."

"I hear you, Andy," said Mary, "but we will lose even more members if we drop the online option."

"I agree," said Harley. "I watch the numbers, and at least half of our congregation is still worshiping from home. And I'm sure some of them give. So, it seems like the hybrid of in-person worship and online worship is here to stay."

"That sounds like a worship committee decision," said Bill, trying to get them on track. "We need to figure out the dollars."

"Before the pandemic," said Mary, "our budget was about two hundred thousand per year. During the pandemic, our giving has dropped to about one hundred and fifty thousand."

"Ouch," said Andy. "A drop of what . . . twenty-five percent?"

"That's right," Harley said, nodding. "I'm hearing the same from other pastors. Fortunately, our program costs have been lower, so we have not spent as much as we did pre-pandemic."

"But those costs will return, right?" asked Andy.

"I hope so," said Harley. "We need to reboot our programs if we are going to come out of this."

"So," said Bill, "the good news is that we have not run a big deficit in recent years. Giving has been down, but spending has been down as well. What is our actual deficit?"

Mary looked at the reports and said, "Looks like we were down twenty thousand in 2020, and eighteen thousand in 2021."

"Thank goodness for our reserves," said Andy.

"So that's the good news," said Bill. "But the bad news is that spending will go up as we return to a full church program. So that could mean an even bigger deficit in 2022."

"Are there cuts we can make?" asked Andy.

"We are already pretty lean," said Harley. "As you know, Andy, I am church secretary as well as pastor."

"And you do it well," said Andy, offering a sly smile.

"So, where can we find additional income?" asked Bill.

"Perhaps we could rent some parking spaces to the Town of Occoquan," said Mary. As postmistress, she knew the official and unofficial business of virtually everyone in town. "The current town parking lot is too small to handle all of the people who come to town to shop and eat and drink."

"Good idea," said Andy. "The lot is virtually empty on weekdays."

"What else?" asked Bill, looking for creative ideas. The room went quiet and Andy put his nose in the financial report.

"I did get a request from Abdul Ali," Harley said, sounding tentative. "His mosque would like to rent space in our social hall. For Friday prayers."

"What?" said Andy, looking up. "A mosque in our basement?"

"Yes," said Harley. "For one prayer service, on Friday."

Andy glared at him. "Shouldn't we be trying to convert Muslims?"

A tense silence filled the room. Harley looked around, trying to gauge if the other members of the finance committee were in agreement with Andy. He suspected that they were not, but were too surprised and timid to speak up.

Finally, Mary said, "That will be a decision for the church council. Way above our pay grade. But if they approve it, the income will help."

Bill seemed relieved that the tension had been cut. "Here is something else, Harley." The pastor shifted his focus, turning away from angry Andy. "When I count the offerings, I try to maintain confidentiality."

"I appreciate that, Bill," said Harley. "I don't want to know what anyone gives."

"A good policy," said Bill. "You shouldn't be deferential to big givers or upset at small ones."

"I try to treat everyone equally," said the pastor.

"But we have a visitor who might benefit from a pastoral call," said Bill.

"Oh, really?" said Harley. He was aware of Nanette Glebesman's visits to the church, but he was not aware that she had any needs. "I assume you are talking about Nanette. Is she sick?"

"No, not sick," said Bill. "Generous. On her first Sunday, she gave an offering of four hundred dollars. Every week since, she has given four hundred dollars."

Harley was impressed.

"That's quite a pattern," said Mary, punching some numbers into a calculator. "If she continues at that pace, she'll make an annual gift of twenty thousand eight hundred dollars."

"That would help with the deficit," said Bill. "Probably eliminate it."

"Visit her!" said Andy, suddenly much more chipper. "Get that woman to join the church!"

Harley stood outside the sanctuary, welcoming people to worship under a sky that was pale blue and filled with soft winter light. After two days of fifty-mile-per-hour winds, the air was still but cold as a tomb, and Harley was glad he had chosen to wear his long, black preaching robe. *That's why they were invented, to keep priests warm in cold cathedrals.* Looking north, he could see that the river was a mirror, offering a reflection of the ancient rocks and hulking trees on the opposite bank. He saw a tall, blond-haired man walking south on Washington Street, but the man never looked at Harley. Clearly, he was not interested in coming to church.

"Good morning, Gretchen," Harley said to the kind-hearted nurse with large brown eyes.

"Hope the heat is on," she said as she scurried into church. A small crowd of people arrived at the last minute, including the visitor, Nanette. Harley greeted her and made a mental note to arrange a visit after worship. The service went fairly well, with Harley preaching on the importance of welcoming people and connecting with them, just as Jesus did throughout his ministry. Quoting the apostle Paul in his letter to the Romans, Harley ended with the words, "Welcome one another, therefore, just as Christ has welcomed you, for the glory of God."

*Not my best sermon,* he thought as the offering plates were passed, *but not a bad message.* The country was being splintered by political polarization and community breakdown, and even little Occoquan—which had a non-partisan mayor and town council—was being pulled into national fights over immigration policies and police reform. Harley was beginning to wonder if the country was moving toward another Civil War, one that would shatter his church and his community. He knew that divisions in denominations across the country had preceded the war between the states, and he worried that the same was happening today.

*So, what's the solution? Church dinners? Small group conversations? Christian hospitality? Welcome one another—Red, Blue, Northern, Southern,*

*Black, White—just as Christ has welcomed you? Hospitality seems kind of anemic,* he sighed, *but better than nothing.* Then, he gave the benediction and walked to the church entrance, anxious to speak to Nanette and arrange a meeting.

A stream of people walked out the door, shaking his hand and offering thanks for the service. One of them was Juan Erazo, the Honduran immigrant.

"*Buenos días,*" said the man. "*Buen sermón, pastor.*" Harley knew enough Spanish to receive the compliment. But Juan's tone quickly became serious, and he switched to English. "I need to talk with you, Harley, about the increase in gang activity around here."

"I'm sorry to hear it," said Harley. He was concerned, but really did not want to be sucked into a serious conversation. Nanette was still inside the church, talking with a couple of people at the back of the sanctuary.

Juan looked behind him, did not see anyone in line, so he dove in. "Things quieted down during the pandemic, but gang members are now out and about."

Harley nodded and said, "That's not good."

"Kids in the Latino Student Association are feeling nervous again," said Juan. He was retired from work in the construction industry, and volunteered at the local high school. "There was gunfire a week ago outside the Lake Ridge community center. Some kind of beef between MS-13 and *Los Gatos.*"

"Too close," said Harley, shaking his head. He recalled that the dead man in the debris after the flood had been identified as a leader of *Los Gatos.*

"A security guard and a bystander were injured. Could have been one of my kids."

"That's got to make you angry," said Harley.

"*Furioso.*"

Looking at Juan's muscular arms, rock-solid from years of manual labor, Harley imagined him doing real damage to anyone who threatened one of his students. Harley wondered if Juan had anything to do with the death of the man in the debris. The case had never been solved, but Harley always had a suspicion about Juan, as well as about the witch John Jonas. Both had lost family members, and both had good reasons to despise the members of these gangs.

"I appreciate what you are doing for the students," said Harley. "They need you."

"Someone has to do something," said Juan. "They need protection."

"You are right," said Harley. "The danger is everywhere."

"I thought Honduras was bad, but this is getting out of control."

"But what can you do, really?" asked Harley. "What can any one person do?"

Juan paused for a moment, looking as though he wanted to answer. He reached over to a holly bush that was growing by the door of the church, one that bore green leaves all winter. In the middle of the leaves were bunches of bright berries, red as blood. Then Juan shifted his attention to Harley and said, "Just wanted you to know, pastor. Be aware." With that, he walked away.

When Harley looked back into the church, Nanette Glebesman was gone.

# 7

# Washington's Birthday 1862

ON GEORGE WASHINGTON'S BIRTHDAY, February 22, the U.S.S. *Stepping Stones* returned to Occoquan, traveling slowly up the river on a misty morning. The river was dark and peaceful, and the hulking Union ship glided quietly into place, southeast of the town wharf. She was one hundred feet in length, weighing two hundred and twenty-six tons, with a steam engine that drove two large sidewheels. Although built in New York as a ferryboat, she had been transformed quickly into a gunboat by the Union Navy. Now, she was on a mission of patrolling Confederate waterways and searching for enemy troops, ready to engage them with her twelve-pounder Howitzer gun.

"Did you see her?" asked Bushrod when he arrived at the mill that morning. His red hair was unkempt and seemed to be flaming.

"How could I miss her?" said Samuel. *Stepping Stones* was twice as long as any of the barges that made their way up and down the waterway. When the steamer dropped anchor, it dominated the town.

"Damn those Yankees!" said Bushrod. "Invading on the President's birthday!"

Samuel paused for a moment, and then said, "They have not invaded, actually."

"They may as well. Sitting in the river as though this town belongs to them."

"She is part of the Potomac Flotilla," said Samuel. "Trying to disrupt communications and shipping."

"Well, they seem to be succeeding," said Bushrod. "I doubt any barges will be able to make it to the mill while she is blocking the channel."

"What dost thou expect?" asked Samuel. "We are in a war."

"You Quakers," said Bushrod, "You do nothing to defend our town. Nothing to protect our citizens. You just go about your business."

"What is wrong with that? Dost thou not want to work and be paid?"

"Of course. But some things are worth fighting for."

"Thou hast caught the war bug, Bushrod."

At that moment, the sound of cannon-fire ripped through the air. Bushrod and Samuel ran up the rough wooden staircase to the top of the mill, and threw open the shutters on the window that faced downriver. They saw dozens of large shells plunging into the river near the ship. As best as they could tell, none of the Confederate shots hit their mark. Samuel craned his neck to see if there were any soldiers on the wharves to the east of them. He saw no one. The cannon-fire must have been coming from the encampment that had been established southeast of the town.

"Wade Hampton is shooting," said Bushrod.

Then, a launch was dropped from the *Stepping Stones*, and on it rode the fearsome Howitzer gun. Four men rowed the launch, while three others manned this powerful piece of artillery, which could launch a heavy shell over one thousand yards. As the launch moved toward the shore, it began to return fire. The two young men in the mill covered their ears as the gun was fired, hoping that the shells were missing the houses and shops of Occoquan.

"They are trying to hit the encampment, are they not?" asked Samuel between shots.

"I think so," said Bushrod, shaken by the gunfire.

"Why are they shooting from a launch?"

"To get closer, I suppose."

The Howitzer was fired a dozen times, with no response from the Confederate cannons. Then a group of Confederate soldiers appeared on the shore and began to shoot at the launch with rifles. Union solders on the *Stepping Stones* returned fire, and the oarsmen on the launch pulled hard to get the boat back to the mother ship. In the exchange of gunfire, one of the artillery men took a bullet and fell into the bottom of the boat. In a few moments, the launch returned to the safety of the far side of the *Stepping Stones*, and the shooting stopped. The Confederate soldiers vanished from the shore as quickly as they had appeared, leaving nothing but the smoke of gunfire.

"Is it over?" asked Bushrod. He began to regain his confidence when the shooting stopped.

"Seems to be," said Samuel.

"I wish one of our soldiers had hit their captain."

Samuel did not know how to respond. That would have seemed to him to be a senseless loss of life.

"Last summer, a Union commander was killed at Mathias Point," said Bushrod. "He was sighting his bow gun, and a Confederate soldier shot him through the abdomen."

Samuel nodded. He had read about that death, the first Union Navy officer to be killed in the war. "Yes, that was a loss," he said, feeling a sense of sadness. He said nothing more, not wanting to show a lack of allegiance to Virginia.

"May there be many more," said Bushrod.

On the last day of Second Month, 1862, a letter was delivered to the Bagley house. Ann immediately recognized William's handwriting on the envelope and ripped it open with trembling hands. She was thrilled to see the letter after two full months of silence, but was anxious about the message it might contain.

> *Saturday, Feb. 15th, 1862*
> *Dearest mother and brother,*
>
> *Most sincere apologies for my sudden departure from Occoquan. I knew full well you would not support my enlistment in the army. But I believe that I must fight for our beloved Virginia, if we are to know any peace in future days. I am serving in Richmond at present, but cannot reveal details to you except to say that I am healthy and well-fed, and am beginning to train on artillery. The population of Richmond is made up of the strangest elements. Many visitors are presenting themselves as officers, with a desire to offer their services at large salaries. One man, who had been engaged all his life in the leather business somewhere in Georgia, offered his services as a General. Another man said that he was a Colonel, although his home was in some swamp in the Carolinas. He came to Richmond to have a private talk with the President, to let him know what he thought of General McClellan! I now realize that I severely underestimated*

*my potential when I enlisted as a Private. I should have set humility aside and offered my services as an officer. Until I write again, I remain your loving son and brother, William.*

*P.S. I should be home on leave in the middle of March. I look forward to your embraces!*

Ann read the letter twice, and then laid it down on the kitchen table. She pushed it across the surface to Samuel, who quickly devoured it. Then he locked eyes with her, awaiting her reaction.

"This is not a message from William," she said.

"What dost thou mean?" asked Samuel. "The handwriting belongs to him. His jests about the officers are words he would likely use."

"But he speaks not as a Friend," she pointed out, pulling the letter towards herself. "Look at this: 'I knew full well *you* would not support my enlistment in the army.' He says, 'you,' not 'thou.' And this: 'I remain *your* loving son and brother.' Such talk! He should have written, '*thy* loving son and brother.'"

Samuel pondered this for a moment, and then said, "Men do not talk like Friends in the army."

"And the date on the top! 'Saturday . . . February 15.' We do not honor heathen gods! What is this acknowledgement of 'Saturn's Day'? And 'February,' a month of pagan purification? William should be writing 'Seventh Day' and 'Second Month.'"

"Thou art correct, mother."

"We have lost him," said, shaking her head. "We 'thee' and 'thou' all people."

"All are equal in God's eyes."

"And pagan practices have no standing amongst us."

"Thou speakest the truth," said Samuel, standing up to walk around the table. "But William is not lost." Putting his arms around his mother's shoulders, he said, "He is alive! And will be home on leave soon!"

"In the middle of 'March'! How fitting: The month of Mars, the god of war!"

"Mother," said Samuel, squeezing her hard. "Thou art too vexed. He is not with Friends. I am not surprised that he is speaking the language of the world."

"I fear he is lost," said Ann, her eyes welling with tears. "As the Bible says, 'For what is a man profited, if he shall gain the whole world, and lose his own soul?'"

Word quickly spread through Occoquan about the letter from William, person to person and house to house, until if made it to the dinner table of the Washington home on Commerce Street. "I hear that your Quaker friend is now a fighter," said Thomas, the red-haired and rotund father of Abigail and Bushrod, as he carved a roasted chicken on their table. Thomas and his wife Martha ran the dry-goods store in Occoquan, and lived in a white Gothic Revival House with pointed windows and steeply pitched gables. They were well-to-do by Occoquan standards, and were proud of their connection to George Washington, the country's first Commander-in-Chief.

Abigail blushed and said, "Yes. I understand that he wrote a letter from Richmond." She had been secretly admiring William for years.

"Good for him!" said Thomas, holding up the carving knife. "He has summoned the courage to fight for what is right."

"I, too, have courage," said Bushrod.

"Yes, you do, son."

"And I am ready to fight."

"Not yet," said his father. "You have work to do right here."

"But the army needs me," said Bushrod. "There is much talk at the mill about the success that the Union forces are having."

"Such as?" asked Thomas.

"The Battle of Mill Springs in Eastern Kentucky."

"Yes, that was a Union victory," said Thomas, "but it did not succeed in securing the area for the Union. Our side is still very strong there."

"How about the capture of Fort Henry, in Tennessee?"

"Yes, that damned U.S. Grant had success," admitted Thomas. "Forced a retreat of our boys to Fort Donelson." As a shop-keeper in Occoquan, Thomas read the newspaper every day, and knew the progress of the war better than most. "But Kentucky and Tennessee are so far from us."

"What about North Carolina? That is very close."

"True."

"The Union has seized Roanoke Island," said Bushrod. "They now control Albemarle Sound."

Thomas put a piece of chicken in his mouth and nodded.

"And the Battle of Elizabeth City," Bushrod continued. "That battle led to the destruction of a number of our ships."

"It sounds like the war is not going well for us," said mouselike Abigail. She was beginning to worry that William was in danger.

"Father, you spoke of the retreat of our troops to Fort Donelson," Bushrod said. "That was a disaster."

"What happened there?" asked Martha, blond and petite like her daughter. She spooned vegetables on to each of the plates around the table.

"Sadly, our men were overwhelmed," said Thomas. "Our twelve thousand were faced by Grant's army of twenty-five thousand. The fort surrendered, setting the stage for the capture of Nashville."

"Nashville has fallen?" asked Martha.

"Yes, I am sorry to report it," said Thomas, wiping his mouth with a napkin. "Just last week. When our forces evacuated, Nashville became the first of our state capitals to fall."

"So, you see, father," said Bushrod, "I need to join the army and fight!"

"Not yet, son," said Thomas.

"Your father and I need you here," said Martha. "Your work in the mill is important, and we need your help in the store as well." She tried to hand him a piece of buttered bread.

"There may be no work in the mill," said Bushrod, waving off her offer, "with *Stepping Stones* blocking the wharf."

"The ship will leave," said Thomas. "It is simply passing through."

Bushrod put his napkin over his plate and stared at his father. "Passing through? Was the barrage from its Howitzer a sign that it is just 'passing through'?"

"That was an engagement with Hampton's troops. Nothing that we need to get involved in."

"Should we not protect our home?"

"That is the business of soldiers," said Thomas. "Our business is at the mill and the store."

"I cannot simply stand by and watch our town be shelled."

"You are not standing by, son. You are working. Grinding grain to feed the soldiers. Helping your mother and me to run the store. We each support the war in our own way."

Bushrod could not accept his father's logic.

"Soon," said Thomas, "normal activities will resume. The barges and flatboats will return. We'll see the transport of flour and grain, coal and lumber, and—of importance to us—all manner of general merchandise."

Such an optimistic outlook seemed wrongheaded to Bushrod, and his anger began to rise. "You commend William Bagley for being a fighter," he said, "even though it goes against his religious principles."

"A noble choice," said Thomas.

"Noble choice? What do you mean by that?"

"That it is noble to fight for our home and our way of life."

"But he has been removed from the Quaker meeting," said Bushrod. "His own people consider him to be a heretic. He has made a great sacrifice to support our cause."

"That is true," said Thomas. Abigail's eyes were beginning to tear up, as she thought about William being an outcast and a heretic.

"So why will you not support my desire to fight," said Bushrod, "when you say that this cause is so noble? I am no heretic; I am taking a stand for our beliefs!"

Thomas looked at Martha, unsure of what to say. He knew that her greatest fear was the loss of her son in battle, but he could not give voice to it. "You are still under my roof, so you abide by my rules," he said. "For now, we need you here."

Bushrod pushed away from the table violently, stood up, and loomed over his parents and sister. "I do not understand you," he shouted. "You say this war matters, but you will not allow me to do what I need to do." Abigail stared at him wide-eyed, shocked by his disrespect for their parents.

"Hypocrites," said Bushrod, stomping out of the dining room.

# 8

## Ash Wednesday 2022

ASH WEDNESDAY FELL ON March 2, a day that started with bright sunshine and morning temperatures in the thirties. Harley began his commute to church by descending the cast iron steps outside his kitchen, stepping carefully to avoid slipping on any ice that might have developed over night. Then he took a looping route to Riverside Methodist via the boardwalk, looking out over the mist on the river, which was quickly being burned off by the morning sun. Pausing outside Maxine's seafood restaurant, he put his hands on the railing and looked toward what he called Turtle Island, a pile of stones that had been dumped in the water to prevent the river from being filled with silt. In the summer, he would paddle his kayak close to the rocks and count the turtles who climbed on to the rocks to sun themselves. Today, no turtles.

*Buried in the mud,* thought Harley, shivering. He knew that lower temperatures made their metabolisms slow down, so they would dig into the mud below the river and rest through the winter. Their decreased metabolic rate meant that they did not need much oxygen, so they could stay underwater for extended periods of time. When springtime came, the warmer weather would bring them back to the surface. *Wonder if my missing church members will reappear as well.*

Turning to his right, he began to walk down Washington Street toward the church. He had a nine o'clock appointment with Andy Stackhouse, the retired Navy man. Andy had said he wanted to talk with Harley about the drift of the Methodist Church, away from the Bible and toward progressive theology. Harley was not particularly anxious to have the conversation, but he had to give Andy credit for not being a hibernating church member.

Just as Harley got settled into his office and poured himself a cup of coffee, a knock came on his door. He glanced at his clock and saw that it was 8:45. *Who could that be?*

Then he figured it out. "Andy, good to see you," he said, opening the door. "Right on time."

"*Fifteen minutes early is on time . . .*" said the church member.

"*And on time is late,*" added Harley, completing Andy's favorite saying. "Wish that more members had that attitude toward the Sunday service."

"Cold one, isn't it?" said Andy, taking off a wool cap.

"Sure is. Let me take your coat and hat. How about a cup of coffee?"

"Sounds good. Black, please."

"Have a seat," said Harley, pointing him to one of the two oak chairs in front of his desk.

"Boiler working okay?"

"Perfect. As you can see, my office is toasty." Harley handed him a steaming cup and took a seat in the chair across from him.

"Thanks for seeing me," said Andy, taking a sip. "I know you're busy, with Ash Wednesday and whatnot."

"No problem. I like these talks." *Well, not exactly.*

"Anyway, I'll get to the point. You know I am a law-and-order guy. I take rules seriously. And I'm just concerned that our church—and even more so, our denomination—is getting away from the Bible."

"Say more," said Harley, shifting in his seat and trying not to move immediately into a defensive posture.

"You know. The Bible says that homosexual activity is an abomination, but some Methodists are now doing gay marriages. The Book of Genesis says that we are supposed to subdue the earth, but you've established a Green Team here at Riverside. Can't we just go by the words of the Bible?"

Harley took a drink of coffee and swallowed it slowly, giving himself time to think. "I hear you, Andy," he said. "And you're not alone. A lot of Christians say that the scriptures consider homosexuality to be a sin. And some people believe that it is wrong to try to preserve the planet, since Jesus is going to come back and replace it."

"Exactly," said Andy. "The Bible says it, and I believe it. I hate to see our denomination splitting over this stuff."

"Me too," said Harley, sighing. *Never thought I'd see the United Methodist denomination come apart like this. Or my own congregation.*

"Men marrying men and women marrying women. I was raised with one man, one woman. Period."

"That was certainly true for me," said Harley, taking another sip. "I know what you are saying. But understandings change, and interpretations change." Then he had an inspiration, which caused him to shift direction. "Andy, I know that you are a Civil War buff."

"Absolutely."

"Think back to the 1860s," said Harley, warming to the topic. "One hundred and sixty years ago. Southern preachers took the Bible literally, and they defended slavery. They asked who could question the Word of God when it said, 'slaves, obey your earthly masters with fear and trembling.' That's from Paul's letter to the Ephesians."

"Yes, I guess that made sense to them, at the time."

"And in Paul's letter to Titus: 'tell slaves to be submissive to their masters and to give satisfaction in every respect.' You don't believe that, do you?"

"No, I don't. Of course not."

"The Christians who wanted to preserve slavery had the literal words of the Bible to back them up. They had all of the clearest scripture verses."

Andy sat silently for a moment, looking at his coffee. Then he asked, "What did the Northern preachers say?"

"They had to be creative," said Harley, glad that he had been doing some reading on the topic. The archaeological dig in River Mill Park had reawakened his interest in the war, so he had borrowed a number of books from the library. "Some emphasized that the Union had to be preserved, so the advance of liberty around the world would not be slowed. One Boston preacher said, 'If America is lost, the world is lost.'"

"I would certainly agree with that," said Andy.

"And, of course, you know *The Battle Hymn of the Republic*. Not a sermon, but a very religious summary of what Christians in the North believed."

"*Glory, glory, hallelujah*?" asked Andy.

"Yes, but more specifically, the verse: '*In the beauty of the lilies Christ was born across the sea, with a glory in His bosom that transfigures you and me: As He died to make men holy, let us die to make men free, while God is marching on.*'"

"I love that hymn," said Andy. "Wish we sang it more."

"We can certainly do that," agreed Harley. "But my point is that religious messages were being delivered from both the South and the North. Both sides were reading the same Bible, but interpreting it in very different ways."

"There were certainly a lot of Christians on both sides," said Andy. "I guess they had completely different views of slavery."

"Slaves, obey your earthly masters," said Harley, circling back to scripture. "As Christ died to make men holy, let us die to make men free. Both very biblical."

Andy paused again, and then said, "One thing I learned in the Navy is that we want God to be on our side. And we assume that God *is* on our side."

"So true," said Harley. "Think back to the fighting in Europe, in both World Wars. Mostly Christians fighting Christians."

"Even today," observed Andy, "you've got Russia invading Ukraine, with the head of the Russian Church supporting Putin."

"I'm sure the leaders of the Ukrainian Church see things very differently," said Harley.

"No doubt," said Andy, smiling. "They don't want Russian Christianity. They want bullets."

Harley was glad that they were finding common ground. "I like what Lincoln said: 'My concern is not whether God is on our side. My greatest concern is to be on God's side.'"

"Amen to that," said Andy. "But how do we know whether we're on God's side?"

"That's the big question," said Harley, taking another drink of coffee. "I don't think we can answer it by assuming that the Bible is going to give us clear guidance on every moral and political issue. The Civil War shows us that the words of the Bible can be used to defend slavery—which is indefensible."

"So, where do we turn?"

"Maybe to some fresh interpretations of the Bible," suggested Harley. "Back in Civil War times, there were African American Christians who had the right ideas, but their perspectives were largely ignored. They were quick to see slavery as a sin and as a defilement of New Testament values. But many in the white world were not listening."

"So, the words of the Bible remain the same, but the interpretations change."

"Exactly," said Harley. "New biblical perspectives are needed. Take a look at what the Bible says about men having sex with men. It is an abomination, according to Leviticus. Why? Because these relationships do not produce children. The Israelites needed to multiply if they were going to survive. Same for God killing Onan in the Book of Genesis. You know what he did? He masturbated. Didn't lead to a child."

"That's pretty harsh," said Andy.

"Indeed," said Harley. "Do you think God wants to kill us for masturbating today?"

"Hope not."

"This is why we need fresh interpretations. I don't think today, in a world of around eight billion people, that we need to make reproduction the goal of every person and every marriage."

"My son and his wife chose not to have children," said Andy. "And when I remarried, my wife and I were too old to have children."

"The New Testament values other things," said Harley: "Faithfulness, love, sacrifice, commitment. These values can be practiced by heterosexual couples without children, and by same-sex couples as well."

"I hear you, Harley. I know we have to change sometimes. I just don't want us to stray from the Bible."

"Neither do I," said the pastor, continuing to push his perspective. "With regard to the environment, I don't think that we live today in a world in which we need to subdue the earth in order to survive in it."

"That's true," said Andy.

"Instead, the time has come to reclaim the biblical value of stewardship. That's what God was instructing Adam to do in Genesis, when he put him in the garden of Eden 'to till it and keep it.' We have mastered the technology of tilling the earth. The challenge now is to keep it."

Andy drained his coffee cup and then said, "You've given me a lot to think about." Harley wondered if he had come on too strong. Then Andy glanced at his watch and said, "I think I better be going."

"Keep the question of Lincoln in mind," said Harley: "Are we on God's side? That's the key. As long as we keep talking, we'll be able to figure it out."

"I hope so," said Andy, getting up and reaching for his coat. "I certainly hope so."

Clouds rolled silently across the sky in the afternoon, blotting out the bright morning sunshine and putting a filter on the colors of the buildings in town. So many winter days had been grey and lifeless, and Harley had grown weary of looking out his office window at the same bare trees and drab buildings. But on that particular afternoon, the arrival of clouds was accompanied by a rise in temperature, from the thirties to the sixties. Having put the finishing touches on the Ash Wednesday service for that evening, Harley got up from his desk, stretched his arms, and decided to go for a walk. When he opened his office door to the warmer air, he was glad he had decided to step outside.

Commerce Street took him up to the concrete bridge which spanned the Occoquan River. Walking north on the pedestrian walkway, he saw the water rippling below him and he felt a breeze moving over the water. *The first day of creation: A wind from God swept over the face of the waters.* The water had been complete chaos in 2018, when the town flooded and the dead body was found in the debris. But today it seemed calm and life-giving. *God said, "Let the waters bring forth swarms of living creatures, and let birds fly above the earth across the dome of the sky."* Harley looked forward to the arrival of spring, with the jumping of fish and the soaring of birds. In the breeze, he thought he caught a whiff of a flower's aroma. He sniffed again. *No, too early. Must be my imagination.*

Reaching the northern end of the bridge, he looked down at *el Castillo* and remembered that he still needed to bring Abdul Ali's request to the church council. He knew that Abdul wanted to move forward with prayers in the church basement, just as he was determined to turn *el Castillo* into a county visitor's center with exhibits on the suffragists. Feeling badly about his inaction, Harley picked up his pace and turned left on the road that ran through the woods on the north side of the river. The ancient rocks that lined the roadway took his mind back to the sermon he had preached on Martin Luther King Weekend. *Rocky God,* he thought to himself. *When life becomes chaotic, we can find stability in a Rocky God.* He felt good about that sermon, and was enjoying the memory, but then he recalled what had been the most important part of that particular Sunday: Shaking hands with Nanette Glebesman at the door.

Harley was grinning as he rounded a bend, and his expression must have looked ridiculous to the tall, blond-haired man he encountered in the road. Harley quickly changed his expression, slowed to a stop, and said, "Good afternoon."

The man stopped his walk as well. "Same to you."

"Have we met?" Harley asked.

"I don't think so," said the man, looking down at him.

"You just seem very familiar," said Harley, looking at the man's dark brown eyes. He was rail-thin and clean-shaven, with an angular face disfigured by a long scar that ran from his temple to his chin. Harley guessed that he was in his mid-forties, but his shoulder-length blond hair made him look younger.

"I get that a lot," the man said.

"I'm Harley Camden, pastor of the Methodist church in town. I've lived here in Occoquan for about five years."

"Don Abad," said the man, putting out his hand for a shake. "Just moved into the new apartments at the end of Mill Street. I work in IT."

"You are not alone," said Harley, shaking his hand. "Lots of folks around here are in tech. Do you work from home?"

"One hundred percent," said Don.

"And you've got a great place to work from."

"You're right," Don said, nodding. "I have a third-floor apartment overlooking the river. Could not be happier."

"I was really glad to see those apartments go in. I remember the empty lot, when it was first being developed."

"Abdul Ali," said Don.

"And before him, Jefferson Jones," said Harley, remembering the day he first saw the two developers walking the lot. *Jefferson was in a seersucker suit; Abdul in a form-fitting t-shirt and warm-up pants. They were standing by the water, looking up and down the river. They had a vision, and it became reality.*

"Well, they did a great job," said Don, beginning to move again. "Nice to meet you, Harley."

"And you, Don," said Harley. Then he realized where he had seen him before: Walking on Washington Street, in front of the church. "Hope to see you around town," said Harley, as they passed each other. But as Don disappeared up the hill, Harley could not shake his feeling of déjà vu. He knew the guy. And not just from seeing him outside the church.

The roadway ended at the pedestrian bridge, which crossed over the river into the town. As Harley walked it, he noticed that some activity was going on at the Quaker Village archaeological site in River Mill Park. Pulling out his smartphone, he glanced at the time and saw that he had a few minutes to spare before he had to return to church for the Ash Wednesday service. Picking up his pace, he hustled over to the site. Several professors were preparing it for the return of student diggers during their spring break.

"Jim!" said Harley as he stepped under yellow rope that ringed the site. "What's going on?" Harley had been volunteering with Jim Dotson, a professor from the College of William and Mary.

"Found something!" said Jim, waving Harley over. Dotson had appreciated having Harley around, especially when no students were available to assist him. While Harley was not completely up-to-date on archaeological techniques, he could sift dirt just as well as he did at Sepphoris in 1985.

"Show me," said Harley, getting his dress shoes muddy as he went deep into the site. Dotson was a rotund man with a bushy brown beard, and he was smiling broadly.

"We pulled off the tarps this morning, and were cleaning up the site," said Jim. "As you know, the excavation of the interior has reached a depth of about two feet. Well, guess what is lying right under the surface?"

"I have no idea."

"You know that the Quakers had a cemetery up the hill, right?"

"Yes," said Harley.

"And that they don't typically bury bodies inside their homes?"

"Right."

"Well, this is why I'm so excited," said Jim.

"Why?"

"We found a grave."

"A grave?"

"Yes," said Jim. "It seems that the Quakers buried someone in the corner of the house."

Harley stood in silence, looking down at the ground. *Ashes to ashes. Dust to dust. A perfect Ash Wednesday discovery.*

# 9

## March 1862

THE SKY WAS CLEAR and the moon was just a sliver of light as three Union soldiers passed the Quaker burial ground and crested the ridge overlooking the Rebel camp. The March night was cold, so the men wore heavy flannel shirts, coats made of dark-blue sackcloth, and baggy wool trousers. Charcoal covered their faces, and all wore dark forage caps with floppy crowns. The three were lightly armed, with just pistols and knives, since they were on a reconnaissance mission. Looking down on the Town of Occoquan and the camp to the southeast, they made every effort to remain invisible.

"Seven, eight, nine, ten." One man counted the campfires that were burning below them, and the second made notes in a small journal, using a stubby pencil to scratch calculations of the number of soldiers. The third soldier remained behind the first two, looking toward the dark woods and watching for signs of any Rebels who might be patrolling the area. "Four, five . . . six," said the first man, looking through a collapsible telescope. "I cannot be sure, but it looks like they have six pieces of artillery."

"We heard reports of artillery," whispered the second man, "along with cavalry and infantry."

"If the moon were brighter, I could see more clearly," said the first. "But yes, it looks as though that assessment was correct."

"What is that movement?" said the second man, pointing toward town. The first man shifted his telescope. A group of men was leaving the Hammill Hotel, carrying torches. "Who is it?"

"Civilians, enlisted men . . . and at least one officer."

"Which one?"

"Looks like the colonel," said the first man. "Based on his coat and hat."

"Wade Hampton," said the second. "Wish I had my rifle."

"Would be a long shot."

"I could make it."

The first man smiled at his comrade's confidence. "Of course, your shot would expose us."

"Would be worth it."

"So, why do you think Hampton has been to the hotel?"

"To have dinner?"

"Rather late for that."

"Perhaps he has made his headquarters there," said the second man.

"Good thought," said the first. "Put that in your report."

At that moment, a sharp cracking sound came from the woods. The third man, acting as lookout, motioned for them to lie down. Keeping his eyes on the tree-line, he carefully removed his pistol from its holster. The wind stirred the bare branches of the trees, but no threats emerged. In a few moments, the lookout gave an all-clear sign and whispered, "Must have been an animal." Then he holstered his pistol and began to scan the woods behind them and the rocky slope in front of them.

The first two soldiers returned to their observation positions and watched the colonel and his entourage return to the camp by torchlight. "Do you see anything else?" asked the second man.

Scanning the edges of the camp with his telescope, the first said, "Just a lot of wagons."

"Does that seem odd?"

"More than the usual number, I would think."

"What could it mean?" asked the second man.

"Could be that they are getting ready to move."

"I wonder where?"

"I don't know."

"I'll make a note."

The third man crept closer to them and whispered, "I think we should head back."

"Why?" asked the first.

"I see movement."

"Where?" asked the second.

"Down below," said the third.

The three peeked over the edge of the rocks, down into the darkness below.

"I do not see anything," said the first man.

"You have been looking at the lights of the camp," said the third. "Let your eyes adjust."

For a few moments, all was silent except for the sound of their breathing. Then the first said, "I see it."

"What?" asked the second.

"Movement," said the first, collapsing his telescope and slipping it into his coat pocket. "Men on horseback."

"Let us go," said the lookout. The second man stowed his journal and pencil and began to move.

Hunching to avoid detection, they snaked through the Quaker gravestones and moved toward the tree-line. Once behind the cover of the woods, they stood up and walked as quickly as they could toward the slope that dropped toward the river. Several times they stumbled, unable to see the rocks beneath them.

"I wish we had better moonlight," said the second man.

"Not me," said the first. "It would reveal us."

"Damn these rocks," grumbled the second, right before the first man tripped and fell to the ground, rolling for a few yards over stones and branches before hitting the trunk of a tree.

"Damn right," he said, after catching his breath. "Help me up."

The three continued their perilous descent until they reached the rocky shore of the Occoquan River. "Almost there," said the third man, pointing to a set of shrubs in which they had hidden their canoe.

"Almost home," said the second.

But then, without warning, two men on horseback exploded from the trees to the east. Two others came from the woods to the west. The rocky hill formed a barrier to the south and the river prevented escape to the north. The Union soldiers were trapped.

"Drop your weapons," shouted a man in a long grey coat and a wide-brimmed Hardee hat. He jabbed his sword at them, while the other three men on horseback brandished their pistols.

In a matter of minutes, the three Union men were prisoners of the Night Riders.

As Samuel Bagley walked to work on the eighth day of Third Month, he stopped to look at a cluster of spring crocuses that had courageously emerged from the hard winter ground. *Purple splendor.* Since childhood, Samuel had delighted in the change of seasons, and he especially loved to look for signs of spring. *Daffodils, Grape Hyacinth, Star Magnolia . . . all would soon appear.* Although his mother was still suffering terribly from William's absence, he had taken comfort from his brother's letter and was looking forward to his return. He did not care that neighbors were gossiping about William and accusing him of abandoning their Quaker faith. He would always be his brother. Nothing could change that. *New life,* he said to himself, thinking of William's return. *New hope. Another sign of spring.*

Then he looked from the ground to the sky and saw a cloud of dust above the housetops. The haze was like nothing he had ever seen before. Reaching the heavy wooden door of the mill, he saw Josiah Farlow standing with arms crossed and looking up. "What is happening?" Samuel asked.

"Wagons are moving," said the miller.

"What wagons?"

"The ones carrying Wade Hampton's troops," said Josiah.

"Where are they going?"

"Not sure. Some are saying that they are heading south, toward Fredericksburg."

Samuel was perplexed. He had assumed that the Rebels would remain focused on Washington. "Do they not want to invade the capital?"

"I do not know their strategy," said Josiah. "Nor do I care. But I suspect that the city is now well fortified."

"Yes," said Bushrod Washington, who had appeared behind them and overheard the last portion of their conversation. "McClellan has been hard at work."

"What has he done?" asked Samuel.

"Last summer, Lincoln put him in charge of the capital's defense," said Bushrod, loving to show off his knowledge. "He began by laying out a complete ring of trenches and fortifications, all around the city. His men are building enclosed forts on hills on every side, and they are putting batteries of field artillery between the forts. My cousin in Alexandria says he has never seen anything like it."

"That should make the city unassailable," said Josiah.

"Unfortunately, yes," said Bushrod.

"Until now, there has been very little protection," said Samuel.

"True," said Bushrod. "Only Fort Washington, across from Mount Vernon." Samuel had passed it once, when he was a passenger on a ship that took a load of flour up the Potomac River to Alexandria. Having never seen structures larger than the buildings of Occoquan, he had stood in awe of George Washington's hilltop mansion on the Virginia side, and the towering stone Fort Washington on the Maryland side. As they passed the fort, a member of the ship's crew mentioned to Samuel that Fort Washington had failed its one and only test in the War of 1812, when the advance of British troops caused the Americans to panic and destroy their own fort. "The captain was found guilty of abandoning his post," the crewman said, as the two of them looked over the gunwale. "He was dismissed from the service, but received no other punishment." Then he added, with a smirk, "You can be sure that a sailor like me would get a flogging."

Fortifications were a foreign world to Samuel, but he found them to be fascinating: Entrenchments, forts, batteries, rifle pits. "It appears that General McClellan knows what he is doing," said Samuel.

"I have to give him credit," admitted Bushrod. "He already has eighty-eight guns on the defensive line facing Virginia. Now he will add additional guns to this ring around the city. I believe that Washington will be one of the most secure locations in the world."

"General McClellan is a relative of mine," boasted Samuel.

"Really?" said Bushrod, running a finger along the scar on his face.

"A distant relative," Samuel added, suddenly regretting his statement. "On my father's side."

"I recommend you keep that information to yourself," said Bushrod. "The people of Occoquan do not like traitors."

Several days later, while Josiah Farlow supervised the work of Samuel in the gristmill, his wife Sarah visited with Ann at the Bagley home. Sarah sensed that Ann was feeling burdened, so she offered to sit with her and work on their mending together. All the curtains in the small house were pulled back to allow the late winter sunlight to enter, and candles sat on tables next to their chairs to give additional light to their needlework. The logs in the fireplace popped and sputtered, throwing much-needed heat into the room, and the two women warmed themselves with cups of tea as they worked.

"What was the poem thou recited at Rockledge?" Ann asked, looking up from her work.

Sarah was not sure that she should repeat that particular poem, in light of Ann's sadness. "About the war?" she asked, pushing a strand of her long black hair behind an ear.

"Yes, that is the one."

"Art thou sure thou wantest to hear it?"

"Yes," said Ann.

"*War's fierce tread upon our land*," said Sarah, slowly. "*Severing once a kindred band.*"

"So true."

"*Child and father ranged for strife, / Brother seeking brother's life!*"

Ann sighed, looked down at her mending, and then said, "It fits my spirit."

Sarah's green eyes looked mournful. "There is truth to it," she said.

They sat in silence, working, and then Ann said, "I do not want the Rebels to have success. But I do desire that William return home safely."

"As do I," nodded Sarah.

"I am deeply vexed," said Ann. "I do not know how to pray about this."

"Thou wantest peace. But not through the annihilation of the Rebels."

"Precisely," said Ann. "I want the Confederate Army to be strong enough to protect William."

"I understand."

"At the start of the year," said Ann, "the Rebels seemed to be doing well."

"Yes, that is what I was hearing."

"But now?" said Ann. "I am concerned."

"Josiah gathers much at the mill," said Sarah. "Over supper, he tells me of the progress of the fighting."

"The war bug," said Ann. "We cannot ignore it."

"February was not a good month for the Rebels," said Sarah, taking a sip of tea. "The capture of Fort Henry on the Tennessee River. The fall of Fort Donelson, on the Cumberland."

"That seems so far away," said Ann.

"Josiah tells me that that these forts were important gateways. Their fall was the first break in the Rebel line."

"I see," said Ann, trying to picture the vast land that spread out to the south and the west.

"Now the Union can challenge Rebel control of the Mississippi and New Orleans," said Sarah. "They have already taken Nashville."

"Which is good," said Ann.

Sarah nodded, but whispered, "Do not say that too loudly."

"I do not know how to feel," admitted Ann.

The two worked in silence, needles moving silently, until Sarah began to recite along with her stitches, "*Then up the sluggish Cumberland came boats / With mighty guns—death in their iron throats / And hosts of armed men, all bent upon / The glorious capture of Fort Donelson.*"

"What is that?" asked Ann.

"Another poem."

"Where didst thou find it?"

"In the newspaper," said Sarah. "It is warlike, I confess it. Not fit for Friends like thee and me. But the verses capture me . . . capture my imagination."

"Such worldly sentiments often do."

"What can we do? Such words speak the truth about our world."

"Verily, they do. But let us not dwell on them."

After another few moments of silent working, Sarah said, "Josiah tells me that McClellan is planning a Peninsula campaign."

"So I hear," said Ann, nodding. "President Lincoln has commanded, 'On to Richmond!'"

"Yes, 'On to Richmond!'"

Ann put down her stitching and said, "Which is where William is serving." Her eyes filled with tears.

"I am sorry," said Sarah, stopping her work. "So very sorry."

"May God allow the lines to hold."

"Indeed."

"I feel guilty saying that," said Ann. "A Quaker, asking for Rebel lines to hold."

"But he is thy son," said Sarah.

"I want only his life."

"That is a worthy desire," said Sarah. "And the Rebel forces may be strong enough. Just a few days ago, an ironclad ship had success. It sank two Union ships."

"The *Congress* and the *Cumberland*," said Ann, taking a sip of tea.

"Sister, thou art highly informed!" said Sarah, smiling.

"We cannot afford to be ignorant," said Ann.

"Thou art correct."

Then, with eyes flashing, Ann said, "Nor can we support McClellan's march to Richmond!"

# 10

## Lent 2022

PW Outlets is a sprawling mall in Prince William County, just four miles south of the Town of Occoquan. It contains over two hundred stores, ranging from Nordstrom Rack to IKEA, and for decades it has been one of the top tourist attractions in the state, drawing hordes of shoppers throughout the year. Built on land that was once gently rolling farmland and thick old-growth forests, the mall has transformed the area into a retail amusement park, with stores and restaurants surrounded by acres of blacktopped parking lots. *Six Flags Over Virginia,* you might call it, except that the excitement of the place comes from deep discounts instead of thrill rides.

On the second Saturday in March, the temperature dropped thirty degrees and an unexpected amount of snow began to fall, blanketing the parking areas. But snow was not the only surprise that day. Just before noon, as customers were streaming through the main entrance, the unthinkable happened: Shots were fired on the wide sidewalk that connects the shopping mall to the multi-screen movie theater. Although the gunshots were muffled by falling snow, the crowd immediately reacted with panic. Customers screamed and pushed past each other, slipping and flailing their arms, struggling to enter the safety of the mall or find refuge behind parked cars. In a matter of seconds, PW Outlets had changed from retail paradise to crime scene, with bright red blood sprayed across the freshly-fallen snow. Two men lay dead on the sidewalk, and a third man stood in front of the mall, making sweeping motions with a handgun.

Then, another shot rang out and the man with the handgun fell to the ground. *Where did that shot come from?* Although the swirling snow reduced visibility for everyone in the area, witnesses said they saw a tall man with a hat and sunglasses put a gun back in his coat pocket and then follow the fleeing crowd into the mall.

No more shots were fired. When police arrived, they found three men dead on the ground. Two young men, later identified as members of the MS-13 gang, had been killed by the first gunshots. The third dead man, found with his handgun by his side, was linked to a rival gang called *Los Gatos*. Police suspect that he would have killed others, if he had been given the chance. He may have taken down other rival gang members or innocent people in the crowd. The carnage was cut short by one bullet from the mysterious tall man.

"Someone we are calling the 'Good Samaritan' was able to shoot the assailant and stop further bloodshed," said the county's Chief of Police on the local news that night. "We don't know who he is, but we believe he saved lives today. On behalf of Prince William County, I am grateful for his quick action and heroism in this situation."

*Good Samaritan.* Harley pondered the description as he put on his robe for worship the next day, the Second Sunday in Lent. He recalled the story of the first-century Samaritan who took pity on a man who was a victim of robbers, cleaned his wounds, bandaged him, and then took him to an inn for further recovery. Looking out his office window at the dark and swirling river to the north, he could not make the connection. *Maybe if the Samaritan had hunted down the robbers and thrashed them.* But that is not the parable that Jesus told.

"One hundred and sixty years ago, there was some shooting in Occoquan," said Harley, after clearing his throat at the beginning of his sermon. "Union troops and Confederate troops exchanged gunfire across the river." He pointed to his right, toward the water. The gloom of the day seemed to fit the Lenten season, and he was surprised by the number of people who had shown up for church. *Bad weather can fill the pews, of course. Sunny days give them plenty of other things to do.* Scanning the Sanctuary, he saw that Juan Erazo was there, looking up from the second row. Nanette Glebesman was on the aisle in the middle of the Sanctuary, a hymnal on her lap. And Andy Stackhouse was sitting by the entrance door, ready to hand a bulletin to any latecomers who might wander in.

"As we look back on the Civil War, let's consider what this conflict can teach us as we face the wars going on in our denomination, our community, and our country today. There has been a lot of vitriol in the Methodist Church in recent years, and the divisiveness in politics—both local and national—has been discouraging to us all. Shots were fired again yesterday at PW Outlets in Woodbridge, just a few miles from here. Two men were shot dead by an assailant, and then the shooter was killed by a man that some are describing as a 'Good Samaritan.' Yes, some are saying that God was *with* this man, working through him to save innocent lives." Harley paused and looked out over the congregation to gauge their reaction. He sensed that he had their attention.

"So, was God with this man? Was God on his side?" He saw a couple of people nodding. "One remarkable thing about the Civil War was that both the North and the South assumed that God was on their side. Both felt that the Lord was speaking of them when they heard the words of Isaiah, our Scripture lesson for today: 'Here is my servant, whom I uphold, my chosen, in whom my soul delights; I have put my spirit upon him.'" Recalling his conversation with Andy, Harley said, "The South, in particular, had some powerful and persuasive preachers, and they used the Bible to defend the institution of slavery. It was all right there in scripture, clear as can be. No wonder the people of the South believed that God was on their side."

After taking a sip of water, Harley continued, "The preachers of the North had to be more creative, but they too found a way to defend their cause. Some drew on the Book of Revelation, and suggested that a Northern victory might prepare the way for the coming of the Kingdom of God. Others preached that God would not allow the North to win until it took decisive steps to end slavery." Nodding to the small choir in the loft, Harley said, "Thank you, choir, for singing 'The Battle Hymn of the Republic' today. You captured the beliefs of the Union so well: *As Jesus died to make men holy, let us die to make men free.*"

Turning back to the congregation and placing his hands firmly on either side of the pulpit, Harley said, "Theological shots were being fired, from both the South and the North. And both sides were convinced that they were acting as the Lord's servant, with God right beside them. They were bringing the words of George Washington to life, a warning that had been written seventy years earlier. That's when Washington said, 'Religious controversies are always productive of more acrimony and irreconcilable hatreds than those which spring from any other cause.' Religious controversies. Acrimony. Irreconcilable hatreds. Prophetic words, don't you think? True then. True today." Harley released his grip on the pulpit and scanned the congregation, allowing the members to ponder these words from Washington.

"But then another president, Abraham Lincoln, offered the most constructive of perspectives. Lincoln said, 'My concern is not whether God is on our side; my greatest concern is to be on God's side.' He was right, wasn't he?" Harley saw Nanette smiling and nodding, which pleased him more than it should have. "That's the question that we are left with today," he said, "in the middle of our contemporary civil wars: Are we on *God's* side?"

Once again, he let the congregation sit with these words for a few moments. There was a rhythm to preaching that Harley had spent decades trying to master. A good sermon was more than words, he had learned. It was also silence. The Word of God was delivered not only by speaking, but by hearing and pondering. He needed to give the church members time to absorb what was being said.

At the same time, he did not want to lose them, so he returned to his text. "We will be on God's side if we act like the servant of the Lord in Isaiah, the one who 'will not cry or lift up his voice,' but instead 'will faithfully bring forth justice.' Those who serve the Lord have a mission to be 'a light to the nations, to open the eyes that are blind, to bring out the prisoners from the dungeon.' Christians who do these things are always going to find themselves right where they need to be—on the side of God. That's where *I* want to be. And that's where I want *you* to be." Looking at Juan and Nanette and Andy, he could tell that he was getting through to them.

Harley's pace quickened as he headed toward the finish line. "This is not a North-South issue, nor is it Right-Left, Blue-Red, Gay-Straight, Republican-Democratic. Wherever we find ourselves on the cultural-theological-political spectrum, we are challenged—when shots are being fired—to be the Lord's servant. According to Isaiah, the servant of the Lord is not loud or obnoxious, destructive or domineering. Instead, the servant works quietly and compassionately, with respect for other people, while also standing strong. 'He will not grow faint or be crushed,' predicts Isaiah, 'until he has established justice in the earth.'"

Wanting to drive his point home, Harley said, "This is a passage that should be studied by protesters from the Far Left to the Radical Right. There is a better way than waving signs and screaming insults, firing verbal shots—or bullets—at the opposition. True servants of the Lord always generate more light than heat. In fact, they are sent to be 'a light to the nations, to open the eyes that are blind, to bring out the prisoners from the dungeon.' God's servants bring light into darkness, and help people to see new ways of living together. They work for the liberation of anyone who is trapped—in poverty, in addiction, in homelessness, in loneliness, in despair. The servant of the Lord is constantly working to free the slaves, to free the oppressed." Harley was speaking with conviction, but suddenly he got the sense that he needed to ad-lib something more specific, more tied to the moment. So, he returned to the man with the gun at the outlet mall.

"So, was God on the side of the man who took down the shooter at PW Outlets? I honestly don't know. But the more important question is, 'Was he on God's side?' I think he was, if he was trying to bring forth justice. The primary role of the servant of the Lord is to 'bring forth justice'—to bring the justice of the kingdom of God into the middle of human life. We do this when we protect people who are vulnerable and in danger of being killed by others. We do this when we treat people fairly and respect their rights, seeing them as precious children of God, made in the image and likeness of God. We do this when we arrest and punish terrorists who murder innocent people. That's what it means to be the servant of the Lord. That's what it means to be on God's side. That's where *I* want to be. How about *you*?"

When he closed with an amen, he could see that Andy was nodding at the back of the room. Harley had not mentioned Karen and Jessica when he talked about terrorist murders, but almost everyone knew what he was referencing, and they sympathized. As he turned to sit down, he noticed the face of black Jesus, gazing at him from the stained-glass window. There was no nodding in agreement. Just strength and serenity in the middle of the storm.

"*Gracias, pastor,*" said Juan Erazo at the coffee hour in the church basement. The crowd was light, but there were a number of people chatting in conversation circles. Old religious art hung on the walls, some of it in dusty frames that dated to the 1950s. "You were right to call that man a Good Samaritan."

"Well, that's what the police chief said," corrected Harley.

"He was correct," nodded Juan. "He did what you said in your sermon: *Bring forth justice.*"

Harley still was not sure that the PW Outlets vigilante fit the definition of "the servant of the Lord," but he didn't want to argue with Juan. He had too much respect for him.

"Did I ever tell you about what happened in Chantilly?"

"No, I don't think so," said Harley.

"It was when I first arrived in the States," said Juan. "Long before I moved to Occoquan."

Harley quickly surveyed the room to make sure there was no one waiting to speak with him. Sensing that he was clear, he said, "Tell me."

"I lived in an apartment, worked hard, and sent as much money back to Honduras as I could. My best connection was with a family called the Wellingtons. Met them in church."

"Methodists?" asked Harley.

"Yes," said Juan. "Really good people. "They gave me steady work in their construction and real estate business. And when work at their job sites was slow, they gave me jobs around their house."

"Sounds like they really valued you."

Juan nodded. "They asked me to call them by their first names, but to me they were always *Señor* and *Señora*. I really honored them."

"Beautiful."

"Any kids?"

"Yes, two. Away at college when I was working for them."

"So, what happened?"

"One morning, I was doing some mulching in their back yard. *Señor* and *Señora* were working in the garage. I heard a car pull into the driveway. Loud rumbling. Not a car that one of their friends would drive."

"Huh," said Harley, intrigued.

"They had a four-car garage with big doors facing the driveway, and a small entrance from the back yard. I crept up to the back door to see what was going on, carrying my shovel. When I looked through the glass of the door, I could see that the garage doors were open and a lowrider was parked in the driveway. *Señor* and *Señora* were standing against the side wall. The man from the car had a gun on them."

"My God," said Harley.

"The man was very agitated, and I could hear him yelling at them. He wanted money and jewelry and said he would kill them if they didn't co-operate. *Señora* was sobbing, and *Señor* looked terrified. He said he would cooperate, but he was frozen in place. I was worried that the man would kill them even if they did cooperate."

"So, what did you do?"

"I opened the back door very quietly, and signaled for the Wellingtons to look toward the driveway. I didn't want the intruder to turn around."

"That was smart," said Harley.

"Then I moved quietly toward him, while he continued to rant at them and wave his gun."

"You must have been terrified yourself."

"Not the first time I have confronted a criminal."

"Then what?"

"When I got within striking distance, I swung the shovel as hard as I could. Split his head open and knocked him out cold."

Harley had never before heard such a story in a church coffee hour. "Did you kill him?"

"No," said Juan. "I would not have grieved if he died. But he survived. While he was unconscious on the floor, I took his gun and tied his hands behind his back with an extension cord. *Señor* called the police."

"Who was he?"

"A former employee, angry about being fired. The Wellingtons knew him, and could have identified him. That's why I believe he would have killed them after robbing them."

"What a nightmare," said Harley.

"After that, *Señora* called me their guardian angel," said Juan, smiling. "*Señor* called me *San Juan*."

"Saint John," said Harley.

"*Sí*. It was an honor."

"You deserved it," said Harley. "I like it, *San Juan*."

"Anyway," said Juan, "that's why I can relate to the Good Samaritan of PW Outlets. Sometimes justice requires violence."

Looking at a faded print of a group of children and Jesus on the wall of the social hall, Harley was not sure he could agree. But *San Juan* had a point.

# 11

# Third Month 1862

"YE SHALL HEAR OF wars and rumors of wars," said Jesus in the Gospel of Matthew: "see that ye be not troubled: for all these things must come to pass, but the end is not yet. For nation shall rise against nation, and kingdom against kingdom." The middle of Third Month 1862 brought these words to life for the people of Occoquan, as "wars and rumors of wars" made it impossible for them to avoid being alarmed. The sudden departure of Colonel Wade Hampton and his troops left them feeling defenseless and exposed. Talk of Confederate troop movements made them anxious about where hostilities might next erupt. Even Quaker residents who maintained silent sympathy for the North worried about what an invading Union Army might do to their fragile Southern town. They were trapped in the middle of a brutal conflict, state against state, region against region, nation against nation.

At the end of January, President Lincoln had ordered his military to launch aggressive actions against the Confederacy, using assets on both land and sea. Union forces had been dormant since the previous July, and the president was becoming impatient. In Northern Virginia, Lincoln wanted General McClellan to lead his army in a decisive strike against General Joseph Johnston and the Confederates in Manassas and Centreville. McClellan disagreed with the president, arguing that his army should be moved down the Potomac River and then up the Rappahannock River, with the goal of landing at Urbanna. This would put his Union forces behind the Confederates at Manassas, in a position that was on a direct line to Richmond. Lincoln was skeptical of the Urbanna plan, since it positioned McClellan between Johnston and Richmond, leaving Washington,

D.C., exposed to attack. "*My dear Sir,*" wrote Lincoln to McClellan, "You and I have distinct and different plans for a movement of the Army of the Potomac."

Before these conflicting strategies could be resolved, the Confederates took action in response to "rumors of wars." On March 5, after receiving reports from his scouts that Union troops were active, Johnston ordered the evacuation of Confederate forces from Northern Virginia. Massive warehouses at Manassas Junction were cleaned out and torched. A newly constructed military railroad was dismantled, and any large guns that could not be moved were pushed into the Potomac River. A Confederate private from Georgia wrote, "Manassas was burnt up and it was the greatest destructing I ever saw in my life."

In just four days, the evacuation was complete, including the movement of Wade Hampton's forces away from Occoquan. After a long and muddy retreat, the Confederate Army reassembled south of the Rappahannock River, and began their preparations for future engagements. Choosing not to pursue the Confederates, McClellan marched his army to Centreville and Manassas, to inspect the abandoned entrenchments. Everywhere they looked, they saw signs of a hurried retreat. They also discovered giant logs mounted in such a way that they looked like artillery, a deceptive tactic designed to convince Union scouts that Johnston's forces were much stronger than they were. This fake artillery was known as "Quaker guns."

Yes, *Quaker guns.* A term that Samuel Bagley both loved and hated.

Since the Confederate retreat nullified the Urbanna plan, McClellan quickly devised a new strategy that focused on attacking Richmond. With Lincoln's approval, McClellan began the Peninsula Campaign, which involved the moving of the Army of the Potomac by ship, down the Potomac River to the Chesapeake Bay to Fort Monroe, located in the city of Hampton, Virginia. Once on land, the army would march up the peninsula that was bordered by the York River and the James River, bypassing the Confederate lines. McClellan hoped that by moving with speed from the east, he and his troops would be able to beat Johnston and the Confederates to Richmond. There, he would force a battle.

On March 14, McClellan addressed his soldiers from the headquarters of the Army of the Potomac in Fairfax Court House, Virginia. "For a long time I have kept you inactive," he said, "but not without a purpose; you were to be disciplined, armed and instructed; the formidable artillery you now have, had to be created . . . I have held you back that you might give the death-blow to the rebellion that has distracted our once happy country." The moment for action had arrived, he told them; it was time to move to the battlefield "to gain success with the least possible loss." Saying that he loved them from the depths of his heart, he now demanded of them "heroic exertions, rapid and long marches" and "desperate combats." Confident in the righteousness of his cause, he proclaimed, "God smiles upon us, victory attends us, yet I would not have you think that our aim is to be attained without a manly struggle."

McClellan was anxious to avoid future criticism from Congress and the press. At that moment, they were blasting him for allowing Johnston's forces to slip away unnoticed from Northern Virginia, and for falling victim to the ruse of the harmless Quaker guns. A satirical poem called "Tardy George" had been making the rounds, one which challenged the general to stop planning and start fighting. "*Is the whole matter too heavy a charge?*" it asked. "*What are you waiting for, tardy George?*" So, in the middle of March, the race to Richmond began.

Oddly enough, the opposing generals McClellan and Johnston were good friends, having served together in a cavalry regiment in Kansas before the Civil War. This regiment had been charged with preserving the peace in a territory being torn apart by clashes between free-state and pro-slavery citizens. Now, there was no peace to be preserved. *Child and father ranged for strife, / Brother seeking brother's life!*

"Nation shall rise against nation, and kingdom against kingdom," said the jowly priest at Trinity Episcopal Church. "Our Lord predicted it, and we must expect it."

Abigail sat quietly in the polished oak pews of the whitewashed wooden church, located outside the Town of Occoquan on the road that ran south to Richmond. Sunlight streamed in through the windows, glimmering off motes of dust that floated effortlessly through the air, making the entire world feel very fragile. Abigail was wedged uncomfortably between her mother and her brother, while her father stood like a sentry at the back, serving alongside three other ushers. All were dressed in their finest clothes, with Abigail wearing a hoop skirt covered with printed wool and silk braid. "We should be thankful," said the priest, "that so many Virginia men have risen to defend our Commonwealth. Some are young and unmarried, but many are the heads of their families. What a sacrifice they are making, following a Lord who came not to be served, but to serve!"

Although the church was small, it had seating for about one hundred on the first level, and a balcony that wrapped around three sides of the sanctuary and seated another fifty. The priest was speaking directly to the people on the first level, all of whom were white. Looking down from the balcony were a handful of others, all black. The balcony was reserved for the enslaved people who accompanied their owners to worship on Sunday mornings, resulting in a thoroughly segregated service of worship.

"A number of you have sent members of your family to serve in this noble cause," said the priest, causing Bushrod to turn his head and raise his eyebrows at his mother. Abigail responded by punching him in the thigh. "You have not allowed your wealth or your social status to deter you. You know how important it is for everyone to play a role, and to protect the property that is our gift from God."

Abigail looked up to the balcony when the priest said these words, and met the gaze of an enslaved girl who was about her age. *When he said "property,"* Abigail wondered, *was he talking about her?*

"It is not only men who are serving," said the priest. "Fine women like you are working at home, and in the fields, and in mills, and even in factories. All are supporting the cause." He paused to cough, which caused the saggy flesh of his cheeks and jaws to shake. "Do you know the story of the Cary cousins of Richmond?" He looked around for a response, and saw a couple of nods. "Three fine women: Constance, Hettie, and Jenny Cary. They responded to the call of a Confederate quartermaster to do an important piece of sewing."

Although Abigail often found herself bored in church, she perked up when the priest began to tell stories. "Last summer, at the Battle of Manassas, the smoke from gunfire was so thick that our soldiers could not tell the difference between friends and foes. So, two of our fine generals—Joseph Johnston and Pierre Beauregard—met at Fairfax Court House to design a distinctive war flag. You know it well: A blue X shape on a field of red, with white stars representing each state in our glorious Confederacy."

This square flag was used only on the field of battle, so Abigail had never seen one flying in Occoquan. But she had looked at pictures in the newspaper, and had heard stories about the pride that soldiers felt as they fought beneath it. The priest continued, "After Johnston and Beauregard approved the design, a quartermaster made arrangements with the Cary cousins to sew the first battle flags. They were members of a Baltimore family that had taken refuge in Richmond, wanting to support the Confederacy. They sewed the first silk battle flags and gave them to the generals. Hetty's flag went to General Johnston, and Jenny's flag went to General Beauregard. These women should be proud of their work, especially now that Johnston's army and Beauregard's army are combining into a new Army of Northern Virginia. May God bless this army with success!"

Abigail had heard the battle flag described as "Beauregard's flag," so she began to wonder why it was not called "Johnston's flag." *Maybe his men do not respect him.* A few days earlier, Abigail had heard a customer at the family store call General Johnston a disparaging name: "Retreatin' Joe."

"All of these efforts, by men and women alike, are intended to support our way of life," said the priest. "This way of life is not an earthly institution, but is ordained by God and supported by Holy Scripture. 'Servants, be subject to your masters with all fear,' says the apostle Peter. 'Servants, be obedient to them that are your masters according to the flesh,' says his fellow apostle Paul. Be obedient 'with fear and trembling, in singleness of your heart, as unto Christ.'" Looking up to the balcony for the first time, the priest repeated the last phrase, "in singleness of your heart, as unto Christ."

Looking around, Abigail saw smiles on the faces of some of her fellow white parishioners, but only stoney stares from the blacks in the balcony. Then, knowing that the hour was drawing to a close, the priest concluded his message by saying, "The Confederate States of America is a Christian nation. As such, we have a mission to bring people to Christ. This includes the servants entrusted to our care." Abigail had never heard this particular point made in a sermon before.

"They have been victims of a godless paganism," said the priest, "one that lies at the heart of their African homeland. Brothers and sisters, we have a sacred duty to share the Gospel with them." A few white parishioners nodded, but not all. "I ask you not to withhold the good news of Jesus from your servants. Allow them to hear the stories of the Bible. Allow them to pray. Lead them to faith, as a parent leads a child. If we are to be victorious in the present struggle, we will need the blessing of Almighty God. And to receive God's favor, we will have to do everything we can to treat our servants well. It is your Christian duty, my friends, to bring them to a saving faith in Jesus Christ."

Needing some fresh air after church, Abigail put on a wool jacket and went for a walk up the hill that overlooked the Town of Occoquan. Her parents would not allow her to walk alone, so they always sent Bushrod to be her chaperone. But since the two siblings had no real desire to spend their free time together, they had come to an agreement: As soon as they passed the end of Commerce Street, they would go their separate ways and enjoy a period of time alone. When the church bell rang at three o'clock, they would rendezvous and return home together. Over the course of numerous Sunday afternoons, their plan had worked perfectly, allowing each of them to enjoy some solitude.

Abigail strolled up the hill that overlooked the Town of Occoquan, gazing at the dark clouds that were rolling in from the west. For a while, the clouds and the sun seemed to be locked in a celestial struggle, with the clouds trying to blanket the sun and the sun attempting to burn off the clouds. Strong beams of light would shoot through the clouds, casting sharp shadows on the ground, and then the clouds would blot out the sun, causing a heavily filtered sunlight to cover the landscape. By the time Abigail reached the crest of the hill, the clouds were winning the contest and making everything look very dull and muted all around her.

The Quaker burial ground looked especially lifeless in the afternoon gloom. Abigail walked among the tombstones, reading the family names that were so familiar to her and to the residents of the town: Farlow, Cadwallader, Milhous, Trueblood, Farlow, Sharpless, Wilbur, and finally . . . Bagley. Death had previously seemed so distant to her, but no longer. She paused and looked at the headstone carved for the father of William and Samuel, wondering how she and her family would manage to survive without their father. Looking at the stone, she a felt a hollowness within her, one that was a strange and unexpected combination of emptiness and ache. *How did they do it*, she wondered, *how did William and Samuel find their way?* She had been a child when Mr. Bagley died, and she did not remember very much about him. She had seen him on Mill Street, walking with his wife, and standing at the counter in their store, talking with her father. He was tall like Samuel, but he had blond hair and blue eyes like William. Yes, now she remembered: The two men were speaking quietly and respectfully. Two fathers. Two husbands. Two citizens of Occoquan. And now only one of them was alive.

"Abigail?" said a voice from behind her. She thought she knew the voice. *William?*

Spinning around, she saw Samuel, wearing a broad-brimmed felt hat and carrying a long walking stick. "Samuel," she said, trying not to sound disappointed. "You surprised me."

"Pardon me," he said, blushing. "I did not mean to startle thee."

"Think nothing of it. You are excused, of course."

"I thank thee."

"What brings you here today?" she asked. Abigail looked mouselike, as usual, but was summoning the courage to speak.

"I have been walking the woods," he said. "Enjoying the peace of First Day."

"First Day?"

"You call it Sunday."

"I see," she said. "Yes, it is peaceful today. So much quieter since the soldiers departed."

"Indeed," said Samuel.

Suddenly self-conscious about where she was standing, she said, "This is your father's grave, is it not?"

"Yes. I like to stop here and remember him."

Abigail did not know what to say. Such profound loss had not intruded on her nineteen years of life. Searching for words, she finally said, "I am very sorry."

"Thank thee," said Samuel. Then, with a smile, he said, "My father had blond hair, like thee."

Now it was Abigail's turn to blush. "And like your brother," she said.

"Yes, he and my father shared that trait. My mother and I are alike with our brown hair."

"You know my brother and my father," she said: "The same fiery red!"

"Bushrod is certainly fiery," said Samuel.

"He is a fighter," she admitted. "Indeed, he is. But so is your brother."

Samuel put a hand to his chin, thought for a moment, and then said, "Yes, perhaps. We do not know."

"Many townspeople speak of highly of him."

"No doubt," said Samuel. "But that sentiment is not found in the Society of Friends."

"You *should* be proud of him," said Abigail, feeling emboldened. "He is fighting for a good cause."

Again, Samuel was slow to respond. He did not want to create discord with the Washington family, especially after his altercation with Bushrod. "I am not sure about that," he said, carefully. "Thou art aware, no doubt, that many people in Virginia wanted to remain in the Union, at least at first."

"Yes, I have heard that."

"When Virginia seceded," said Samuel, "there was danger that Maryland would do the same."

"Is that true?"

"Yes. The state was divided between the North and the South. Lincoln feared that Washington would be surrounded by enemy states. Do you know what he did?"

"No, I do not."

"He put Maryland's pro-slavery leaders in jail. Without trial."

"The tyrant!" said Abigail, echoing words she had heard in the family store. "That is unjust."

"Perhaps," said Samuel, "but it saved the capital."

"What are you trying to say?" Abigail did not consider Samuel to be as attractive as William, but she was finding herself intrigued by this debate. He clearly had a sharp mind.

"Simply that it is difficult, in this present conflict, to identify a cause that is nothing but good." Samuel had his own strong feelings about slavery, but he was not ready to share them with a member of a slave-owning family.

"Where do you stand?" asked Abigail, wanting to know more.

"On what?"

"On the war," she said. "My priest said that we must defend our state."

"Against what?" Samuel said. He was enjoying the sparring as well.

"Northern aggression," said Abigail.

"That is what many say," admitted Samuel, "but I do not know it to be true."

"You do not *know* it?" said Abigail, showing a flash of her brother's fire. "Did you not see what *Stepping Stones* did?"

"Yes, of course I did," said Samuel. "But the Union is trying to defend its capital."

"And you support them?"

"I would not say that," said Samuel, weighing his words carefully. "I cannot support aggressive action by either side." He thought of General McClellan, who had put enormous effort into defending the capital through the building of fortifications. Now, the general was being criticized for his failure to attack. Samuel was finding himself sympathetic to defensive actions, but not offensive actions. Especially since his brother was in the line of fire.

"So, whose side are you on?" said Abigail.

*I want to be on your side,* he thought, captivated by her beauty and her fire. But he did not say this. Instead, after pausing for a moment, he said, "On the side of peace."

At that moment, the church bell tolled three times.

# 12

## March 2022

A MAN IN A Hardee hat and long grey coat knocked on the door of a condominium unit on the rocky ridge overlooking the Town of Occoquan. He had cavalry insignia on his uniform, a sword at his side, and a holster on his belt. Rain was falling and temperatures were in the fifties, one week after an unexpected snowfall had briefly plunged the area back into winter. His coat and hat were appropriate coverings for that particular Saturday morning, but he looked like he belonged in March of 1862 instead of March of 2022.

"May I help you?" asked the young woman at the door.

"I'm Andy Stackhouse, one of your neighbors," he said. "Pardon the outfit. I'm dressed for this afternoon's Blue and Grey Day, over in Occoquan Regional Park."

"Blue and Grey Day," she said. "What's that?"

"A Civil War re-enactment," he said. "We get together and recreate what happened here at Occoquan, one hundred and sixty years ago. Wade Hampton's encampment. The volley of shots between Union and Confederate forces across the river. The capture of Union spies by the Night Riders."

"Didn't know about that," said the woman.

"I'm a Night Rider," said Andy.

"Okay," she said, slowly edging back into her house.

"But I'm not here to talk about the Civil War," said Andy, sensing that he was losing her attention. "I'm circulating a petition. I think our schools should not include a particular book in their libraries. Maybe you have heard of it? *Gayboy*?" Reaching into the large pocket of his grey coat, he pulled out a copy.

"Yes, I've heard of it," said the woman.

"And what do think?"

"I think it's fine."

"You don't think it is inappropriate for students?"

"No," she said.

"Really?" he said. "You believe middle school students should read it?"

"Yes," she said. "That's when kids begin to figure these things out."

"But . . ."

"Thanks for stopping by," said the woman, closing the door.

Andy put the book back in his pocket. *Can't win 'em all.* He had found that his Night Riders uniform was a good conversation-starter with many of his neighbors, and when wearing it he had succeeded in acquiring a number of signatures on his petition. But it had not helped with this particular woman. *Maybe someday she'll see the light.* Looking up at the sky, he hoped that the sun would come out and the weather would warm up for the afternoon's Blue and Grey Day.

Another door was knocked on that morning, on the third floor of the Gristmill Luxury Apartments. Don Abad opened the door and welcomed Abdul Ali into his home. The two had an appointment to talk about the one-bedroom unit that Don had recently leased.

"Thank you for agreeing to meet, Mr. Abad," said Abdul. As he entered, he noticed that the living room was sparsely furnished, with nothing hanging on the walls. A sliding glass door opened to a small balcony, with a panoramic view of the river.

"Please, call me Don," said the man.

"And I go by Abdul."

"Coffee?"

"No, thank you."

"Please, have a seat." The only furniture in the living room was a small couch, coffee table, and armchair—all made of tubular steel and red cushions. Abdul sat on the couch and Don in the armchair. Looking across the room, Abdul could see the dining area, the kitchen, and the door to the bedroom. A small round table sat under a chandelier in the dining area, with a single straight-back chair.

"I am visiting with an assortment of new residents," said Abdul, "to see if Gristmill is meeting their needs." He was wearing a blue warm-up jacket that was being strained by his enormous biceps. Reaching into a side pocket, he pulled out a small notebook and a black pen.

"I'm happy," said Don, stroking the chin of his thin face. Abdul was struck by how blond the man's hair was—a stark contrast to his brown eyes—and he wondered how he got his scar. "The appliances are top notch, the kitchen and bathroom fixtures are great, and the view . . . well, as you can see, it is spectacular. Especially on a sunny day."

"Glad to hear it," said Abdul, making a few notes. "How about the quality of construction?"

"Aside from a few nail pops in the drywall, just fine," said Don. "And your maintenance man stopped by to fix them soon after I reported them."

"Was the painting done correctly, and the color what you requested?"

"Yes," said Don. Then, sweeping his hand toward the empty ivory-colored walls, he said, "But you can see that my tastes are simple."

"Mind if I look around?" asked Abdul.

"No problem," said Don, motioning him toward the bedroom.

Abdul poked his head into the room and saw a computer workstation, a single bed, and a dresser. "How's the wi-fi?" he asked.

"Strong," said Don.

They returned to the main room and stepped into the kitchen. Abdul ran his fingers across the countertop and noticed that the place was spot-less. Then they stepped back into the living room and Abdul opened the sliding glass door to make sure that it was operating smoothly. As he did, a blast of moist air came into the room. "Door is sliding nicely," said Abdul, "but I'll keep it closed because of the rain."

"I look forward to using the balcony this spring," said Don.

"Should be nice."

"I've stepped out a few times, but the weather has not been cooperative."

"I agree," said Abdul. "Have you been able to get out and walk?"

"A lot," said Don. "I enjoy the loop that goes over the pedestrian bridge, up the shoreline, and then back across the concrete bridge." Abdul nodded. "I also like walking in town, looking at the mixture of old and new."

"Occoquan has character," said Abdul.

"I just wish some of the neglected buildings would be torn down and replaced," said Don.

Abdul smiled and said, "As a developer, I'm working on it."

"I've got nothing against a historic building," said Don, "one that is well-maintained and put to good use. But some of these old buildings, with peeling paint and rotting windows . . . they seem to get very little use. They need to go!"

"I would have to agree," said Abdul.

"And that Riverside Church?" said Don. "What good is it?" He figured that a Muslim would agree with him. "I see people in there one day a week, at most."

"The church does have a congregation," said Abdul, not wanting to disclose his own interest in the space.

"But they will probably die soon," said Don. "They *should* die. Survival of the fittest."

With that, Abdul put away his pen and notebook. "Thank you, Mr. Abad," he said, taking a step toward the door. "I think I have everything I need. I am glad that you are so happy at Gristmill." He left the apartment wondering if Riverside Church was really so close to death. If so, he could turn the whole building into a mosque.

Having failed to connect with Nanette Glebesman after worship on Sunday, Harley called her at home and asked if he could come to her apartment for a visit. She responded by saying that she would be happy to have him over, any time, but she would prefer to get together for dinner on Saturday night. Harley was delighted by the offer, and found his excitement growing throughout the week. On Saturday evening, he gave himself plenty of time to walk the short distance from his house to the wine bar on Mill Street. As he walked down his wrought-iron stairs, he noticed that the Star Magnolia in front of his townhouse was in full bloom, and that the pear trees along the street were full of delicate white blossoms, bright against the leafless brown branches. The air was warm and there was fragrance all around. *This is not a date, is it? No, cannot be a date. A pastoral visit.*

Date or not, he was thrilled to see Nanette walking east on Mill Street, her long blond hair bouncing as she moved along the brick sidewalk. She had a big smile on her face, and her petite body was covered by a long purple coat. "Good evening, pastor," she said, sticking out her hand for a shake.

"Please, call me Harley," he said, taking her hand.

"Okay, Harley. So glad you were available."

"Me too," he said. "And aren't you happy the rain has stopped?"

"Absolutely," she said. "I thought about bringing an umbrella, but then said 'no.' I like to take chances!"

"Live dangerously," said Harley with a smile.

After being seated, they each ordered a glass of pinot noir. Harley was dressed in a pink dress shirt with open collar, a blue blazer, and gray pants. Nanette was wearing a red sweater, pleated black skirt, and black tights. Dangling silver earrings framed her slender face. Harley thought she looked terrific.

"I saw on the church website that you went to Duke," she said.

"Blue Devils!" he said, raising his glass.

"Well, I went to Clemson, so I guess we are enemies."

"At least you didn't go to Carolina," he said.

"ACC rivalries are intense."

"You always kill us in football," said Harley, "but we usually get you back during basketball season."

"Got us twice this year," she sighed.

"So, where were you before Occoquan?" Harley asked.

"Seattle," she said. "Twenty-five years, working in human resources. Made my way through a series of tech companies and ended up at Amazon. You've heard of it, right?" she said with a wink.

"Think so," said Harley.

"They brought me here to the new East Coast headquarters."

"HQ2," said Harley, aware of the lingo for the facility.

"Indeed," said Nanette.

"Seattle is nice," said Harley. "Do you miss it?"

"Not really," she said. "I grew up in South Carolina, so I'm an East-Coaster at heart." After taking a sip of wine she added, "Also, I had a marriage go bad there."

"I'm sorry," said Harley, hoping he had not hit a nerve. He gave her a moment to say more, but she did not seem to want to go deeper.

"What brought *you* here?" asked Nanette.

"My bishop," said Harley. "I was serving a big church in Sterling, but I was not doing well. Really spiraling down. I lost my wife and daughter in a terrorist attack."

"Oh, God, no," said Nanette, reaching a hand across the table. "That is the absolute worst." No one had mentioned this tragedy to her.

"Yes, it was," Harley nodded. "They were killed by nail bombs in the Brussels airport. A nightmare." Nanette had no words, so she squeezed his hand. "My grief and anger were doing no one any good," Harley said, "including myself." *My rage distracted me when I tried to write sermons at church, made me short-tempered in lines at the grocery store, and took me to very dark places when I was home alone at night. The memories of that period were vivid, but he kept them to himself. I started drinking alone in a recliner at the end of the day, quickly progressing from one drink a night to four. I would nod off in the recliner and be awakened by nightmares. In one, I fell into a hellish pit and found myself trapped in ice, gnawing on the head of one of the terrorists who destroyed my family.*

Harley felt the warmth of Nanette's hand on his, and it was soothing. But he realized that his rush of memories had created an awkward silence. "So," he said, "my bishop sent me here to heal and to recover."

"And, how is it going?" she asked.

"Pretty well, I think."

At that point, Andy Stackhouse and his wife approached the table, causing Nanette to retract her hand. "Good evening, Harley," he said. Then, turning to Nanette, he said, "I think I've seen you in church."

"Nanette Glebesman," she said, offering her hand for a shake. "You are an usher, correct?"

"That's right," he said, sounding pleased to be recognized. "Andy Stackhouse, and this is my wife, Jean."

"Very nice to meet you," said Nanette.

"Look, we don't want to interrupt you," said Andy, "but I heard something today that will interest you, Harley. I was at the dig site in River Mill Park. You know they have been excavating the grave in the house, right?"

"Yes," said Harley. Turning to Nanette, he said, "It's an old Quaker house."

"Well, you will not believe this," said Andy. "The human remains are covered in what seems to be a uniform. It has Confederate buttons. Kind of odd for a Quaker home. But here is the shocker: The remains also contain a Union challenge coin, with the initials G.B.McC."

"What could that mean?" asked Harley.

"Hard to say for sure," said Andy. "But the initials suggest a connection to the Union General, George Brinton McClellan."

"Huh," said Harley, wondering why a Southern soldier would have a Northern general's coin.

At that moment, a waitress approached the table to take the dinner order for Harley and Nanette. "Andy, we should go," said his wife Jean, "and let them eat in peace."

"I'm starting to read some letters at the Library of Congress," said Andy, reluctantly starting to move. "Civil War letters, written *to* people in Occoquan, or written *by* people in Occoquan. I'll let you know what I find." At that point, Jean was actively pulling him away.

"Archaeology," said Nanette, after they placed their order. "That's interesting stuff." Harley agreed, and told her that he had done a fair amount of digging while a student at Duke Divinity School, first in the Galilean city of Sepphoris and then in the Honduran city of Copán Ruinas. The conversation took off, and they chatted without interruption for over an hour, talking about the travels they had done and the historical sites they had visited. Although Nanette was not a student of archaeology, Harley discovered that she had traveled much of the world and was intensely curious about ancient civilizations. She peppered him with so many questions that his food went cold before he could finish it. But he did not mind a bit.

"You know what Agatha Christie said about archaeologists, don't you?" Nanette asked as they sipped an after-dinner drink. She was a big fan of Christie's mysteries.

"No, I don't," said Harley.

"An archaeologist is the best husband a woman can have. The older she gets, the more interested he is in her." Harley laughed and wondered, *is she flirting?*

The check arrived and Nanette grabbed it. "This is on me." Harley could see that the bill was for one hundred and thirty dollars, and Nanette paid with two hundred-dollar bills.

The waitress picked up the check and said, "I'll be back with your change."

Nanette waived her off and said, "Keep it."

*Wow,* thought Harley, *a seventy-dollar tip.*

"Thank you," said the waitress. "I really appreciate it." She had heard rumors about "No-Change Nanette," but this was her first encounter.

Harley helped Nanette to put on her long purple coat, and they walked out of the restaurant together. He did not want the evening to end. Standing together on the sidewalk, he said, "Thank you for that delicious dinner."

"You are welcome. I enjoyed it."

"And I hope you don't mind me asking you something," he said. "I've gotten a little more direct in my old age."

"That's good," she said. Then, drawing out the words with her Low-country accent, she added, "I . . . *think.*"

"I could not help but notice that you left a very generous tip."

She smiled and said, "Are you getting into my business, pastor?"

"I guess so," Harley said. "But I was impressed. Why did you do that?"

After a brief pause, she said, "A tip like that is a small amount to me, but a big amount to a service worker. I guess I like to spread a little joy."

"I think you succeeded."

"I decided a couple of years ago to always tip my change," she said, "and never think twice about it. At the start of the pandemic, when things were so stressful and crazy, I figured one thing I could do, very easily, was be generous."

"It's a great thing," said Harley, remembering that her generosity was being extended to Riverside Church as well.

"Plus, it makes me happy," she said. "I have discovered that there are two keys to happiness for me: Generosity and curiosity."

"Well, you are certainly showing both," he said. "I could barely keep up with your questions tonight!"

"Get used to it, Harley," she said. "I have lots of them!" With that, she reached out with both arms and gave him a hug. "Better say good-night," she said. "You've got to preach in the morning."

On Monday, temperatures were in the sixties and spring was in the air. Sunday worship had been a delight for Harley, especially with Nanette in the congregation, and recollections of their dinner had lifted his spirits throughout the day. *Maybe it was a date,* he thought to himself. *It certainly felt like a date. Nothing wrong with that.*

But the joy of the weekend was snuffed out when he met Leah Silverman for coffee at Occoquan's Grindhouse on Monday morning. As Harley approached their table, Leah asked, "How are you after the attack on Father Black?"

Falling heavily into a seat, he asked, "What are you talking about?"

"I'm sorry," she said, putting an arm on his shoulder. "I assumed you had heard."

"What happened?" said Harley. Black was Harley's running buddy, and the two had worked together on immigration issues.

"He was stabbed last night."

"God, no," said Harley.

"I had some police at the clinic today, and they filled me in," said Leah. "Last night was a Lenten supper at Sacred Heart. A stranger arrived and was welcomed, of course. After the meal, he asked if he could talk with Father Black. The two went to his office. Parishioners said that he was still there when they finished cleaning up and went home."

"Does anyone know what happened?"

"Not exactly. A custodian heard a crashing sound at about nine o'clock, and went to the office to see if there was a problem. He knocked on the door and the stranger rushed out, pushing past him. The custodian saw blood on the man, spotted the priest on the floor, and immediately called nine-one-one."

"Was he hurt badly?"

"Yes, multiple stab wounds," said Leah. "But he's in the hospital, and expected to recover. The police caught the stranger within an hour, walking down Route One with blood on his hands."

"Damn it," said Harley.

"The attacker might have been on drugs. Might have been psychotic. Stabbed Father Black with his own letter opener."

"What a nightmare."

"A trauma for our whole community," said Leah. "A good man, attacked while doing God's work."

"I saw him just a little while ago."

"Harley," said Leah, "we need to make sure that you stay safe."

"What do you mean?"

"Well, you spend a lot of your time alone at church. You see strangers, as Father Black did. You need some kind of an emergency alert."

"I can always call nine-one-one," said Harley.

"Maybe," said Leah. "But what if a person in your office was disturbed, or violent, or angry? They might prevent you from making such a call. How about if you and I have a code?"

"Okay, say more."

"The police have codes. I've learned some when they bring patients to my clinic. Ten-four means 'okay.'"

"Yeah, I've heard that one," said Harley.

"Ten-sixteen is a domestic disturbance. We get a lot of those." Leah pulled out her smartphone and pulled up a list of all of the police codes. Then she said, "Maybe you and I should use ten-thirty-three as our code. That's for an emergency."

"How would it work?"

"Well, you could just text me the number thirty-three. I would know you were in trouble and would call the police."

"Thirty-three. Easy to remember. The age that Jesus was when he died on the cross."

"Don't want you to end up like that," said Leah, gazing down at her phone. "Hey, look at this. Convenient that the numbers are on the top of the keyboard."

"Okay. But how would you know where I am? Maybe I wouldn't be in my office."

"If you allow me," said Leah, "I can track the location of your phone." Harley handed his phone to her, and she made some changes to the settings. "And you can track mine as well," she said. "If either of us gets in trouble, we'll text thirty-three and the other can find us and send help."

"Unless we don't have our cell phones."

"Then," said Leah, "we're out of luck."

Harley took back his phone, slipped it into his pocket, and then reached across the table.

At that moment, Nanette walked by the Grindhouse, looked in the window, and saw Harley holding hands with a woman she had never seen before.

# 13

## Spring 1862

THE FIRST DAY OF spring arrived damp and chilly on the twentieth day of March, 1862. On the Virginia Peninsula, Julius Alexander Robbins was serving as a Confederate soldier in the Army of the Peninsula, wondering when the fighting would begin. About twelve months earlier, he had left his law practice in Selma, Alabama, but he had not yet seen any military action. Waiting to engage with Union forces on the Peninsula, he sat down and put pen to paper in a letter to his cousin Anna.

"We were very near the recent naval battle in Hampton Roads," he wrote, "but were not where we could see the fight; we, however, heard all the guns and I heard very distinctly the explosion when the *Congress* blew up. It is said, Napoleon maintained always that Providence was on the side of the heaviest artillery but I am inclined to believe more that Providence is on the side of *our* boat." Like the priest at Abigail's church, Robbins believed that God's will was being done through service to the Confederacy.

"Most of the troops on the Peninsula are now down at Bethel four miles below here & 20 below Yorktown," he wrote. "Our Regiment went down yesterday morning without any tents. I rode down there and back today—It would amuse you to see the arrangements the soldiers were making to sleep; the weather is wet and cold. They take a common blanket and stretch it over a little pole set up on forks two feet high and then make a little ridge just large enough for the soldier to creep into and roll himself up in another blanket. The arrangement looked to me like a poor one but they told me they were able to keep tolerably dry in this way, and rest well."

Like many Southern soldiers, Robbins had a slave with him. "I have a very sick servant here and on this account I got permission from Col Winston to come up to camp and thus I am comfortably by my fire in my cabin here at our winter quarters. I otherwise would be down at Bethel roughing it with the rest of them." The Confederate Army required owners to lend their slaves to the military, so that they could work as personal servants, cooks, butchers, and blacksmiths. They dug trenches, labored at arsenals, and mined potassium nitrate to make gunpowder. Any money they earned—sixty cents, for example, the daily wage for a cook—would go their masters. In many ways, enslaved laborers were the backbone of the Confederate war effort.

Robbins left his wife and two children when he joined the army, and in March 1862 they were living in Western North Carolina with his father. "It is terribly hard to be so long separated from my precious wife and children," he wrote to Anna, "but I had rather bear it all than submit. Notwithstanding our late reverses I still feel cheerful and hopeful and cannot sustain the idea for a moment that we will ever be conquered. The sunshine of secession never sets in my soul: and, I hope, our country will be purified by the fiery furnace we are passing through."

*The sunshine of secession never sets in my soul.*

A different kind of sunshine was emerging in Occoquan on that particular Thursday afternoon. After a rainy week, the sun had finally driven away the clouds and begun to cast its bright light on the muddy streets and leafless tress of the town. The air was still cold, but the sunshine felt warm on Abigail Washington's face as she walked to Merchants' Mill, carrying a lunch for her brother. She expected to see Samuel, which made her think of William, who had not yet returned from the army on leave. *What is taking him so long? His letter said mid-March.* She was anxious to see his big smile and bright blue eyes under his mop of blond hair, and she looked forward to talking with him about what he had seen and heard in Richmond. As she walked along Mill Street, she noticed that a few pale pink cherry blossoms had appeared on the trees that lined Mill Street, and these blooms gave her a feeling of hope. She began to skip down the street, swinging the bag that contained a meal of cornbread, dried meat, and cheese.

"Abigail Washington," said Samuel, when she pulled open the heavy wooden door of the gristmill, "how art thou?"

"Very well, Samuel Bagley," she said with a smile, mimicking his Quaker practice of using first and last names.

"I am happy to see thee," he said.

"She is here for me," said Bushrod, coming up from behind Samuel. "She has my lunch."

"Thou art fortunate," said Samuel, "to have such a devoted sister." Abigail blushed.

"She plays her part," said Bushrod, taking the bag from his sister.

"I carry my own lunch," said Samuel, sitting down on a bag of corn in the storeroom. "Abigail, will you join us?"

"I do not have a lunch."

"I have more than enough for thee and me," said Samuel, opening his own lunch sack.

"She usually eats at home," said Bushrod, "with our parents."

"I understand," said Samuel. "But perhaps she would like to try something new."

"Lunch in a gristmill?" said Bushrod, looking around at the rough industrial space.

"As I said, something new."

"I would be delighted, Samuel Bagley," said Abigail.

"Then, let me make thee comfortable," said Samuel, arranging several small bags of corn to make a seat for her. "Welcome to our dining room."

She smiled, took a seat, and said, "Thank you." Bushrod looked unimpressed.

"Wouldst thou like a piece of bread and a slice of cheese?" Samuel asked her, giving her a napkin for her lap.

"Yes, please," she said.

"And some dried fruit?"

"Thank you."

After sharing his food, Samuel returned to his corn bag seat. Bushrod sat on another, and the three began to eat. "I wish I had been down in Hampton Roads to see the fight," said Bushrod.

Samuel nodded as he was chewing, then swallowed and said, "First battle of iron-covered warships. That is all that people are talking about."

"Our ironclad *Virginia* was able to destroy two Union ships, *Congress* and *Cumberland*," said Bushrod. "What a conquest!"

"Then the *Monitor* arrived," said Samuel, "the Union's ironclad."

"They fought for three hours," said Bushrod, "and neither could prevail."

"The blockade of Hampton remained in place," said Samuel.

"Unfortunately, yes," said Bushrod, "for now."

"So, why does this blockade matter?" asked Abigail.

"Trade," said Samuel. "It prevents merchant ships from reaching Norfolk and Richmond."

"We will find a way," said Bushrod, with confidence. "The *Virginia* will be repaired. She will sail again."

"Speaking of battles," said Samuel, after taking a bite of his bread. "I hear that there has been fresh fighting in North Carolina."

"Yes," said Bushrod. "Sadly, it has not advanced our cause. Union troops have now captured two sites along the coast, Roanoke Island and New Berne." Samuel was pleased to hear this, but kept his feelings to himself.

"Samuel," said Abigail, wanting to change the subject, "why do you Quakers say 'thee' and 'thou'?"

Samuel chewed a piece of bread for a few seconds, thinking. Then he replied, "We do not show favoritism."

"What do you mean by that?" asked Bushrod.

"All people are equal in Quaker eyes," said Samuel, "as in the eyes of God. We make no distinctions between people based on social rank or wealth or education."

"But what does that have to do with 'thee' and 'thou'?" asked Abigail.

"Thou mayest not be aware," said Samuel, "but the word 'you' was once reserved for people of high class. Back in England, if a poor man approached a rich man, he would say 'you' to him. But the rich man would say 'thou' to the poor man."

"That sounds odd," said Bushrod.

"Yes, I know," said Samuel. "The non-Quakers of Occoquan say 'you' to everyone."

"It is you Quakers who do not speak correctly," Bushrod said.

"To thine ears, it sounds odd," said Samuel. "But let me explain. We 'thee' and 'thou' everyone because we believe that everyone is equal. Everyone is a child of God. No one is higher or lower than anyone else."

"Even a slave?" asked Bushrod.

"Even a slave," said Samuel. "We do not see slaves, only people."

"That is ridiculous," snorted Bushrod.

"Let him speak," said Abigail.

"Our founder was a man named George Fox," said Samuel. "He said that God sent him forth to 'thee' and 'thou' all men and women, without any respect to rich or poor, great or small."

"I like that," said Abigail.

"Wrong," said Bushrod. "God has made people rich and poor, free and slave, for a reason. That's what our priest says, and I believe it."

"Thou art welcome to believe that," said Samuel, "but we disagree."

"And why will you not fight?" asked Abigail. "My father says you are . . . what? . . . *pacificists?*"

"Indeed," said Samuel. "We believe that war and conflict are against God's wishes."

"Even when we have to defend ourselves against a voracious and plundering invader?" said Bushrod. "Even when we have to protect our families and our homes?"

"Yes, even then," said Samuel, although he found himself sympathetic to defensive actions. "We believe that war causes more problems than it solves."

"Your brother William has gone to war," said Bushrod. "He is entering the fiery furnace that will purify us, like a refining fire."

"Perhaps," said Samuel, not really interested in what Bushrod was saying. He was looking at Abigail, and he saw her face light up when Bushrod spoke of William. Embarrassed, he looked down at the floor and said, "We look forward to seeing him and learning more. Soon, I hope."

"Me too," said Abigail. An unexpected and unwanted feeling of jealousy came over Samuel.

"I support what William is doing," said Bushrod. "He is fighting to defend our town, our state, and our way of life. But most of you Quakers: You live in a fantasy world, not the real one."

"Dost thou knowest about William Penn?" asked Samuel, desperate to shift the focus away from his brother.

"Yes," said Bushrod. "Founder of Pennsylvania."

"He lived in the real world," said Samuel. "He was a Quaker, and he said that 'a good end cannot sanctify evil means.' This means that even if it is good to defend thy family and thy home, thou cannot use evil means to achieve this good goal. Thou must find another path."

"Such as what?" asked Bushrod.

"Working to remove the causes of conflict," said Samuel. "Making efforts toward reconciliation. Dispute resolution."

"I believe it is too late for that," said Bushrod, "especially now that McClellan is planning to attack Richmond."

"Perhaps," said Samuel. "But we always try to work for peace."

Abigail found herself being drawn into Samuel's world, and she wanted to learn more. Although she had always been attracted to William's broad shoulders, blond hair, and easy smile, she now found herself intrigued by Samuel's heart and mind, and the vision he had for life. "Why do you use different words for months and days?" she asked.

"That is an unusual practice, I admit," said Samuel.

"I would say, 'strange,'" quipped Bushrod.

"We do not use names that are based on pagan gods," explained Samuel. "We say First Month, not January, since that month is named after Janus, the god of beginnings."

"But why not say Sunday and Monday?" asked Abigail.

"They are named after the sun and the moon," said Samuel.

"Is that bad?" said Abigail.

"Not bad," said Samuel, "but not necessarily Christian." He was thrilled by Abigail's questions and her interest in his Quaker practices. But he knew full well that she was attracted more to his brother than to him. *Could Abigail not love us both? Would that even be possible?* He was feeling conflicted, torn apart by desire for Abigail and loyalty to William.

"You make things so complicated," Bushrod said. *If only he knew,* thought Samuel. "You Quakers," said Bushrod, "can be so difficult and contrary."

"With good reason," said Samuel, "and for a good cause."

"Like abolitionism?" said Bushrod, now wanting to stir up trouble.

Samuel had no desire to fight about this, especially in front of Abigail. But he was compelled to speak the truth. "Yes," he said. "We Quakers were the first to condemn slavery. And, as thou knowest, we do not allow our members to own slaves."

"You are trouble-makers," said Bushrod. "Some of your people help slaves to escape from the South to the North."

"People ride that railroad every day," said Samuel, "all the way to Boston." *Maybe we Quakers are, in fact, contrary. And not in a bad way.*

At that point, Josiah Farlow entered the room and told Samuel and Bushrod that it was time to return to work. He wanted no talk of the Underground Railroad in his place of business.

Knowing that it was time to go, Abigail thanked Samuel for sharing his lunch. Then she stepped into the sunshine. A new light was coming into her world.

# 14

## Spring 2022

THE SEASON OF SPRING was just two days old when a group of seven young men entered Prince William Forest, a heavily wooded area ten miles south of Occoquan. The temperature had hit seventy-one degrees, so conditions were fine for an evening walk. Five of them were in their twenties, and two were teenagers. Two members of the older group carried machetes, one held a pickaxe, one carried a coil of rope, and all of them had knives.

"*Vámonos,*" said one of the twenty-somethings to the teenagers, pushing them down the path. The younger guys were short and wiry, and they looked like children in front of the muscular and tattooed man who was shoving them along. The sun was setting, and an inky darkness was settling on the woods.

"*Dónde está la reunion?*" asked one of the teenagers. He had been told they were going to a gang meeting. No one answered, but one of the older guys, a brute with a scar on his face from ear to mouth, gave a signal to keep moving forward.

When they came to a clearing, the teenagers realized that there would be no meeting. Directly in front of them was a crudely dug grave. One of them whimpered and tried to turn and run back up the path. He was immediately restrained by the muscular guy. The other screamed and bolted into the woods, but was quickly tackled by the man with the scar. In seconds, the two were hog-tied, gagged, and placed next to the grave.

As they struggled with their bonds, the senior member of the group began to speak. He was the tallest in the group, with a shaved head and a rumbling voice. Pointing a machete at the older of the teenagers, he accused him of joining MS-13, a rival gang. Poking the younger, he said that he knew that he was a police informant. Neither behavior was tolerated in *Los Gatos,* so they would have to die.

And how would *el veredicto* be carried out? The gang leader seemed to delight in laying out the procedure. They would be stabbed and chopped with knives, machetes, and the pick-axe. Every slice and blow would remind them of their betrayal. If they did not die from the weapons, they would suffocate in their grave.

The eyes of the teenagers were wide with terror.

Then, a shot rang out and the muscular man clutched his chest before falling in a heap. The one with the scar took a shot to the head, which sprayed blood over the teenagers. The remaining three turned to confront their assailant with the pickaxe and machetes, and two of them were quickly dispatched. The shaved-head gang leader began to run for the woods, and was brought down by a shot to his leg.

A man with black hair walked slowly out of the dark woods, and then stood above the man who was writhing in pain from his gunshot. He ended the gang leader's life with a close-range shot, and tucked his gun into the pocket of his camouflaged coat.

Then he put on sunglasses, although the woods were quite dark. With gloved hands, he picked up the knife that had been carried by the scar-faced man. Approaching the teenagers, he bent down and cut the bonds of the older teenager. Then he gave the knife to him to free the younger boy.

"*Soy San Juan,*" he said, as he disappeared into the woods. *I am Saint John.*

The next day, Harley met Abdul Ali at the door of the social hall, which was on the lowest level of Riverside Methodist Church. The businessman was dressed in a tailored grey suit with a red silk tie. Harley sensed that a man of his musculature could not buy a suit off the rack.

"Any water in the basement?" asked Abdul as he stepped into the room.

"Not since the flood," said Harley. Abdul had a been a huge help to the weak-kneed Riverside volunteers who had used Shop-Vacs to suck up the remnants of the 2018 deluge. "We couldn't have finished the clean-up without you."

"It was a *Sadaqah,*" said Abdul, using the Arabic term for "good deed."

"A blessing to us," said Harley.

"*Sadaqah* holds great value in the eyes of Allah," said Abdul.

"To us as well," said Harley. Then, sweeping his arm across the empty room, he said, "I think you know the space." The floor was tile, yellowed with age. The cinderblock walls were painted light green and the ceiling was sprayed asbestos—which Harley knew he should never disturb. The only natural light came from small rectangular windows near the ceiling. "Nothing fancy."

"It's perfect," said Abdul. "All we need is a clean floor and a northeast orientation for prayer." He pointed to the corner of the room that was directly under Harley's office and said, "We will face this way."

"Why northeast?" asked Harley.

"Shortest path to Mecca," said the big man.

At that moment, Andy Stackhouse poked his head in the door. "Hi, Harley," he said. "Saw the door open."

"Come in, Andy," said Harley, feeling his stomach begin to knot up. He remembered how Andy had objected to having Muslims in the basement. "I want you to meet Abdul Ali."

"Oh, I know him," said Andy, sticking out his hand. "I remember him well."

Abdul offered a firm handshake and said, "Good to see you again, sir."

Harley was confused. "Remind me how you met."

"The flood clean-up, of course," said Andy. "Abdul and I spent a whole day together. We moved a lot of water." Abdul smiled.

"I remember that you both were present," said the pastor, "but I didn't know you worked together."

"Yeah, we were working," said Andy. "Working hard, while you and Jefferson were chewing the fat."

"Abdul is the one who wants to rent the social hall for Friday prayers," said Harley. "Remember how I mentioned that in finance committee?" *You glared at me, Andy,* he was tempted to say. *"Shouldn't we be trying to convert Muslims?"*

"Sure, I remember the request," said Andy. "But I just heard 'mosque.' If Abdul wants it, fine with me."

Harley was stunned. "Really?"

"Of course," said Andy. "I support it. Abdul is good people. He's a *good* Muslim." Abdul tensed his massive shoulders, but remained silent.

"I am glad to hear of your support," said Harley.

"Abdul and I had a good talk at the clean-up," said Andy, oblivious to Abdul's discomfort. "We have a lot in common. Family values. Concerns about cultural decay. Desire to live a righteous life."

"We talked a lot," said Abdul, his shoulders relaxing slightly.

"Well, let's take the request to church council," said Harley.

"I'm on it, pastor," said Andy. "As the finance committee rep on the council, I'll push it through. Lord knows we need the money!"

"I'm grateful to you," said Abdul, giving a bow.

"Happy to help," said Andy, heading for the door. "See you soon."

Once the door closed, Harley said, "Sorry about that, Abdul."

"Could be worse," said the big man. "At least he supports the request."

"But that 'good Muslim' comment?"

"Again," said Abdul. "Could be worse. All's well that ends well."

"I admire your serenity," said Harley.

"The prophet and his companions endured a tremendous amount of adversity," said Abdul. "Verbal abuse, trauma, pain, grief. If they stood strong, so can I."

"Jesus suffered as well," said Harley. "We can learn from such examples."

"My Muslim faith helped me a great deal in prison," said Abdul. "When I was first locked up, I was lost. But as I grew in faith, I found a path."

Harley had always been curious about Abdul's incarceration, but he had never summoned the courage to ask. Now, with Abdul asking for church space, the time seemed right. "What offense put you in prison?" asked Harley. Abdul looked at him, expressionless. For a second, Harley feared he had crossed a line.

"I don't talk about it much," said Abdul. "Not good for business, you know?" Harley smiled. "But I trust you, pastor."

"Thank you," said Harley. "Here, let's take a seat." He pointed to a couple of ancient steel folding chairs, under one off the basement windows. The two men settled into the chairs, shifting their weight to find some measure of comfort.

"I was sent away for crack cocaine," said Abdul. "It was the eighties. Crack was everywhere."

"I remember it well," said Harley.

"Rayful Edmond," said Abdul, looking up to the window. "He was the king of crack. Mixed up with the Medellin cartel. He made three hundred million dollars a year."

"Really?" said Harley.

"An insane amount of money," said Abdul, looking back at Harley. "Which is what hooked me. I grew up poor, in Southeast DC, and it looked like a good path out."

"I can understand the attraction."

"On top of this, Rayful was a likable guy. Handsome, with a good personality. I was never close to him, but I looked up to him."

"I remember he used to sit courtside at Georgetown games."

"That's right. Coach Thompson did not like that one bit. He called Rayful into his office and told him to stay away from his basketball players."

"Brave man," said Harley.

"Absolutely. Probably the only man to ever stand up to Rayful without consequences."

"Much respect."

"But anyway," said Abdul, taking a deep breath. "You want to know about me. I was a peon in Rayful's organization, a delivery boy. I was making drops all over DC, and earned a ton of money. I never used crack myself, but I put it in a lot of hands."

"When was that?" asked Harley.

"1988," said Abdul. "I was eighteen years old."

"Just a kid," said Harley. *Yes, just a kid. But wait a minute . . . eighteen years old in 1988? That means born in 1970.*

"But old enough to know better," said Abdul, the muscles in his face tensing as he spoke. Harley's brain was spinning. *When we first met, I assumed he was in his mid-thirties, but he must have been in his mid-forties. Now he is in his early fifties.*

"The easy money came to an end that summer," Abdul continued. "I was sent with one of Rayful's lieutenants to make a delivery here in Woodbridge, and we walked right into a sting operation. Met up with some guys in a motel on Route One, and everything seemed normal until the DEA crashed through the door. Rayful's guy pulled his piece and they immediately took him down. I fell to the floor with my hands covering my head."

Harley was struggling to take it all in. He had a hard time picturing Abdul in such a vulnerable spot. "You must have been terrified," he said. *But you are so far from being a kid. Look at you now, appearing younger and stronger than your years. How can that be? Must be all the weightlifting and the healthy living. No alcohol. No smoking.*

"I peed my pants," Abdul admitted. "I thought my life was over. I thank Allah that I was not shot dead."

"That would have been horrible," said Harley. *What a waste that would have been.*

"Yes, horrible . . . but understandable," said Abdul. "I was dealing drugs. Crack cocaine. I was a nobody going nowhere. I could have easily been killed."

"I am glad you weren't," said Harley. *I cannot imagine this town without you.*

"Me too," said Abdul. "That bust saved my life. I got five years in prison, the mandatory minimum sentence for first-time possession. Did my time in Lorton, right across the river."

Harley knew it well. The Workhouse had become an arts center, and the Penitentiary was in the process of being transformed into condos and apartments with a cellblock vibe. "The place must be full of memories," he said.

"Indeed," said Abdul. "Lorton was dangerous when I was there. I kept my head down, lifted a lot of weights."

"I believe it."

"It was a dark place," said Abdul. "I came to despise the drug trade and anyone associated with it." His words made Harley wonder if he had anything to do with the deaths of the gang members he had just seen reported on television. *So close: Prince William Forest.* "But even more than drugs, I hate guns," said Abdul. "Don't go near them. They take so many lives, so quickly."

*So maybe he is not the shooter,* thought Harley. *But what do I know? I guessed he was decades younger!* Then, curious about the big man's time in prison, he said, "Five years seems harsh."

"Yes, but it could have been worse. Remember, I was dealing."

"True," said Harley. "But five years for a first offense?"

"That was the law," said Abdul. "Unjust, perhaps, but it didn't hurt me. It *helped* me. Prison is where I discovered Islam."

Harley felt a wave of shame. *Why didn't the Christian chaplains reach him?* "There was no good Christian ministry available?"

"Only Jefferson's group," said Abdul, "from Emanuel Baptist. But by then I was professing to be a Muslim."

"That's right," said Harley. "Your cellmate was Muslim, right?

"Yes, led me to the faith," said Abdul. "Mehmet."

"I am glad you two were put together," said Harley. "Would have been a nightmare without him."

"Lorton was a nightmare, even *with* him," said Abdul, smiling. "Mehmet was a good man, but have you seen those cells? Smaller than your office, if you can believe that. One bunkbed. One toilet. One sink."

"Zero privacy."

"None," said Abdul. "The whole experience was dehumanizing. But that is why Jefferson was so important to me. He came into Lorton with a personal finance class, and I discovered I had a gift. We stayed in touch, and Jefferson hired me as soon as I was released."

"That's good," said Harley.

"More than good," said Abdul. "My salvation." The muscles in his jaw seemed to relax as he spoke. "My incarceration, my conversion to Islam, and my mentoring by Jefferson—these three, together, were nothing less than gifts of Allah."

Harley sat silently for a minute, pondering how God could use an arrest for crack cocaine to turn a man's life around. Then he said, "You were redeemed."

"Indeed," said Abdul. "Rescued and released."

"What about the guy who was shot?" asked Harley.

"He survived and went to prison, along with me. But prison was his damnation, not his salvation. He continued to deal, and when he got out he was killed by a member of a rival gang."

"A senseless loss," said Harley.

"That's the way dealers are dealt with," said Abdul, shrugging his shoulders. Harley wondered if Abdul *did* have something to do with the killings in the forest. *Crack in the 1980s; fentanyl in the 2020s.* "My colleague chose the path that led to his death. The Quran says that anyone who turns away from Allah will have a depressed life."

"Logical consequences," said Harley.

"Yes," said Abdul, nodding. "We are crippled by our sins."

"What ever happened to Rayful?" Harley asked, curious about the consequences of the drug dealer's actions.

"I hear he became a government informant," said Abdul, "which led the authorities to many arrests. Gave up information concerning twenty homicides. He is still locked up, but in an undisclosed location."

"Why is that?"

"Federal Witness Protection Program," said Abdul, smiling. "He is aware of what your Bible says, 'the wages of sin is death.'"

"We take sin seriously," said Harley. "That's what Lent is all about."

"I appreciate what you are doing for me, pastor, especially during this holy season."

Harley pondered Abdul's words, "The wages of sin is death." *Drug dealers are dying. Could he somehow be involved?*

Friday morning, Sheriff Terry Stone made a surprise visit to Andy Stackhouse at his condominium. As he walked up the sidewalk, he noticed that the blooms of the Star Magnolias had exploded and then quickly died, showering white petals against the ground. Stone was a middle-aged man with a close-cropped beard and warm brown eyes, and he knew just about everybody in town. Along with a single deputy, Sharon Madison, he provided all of Occoquan's law enforcement and raised most of its revenue through traffic enforcement.

"Good morning, Andy," he said, as soon as the front door opened.

"Terry!" said Andy. "To what do I owe this pleasure?"

"Was in the neighborhood," said the sheriff. *Not a lie.* "Had something I wanted to run by you."

"Okay," said Andy, running his hand over his close-cropped white hair. "Come on in." The sheriff stepped into the foyer and removed his hat. "Coffee?"

"No thanks," said Terry. "This will only take a minute."

"Want to sit?"

"No. I'm fine right here," he said, resting his right hand on the holster containing his firearm. "Andy, I wanted to let you know that I got a complaint from one of your neighbors."

"Oh, really?"

"She said you showed up at her door with a sword and a gun, asking her to sign a petition."

"Yes, that's right," said Andy. "Sort of. I was dressed for Blue and Grey Day."

"Okay," said Terry. "Tell me more."

"I asked her to sign a petition about a book, one that I don't think should be in the public schools."

"And you had a sword and a gun?"

"A sword, yes," said Andy. "From my Night Riders uniform. But not a gun."

"No gun?"

"No, just the holster."

"All right," said Terry. "She might have assumed that the holster contained a gun."

"I have a permit," said Andy.

"I'm sure you do," said Terry. *Could he be connected to the PW Outlets or Prince William Forest shootings?* The sheriff paused for a moment, thinking, but then assessed that Andy probably did not fit the profile. Returning to the matter at hand, he said, "Andy, think about it. Is it really a good idea to ask for signatures in a Civil War uniform, carrying weapons?"

"Only a sword," said Andy.

"Still," said Terry. "You are really going to turn some people off."

Andy pondered the sheriff's words for a few seconds. Then he said, "I get your point."

"Do me a favor, Andy," said Terry, putting his hat back on. "When you take your petitions around, leave the weapons at home."

# 15

## Late Third Month 1862

His uniform was covered in dust, so completely coated that she could not make out whether it was blue or grey. The setting sun was behind him, so his face was not recognizable, but she saw the outline of his well-developed shoulders and arms. He was not a tall man like her brother, but instead short and compact. Walking toward her on the road that entered Occoquan from the west, he carried a rifle over one shoulder and a knapsack over the other. The corona of light around him made him look angelic. Her heart began to pound as he moved slowly toward her.

"Who goes there?" she asked, feeling both frightened and aroused. She shifted her position to get a better look at his face, but this move to the right did not help. In fact, the setting sun briefly blinded her.

"Friend or foe?" she said, moving back to the center of the road. Although the man was a stranger, his appearance did not make her want to turn and run. Instead, his presence excited her. Against all her mother's instructions in ladylike behavior, she wanted nothing more than to engage him. The silhouette of his broad shoulders, narrow waist, and muscular legs filled her with an attraction that was new to her. She stepped toward him, and he stopped. Her yearning only grew, a feeling that was both frightening and thrilling. For a moment, the two were at a standoff.

"Abigail," he said, his voice low but playful. "Where is my welcome-home parade?"

"William!" she shouted, hiking up her dress and running toward him. Then she awoke.

Soldiers passed through Occoquan later that morning, the twenty-third day of Third Month, but they were not Confederate fighters returning to defend the town. No, they wore the blue of McClellan's Union Army, and the war-weary group of twenty men encountered nothing but hostile stares as they rode through the center of town. Occoquan had been left undefended by the retreat of Wade Hampton's forces, but the locals were determined to muster enough silent antagonism to let the men know that they were not welcome.

"Where is Merchants' Mill?" asked the captain, his uniform covered by dust from the road. He had a rifle slung over his back and a saber at his side, and he appeared to be a man who knew how to use his weapons. Standing in front of the stone façade of the Bank of Occoquan, Abigail pointed northward on Union Street, and then indicated they should turn left on Mill. She was afraid to speak but also feeling disappointed that the dusty soldiers were not from the side that would include William. Her brother Bushrod gave her a withering look and hissed that she should stop helping the enemy.

"And what are *you* doing?" she responded angrily. She wanted him to feel shame for doing nothing to resist or repel the armed travelers.

The group turned the corner and moved slowly along Mill Street, their horses kicking up small clouds of dust as they made their way toward the mill. Bushrod examined each of them carefully, taking stock of their weapons and their military insignia, and at the end of the procession he saw something that shocked him—a black man on horseback. *What is this?* He was not dressed in a soldier's uniform, but he had a rifle over his shoulder. *How can this be? Blacks are not allowed to fight!* Bushrod knew that there were slaves in the Confederate Army and black camp workers in the Union forces, but in neither army were blacks permitted to use weapons. He felt a burning rage.

"Did you see that black man?" Bushrod said to Abigail, once the group had passed. "The arrogance: Riding like a white man and carrying a weapon. The world is going to hell!" He spat towards the group, then spun around quickly and marched toward his home. *Coward,* thought Abigail. *All words, no action.*

When the group reached Merchants' Mill, the captain dismounted and banged on the door of the storage room with his gloved fist. No one answered, since it was First Day and the mill was not in operation. In a moment, however, Josiah Farlow emerged from the Mill House, rubbing his large hands together and looking concerned. He was reluctant to engage with Union soldiers and incur the wrath of his neighbors.

"Are you the miller?" asked the captain.

"I am."

"We hear that this is a Quaker operation."

"That is true," said Josiah. He shifted his eyes toward town, trying to assess the risk. Except for a couple of onlookers, the locals had dispersed.

"We need water for our horses and a place to rest," said the captain. "Can you provide this?"

Josiah paused for a moment, took a deep breath, and then said, loud enough for the onlookers to hear, "Our Lord requires that we offer hospitality to strangers."

"Good man," said the captain, knowing that Josiah was in a tough spot. "We will not disturb your community, and will take no more than water." He gave a signal for his men to dismount and to lead their horses to the troughs alongside the mill.

"Union soldiers at the mill!" was the message Samuel heard from his next-door neighbor, causing him to put down the book he was reading outside his front door. *That is unexpected. Union soldiers? What are they doing here?* Getting up from his stool, he made his way to the mill, to see what was going on and to figure out what he could do to help Josiah. Feeling excited about the visitors, and a little bit guilty about wanting to see Union forces up close, Samuel walked quickly and with purpose. As soon as he rounded the corner of the mill, he could see that the horses were quickly emptying the troughs, so he grabbed a bucket and began to refill them from the well. Finding the soldiers to be intimidating, he did not try to engage them in conversation, but made every effort to listen to what they were saying. One man said that he was anxious to get across the river and return to friendlier territory. Another agreed, saying that only two rivers now stood between him and his wife in Maryland. A third spat on the ground and said that if he ever touched Virginia soil again, it would be too soon.

Then, Samuel saw the black man, standing at the back of the group and waiting patiently to water his horse. His skin was very dark, and he had a strikingly handsome—even regal—face. When his turn came, Samuel poured a fresh bucket of water into the trough and said that he would fetch some more.

"Thank you," said the man. "Much obliged."

"Thou art welcome," said Samuel. The man looked at him and offered a knowing smile.

Samuel was mystified by the expression and pondered it while filling his bucket. When he returned from the well, the horse was still drinking. The man turned to Samuel and said, "You are a Friend, right?"

"Yes, I am."

"We have Friends where I live. Good people."

"Thou art kind," said Samuel.

"Many are abolitionists."

Samuel was afraid to answer out loud, but gave a small nod.

"My name is Lewis Bell," said the man. "I was born into freedom in Washington, DC."

"I am pleased to meet thee," said Samuel. Then, not knowing what to say, he lowered his head and watched the water level dropping in the trough. The two men stood in silence.

When his horse was finished drinking, Lewis led the animal to a tree across the street, where he tied her up. The man lowered his body to the ground, clearly tired of riding. Samuel, feeling shy but curious, asked if he could join him.

"Be my guest," said Lewis, pointing to a spot next to him.

Samuel sat down and pulled out a cloth bag. "Wouldst thou care for some bread and cheese?"

"Oh, yes," said Lewis. "I have had nothing but hardtack and water today." He accepted Samuel's offering with his large, calloused hands and ate it slowly, with great pleasure. The sun broke through the clouds and began to warm the cool spring day. Samuel looked up at the delicate blossoms on the tree above them, and felt an unexpected sense of peace. *I should feel threatened by these soldiers, but I do not. How odd.* Then he turned his attention to his companion.

"What bringest thee to Occoquan?" he asked him.

Lewis swallowed and then said, "A prisoner exchange."

Samuel nodded, but did not really understand.

"Except for the captain and his lieutenant," said Lewis, "all of us were prisoners of the Rebels. Down in Richmond."

"So, the Union exchanged some Confederate prisoners for thee?"

"That is right," said Lewis. "We were taken down to Fort Monroe, in Hampton. There we were exchanged."

"I am glad thou art free again."

"Me too," said Lewis, smiling again. "Working as a kitchen attendant in that Richmond prison was like being a slave."

"Didst thou ride all the way from Hampton?"

"No," said Lewis. "We left the fort on a steamboat, headed for Washington. But it began to take on water near Kilmarnock. We came ashore there with our horses, and decided to complete the trip by land."

"Wast thou not worried," asked Samuel, "about the Confederates?"

"Somewhat. But we knew that their army had moved to a point south of the Rappahannock River, and we landed to the north. We made sure that we had arms and ammunition, in case we ran into any scouting parties."

"That sounds dangerous."

"Could have been," said Lewis, adjusting the rifle at his side. "But we have made it this far without trouble."

"I am glad to hear that."

"Although I am not a soldier, I am ready to defend myself. And to protect my companions as well."

Samuel had never seen a black man like this before, armed and riding alongside a group of white soldiers. He felt a rush of concern that one of the residents of Occoquan might take a shot at him, to punish him for his arrogance. But then he realized that a single assailant would have no chance against this heavily armed group. Such an act would be suicidal.

"How wast thee captured in the first place?" asked Samuel. Then, concerned that he was being inappropriate, he added, "If thou dost not mind the question."

"Not at all," said Lewis. "I was captured in a battle."

"Do tell," said Samuel.

"I was a camp worker for the Union," said Lewis, "Stationed in Poolesville, Maryland. Helping with food service. Carrying gear. Helping the cause." He put another piece of bread and cheese in his mouth and chewed slowly, savoring the taste. Then he continued, "Colonel Edward Baker was our commander. You may have heard of him: He is a United States Senator."

Samuel did not know the name, but he nodded so that Lewis would continue.

"Last October, our soldiers crossed the Potomac River into Virginia, in pursuit of the Rebels. The place was called Ball's Bluff, up near Leesburg. We thought we would overtake them quickly, but they fought back fiercely. Those Rebels were battle-hardened, having been victorious at Bull Run.

They pushed our soldiers down the bluffs and back to their boats, and a lot of good men died in the river."

Samuel was captivated by the story, imagining the drama taking place on the Potomac. "Where wast thou?" he asked.

"I was on the Maryland side," said Lewis, "watching the horror unfold. And then I did what any good man would do. I picked up a rifle and started shooting."

"Truly?" said Samuel. "I thought only white men could fight."

"That is true," said Lewis. "But how could I not? I had to defend the retreating soldiers. I was standing right next to a lieutenant, and he said nothing to discourage me. I considered myself part of the Fifteenth Massachusetts Regiment, so I loaded and fired with great spirit. Think I even hit a few of the Rebs."

"I have never heard of a black man being allowed to fight," said Samuel.

"I may have been the first," Lewis said. Then, after a pause, he added, "But I will not be the last."

Samuel nodded and asked, "So, what happened next?"

"The Rebels captured us," said Lewis. "Captured the whole Fifteenth Regiment. Took us all to prison."

"For how long?"

"Let me see," said Lewis. "Captured in October. In prison in November, December, January, and part of February. Four months. But I consider myself fortunate to be part of this exchange."

"Indeed," said Samuel. "And now thou art going home?"

"Yes," Lewis said, "back to Washington. Back to freedom. But if I get a chance to fight again, you know I will."

A breeze blew through a stand of pines at the top of the hill, causing the trees to sway like dancers. Their green needles were the only color in the forest, since the other trees had not yet gained their spring leaves. It seemed to Samuel that the pines were showing off. As a Quaker, he always wore clothing of subdued colors, not wanting to draw attention to himself, and in the colder months he particularly enjoyed taking hikes because it seemed that nature shared his modest color scheme. He had recently read a line by the New England writer Henry David Thoreau, who said that late fall was a time in which nature wore "Quaker colors, sober ornaments, beauty that quite satisfies the eye." Samuel liked that. *Quaker colors.*

But Samuel's eyes were not focused only on pine trees as he walked past the Quaker cemetery. He was also looking for Abigail, whom he expected to be out for her Sunday afternoon walk. Samuel had found that she was dominating his thoughts as of late, and he felt his heart racing whenever he ran into her on the street or had a chance to talk with her at the mill. He was conflicted, of course, since Abigail was from a loyal Southern family and her feisty brother rarely missed an opportunity to provoke him. On top of this, he knew that Abigail had feelings for his brother William, so his own attraction to her made him feel disloyal to his family. But he could not deny that the heart wants what the heart wants. And that afternoon, he wanted to see Abigail and to speak from his heart.

Hearing the sound of honking above him, Samuel looked up and saw a v-formation of geese, crossing the sky from west to east. They were like a giant arrow, pointing him eastward, and as he followed their guidance his gaze fell on a figure cresting the eastern edge of the ridge. *Abigail!* She had a white bonnet over her long blond hair, and she was wearing a white dress with yellow stripes.

Samuel waved to her and called her name. She responded by waving back and striding across the grassy field that was just beginning to come to life. Although she had been thinking of William, she was very happy to encounter Samuel.

"Did you see the soldiers?" she asked him, out of breath from the climb up the hill.

"Indeed," said Samuel.

"What a shock," she said. "So soon after the departure of Colonel Hampton."

"The tide of war turns quickly, does it not?"

"Do you feel we are in danger?" Abigail asked. Samuel was jarred by the question, since it made clear to him how differently they felt about the war.

"Not from these soldiers," he said. "They were former prisoners, returning home."

"Really?" said Abigail.

"Exchanged for Confederate prisoners, down in Hampton." He wanted to say "Rebel prisoners," but dared not use that term in front of Abigail.

"So many Hamptons," she said, smiling for the first time. "Colonel Hampton. Hampton, Virginia."

"It can be confusing," said Samuel. Then he pointed his hand to the south and suggested that they walk down that side of the hill, on which a grassy path led to a gentle stream.

"I hear that you helped them," she said.

"Yes," said Samuel. "Watered their horses. Shared some food." He could see that she was skeptical of his actions. "Basic Christan hospitality," he concluded.

She pondered this, looking down at her footing on the path, and realized that it made sense. Then she asked, "So, what is going on with the war?"

"I hear that General McClellen is gathering his forces down at Fort Monroe. Once again: Hampton. He now has over one hundred and twenty thousand men."

"That is a considerable force."

"Yes, it is," Samuel said. "He intends to march up the Peninsula and capture Richmond. He wants the Union Navy to sail up the rivers on either side, to protect his flanks."

"Frightening," said Abigail. "I fear for our army, and for our capital. When will this begin?"

"Early April is what I hear."

"My brother tells me that there is fighting in the Shenandoah Valley, as well."

"Yes," said Samuel. "Stonewall Jackson is attacking the Union forces. I do not know the outcome."

"May he have success," said Abigail. "To protect our commonwealth."

Once again, Samuel felt a deep divide. "It is in God's hands," he sighed.

"Yes, it is," she agreed. Walking in silence, they reached the bottom of the hill, where they could hear the gently babbling of the stream.

"The water is calling," said Samuel.

Abigail winked at him, which lifted his spirits. "Look," she said, pointing ahead. "The bluebells have emerged."

Abigail took his hand and led him toward the stream, into a marshy area covered with smooth gray-green foliage. Nodding clusters of pink buds opened into sky-blue, trumpet-shaped flowers. They were lovely, delicate, and everywhere throughout the marsh. "Spring is here," said Abigail, squeezing his hand.

Samuel felt a warmth come over him that he had not felt in years. In fact, he had not experienced such serenity since before his father died. His mind traveled back to a picnic his family had enjoyed in a similar spot when he and William were children, and he suddenly remembered what complete peace and security felt like. Once, he had known this kind of calm. It was effortless and unconditional. But since his father's death, life had been nothing but striving.

Then, in a flash, the mood was broken. Abigail said, "How I wish William were here."

Samuel jerked his hand away. Abigail looked startled.

"William?" he said.

"Yes, William. He would enjoy this beautiful, peaceful place."

Once again, Samuel realized that he and Abigail were looking at each other from positions across a deep divide. He sensed that she had feelings for him, and was hoping the attraction would grow. But he could not, in good conscience, undermine his brother. "I suppose you are right," he said.

"I do miss him," said Abigail, "I dreamed of him last night." Samuel did not respond. "I'm sure you do as well."

"Of course," he said, looking down at the flowers. "My mother, especially, is terribly upset by his absence."

"Do you think he is safe?" Abigail asked. Although frustrated, Samuel was moved by her concern.

"Yes, as far as I know," he said.

"I am so proud of him," she gushed. "A Son of Occoquan, fighting for what he believes in. He has such strength, such heart, such courage."

*Yes, he has always been quite contrary.* Samuel kept that thought to himself, saying instead, "We hope to see him any day now."

"That will be wonderful," said Abigail. "You must fetch me as soon as he arrives."

"I shall, of course," Samuel said. He had planned on confessing his love for Abigail that afternoon, but their talk among the bluebells had revealed that intention to be folly. "You know that I want nothing but the best for thee," he said. "And for William."

# 16

## Late March 2022

"THERE WAS ONCE A cotton factory here," said Harley to Nanette, standing at the edge of River Mill Park. "Constructed by Samuel Janney, a member of the Quaker community."

"Nothing but grass now," she said, sounding unimpressed. "I have to use my imagination."

Harley and Nanette were taking a stroll on the afternoon of Sunday, March 27, the Fourth Sunday in Lent. Cherry blossoms were at their delicate peak, and it would have been a lovely spring day except for the fact that temperatures had plummeted overnight into the twenties. The air had warmed slightly throughout the day, but winter was fighting to return as dark clouds sailed across the sky, backlit by brilliant sunshine. At one point, when a cluster of particularly ominous clouds passed over Occoquan, snow began to fall.

"Yes," said Harley, "the factory had a picking house, a cotton house, and even a wharf on the river. It was quite an operation." He had offered to take Nanette on a walking tour of the buildings of Occoquan, and had been looking forward to their afternoon together. They had looked at the Hammill Hotel, which had once been Wade Hampton's headquarters, and had stopped at the Town Hall building, which had started its life as a church. Harley had told the story of the Liberty Pole in front of the Rockledge Mansion, and had taken her by the Mill Street Museum, which was the only remnant of Merchants' Mill. Now, the tour seemed to be coming to an end, since they had arrived at the western end of Mill Street and were running out of buildings.

"You can see the excavation of the Quaker village," said Harley, pointing across the park. "I've really enjoyed being a part of it."

"Sounds interesting," she said, sounding anything but interested. Harley wondered what was going on, since she had been so affectionate and enthusiastic at their dinner.

"Yes, it has been," he said, expecting a follow-up question.

She remained silent.

A break in the awkwardness came in the form of Tim Underwood, the town maintenance man. He rolled up in his official town golf cart, picking up trash from the town barrels at the end of the weekend. Tim was wearing navy-blue coveralls under his official town work coat, and his cheeks were bright red around his gray beard. "Pastor!" he said. "You have a celebrity with you."

Harley and Nanette looked at each other, and then back at Tim. "Who, me?" she said.

"No-Change!" Tim said, smiling broadly. "Very pleased to meet you."

"This is Tim Underwood," said Harley, making the introduction. "Town Maintenance Man. People call him 'Tye-Dye.'"

"You'll understand, once the weather warms up," said Tim. His bright summer t-shirts were legendary.

"Well, nice to meet you," said Nanette. "I'm Nanette Glebesman." Having noticed that he was picking up trash, she did not extend her hand.

"You are developing a reputation," said Tim. "A good one."

"Nice to hear," said Nanette.

"Tim is part of an old Occoquan family," said Harley. "He knows more about Occoquan than anyone."

"Don't embarrass me, Harley," said Tim. "But he's right about my family."

"We were just on a bit of a history tour," said Nanette. "But we've run out of buildings."

"There are many stories in this town," said Tim, "aside from the structures." He turned off his ignition, prepared to sit and talk. "You've heard about the Liberty Pole, I assume?"

"Yes," said Nanette, looking up toward the Rockledge Mansion.

"Well," said Tim, "that was a notable example of abolitionist sentiment here in Occoquan. A position held mainly by Quakers and Presbyterians."

"No Methodists?" asked Harley.

"Not that I know of," said Tim. "But there may have been a few. The war was particularly hard on the Quakers, and it split many families. This was not because they supported slavery. No, they despised it. The families were divided over whether good Christians should take up arms to free the slaves. In one family, a young man named Amos Cadwallader caused a stir when he left Occoquan to join the Union Army."

"What a tough choice," said Nanette. "If there was ever a good reason to join the army and fight, it would be to free the slaves."

"For sure," said Tim. "But his decision caused him to be kicked out of the Quaker meeting. And it made life hard for the Cadwallader family, who had to do what they could to stay on good terms with their Confederate neighbors."

"And we think we have divisions now!" said Harley, shaking his head. He hoped that Nanette would agree with him, but she remained focused on Tim. After an awkward moment, Harley asked, "Do you know what happened to Amos?"

"He survived the war and returned to Occoquan. But he had to become a Presbyterian—there was no room for a veteran of war in the Quaker meeting."

"Imagine that," said Nanette. "Being kicked out of church for joining the army."

"As for my family," said Tim, "John Underwood was one of the most outspoken of the abolitionists, and he was considered a traitor to the Confederacy. Makes me kind of proud."

"You should be," said Nanette.

"In December of 1862, Wade Hampton led a raid through Occoquan, and he arrested John. Threw him in prison."

"The same Confederate who stayed at the hotel?" asked Nanette.

"Yes," said Tim. "The very same. He left with his troops in March, but then returned in December."

"Exactly one hundred and sixty years ago," said Harley, wanting to be part of the conversation.

"Yes, one hundred and sixty years ago this December," said Tim. "John remained in prison until 1863, when he was released in a prisoner swap. Then he became a United States Marshall, and lived at 314 Mill Street."

"Is the house still there?" asked Nanette.

"No, it was destroyed in the fire of 1916," said John. "Now it is the site of Town Hall."

"Must make you feel at home," said Harley, knowing that Tim spent a lot of time at that location.

"I suppose," said Tim. "But I do wish the family home was still intact."

"What else happened in Occoquan?" asked Nanette.

"Wade Hampton came back to Occoquan after arresting John," said Tim. "Later in December, he captured twenty Union supply wagons that were attempting to cross the river by ferry. Then, Jeb Stuart raided Occoquan and drove two hundred members of the Second Pennsylvania Calvary out of town. He did that right before heading north and raiding Fairfax."

"Lots of action," said Harley.

"And that's not all," said Tim. "A Confederate Major name John Pelham took his horse artillery across the river and chased Union troops into Fairfax. Same day as Jeb Stuart's raid."

"This was not a sleepy town," said Nanette.

"Not at all," said Tim. "Confederate and Union forces were in and out, especially in 1862 and 1863. I think of it as a microcosm of the Civil War. A house divided." Wanting to contribute something, Harley took out his phone and plugged "Occoquan cotton factory" into the search bar. He had a sense that the factory had been destroyed, but he could not remember the details. "I'm curious about the cotton factory," he said as he was waiting for the search results.

"What happened to the factory?" Nanette asked Tim, bypassing Harley.

"Good question," said Tim, warming to the subject. Harley slipped his phone back into his coat pocket. "It was burned to the ground in 1862. Arson."

"By whom?" asked Nanette. "Rebels?"

"Probably," said Tim. "May have been destroyed to prevent textiles from falling into Union hands. The loyal Southerners in Occoquan never trusted the Quakers."

"The Quakers were on the right side of history," said Harley. "But it cost them."

"Did you know," said Tim, looking at Nanette, "that Harley's house is located on the spot where the Underground Railroad had a station?"

"No, I did not," she said. Harly appreciated that Tim was throwing him a bone.

"Yes," said Tim. "Was a warehouse owned by Quakers."

Harley opened his mouth to speak, but was interrupted by the ringing of his cell phone. He pulled it out, saw Leah's number, and asked Tim and Nanette to excuse him. He turned his back to them to take the call.

"Harley!" shouted Leah. "Are you okay?"

"Uh, yes," said Harley, confused. "I'm standing near the park, with Nanette and Tim."

"You texted me the code," said Leah. "Sort of."

"What do you mean?"

"I got a text: 3333." Harley changed the screen from phone to text messages, and saw that she was right.

"My bad," he said. "Pocket text."

"Well, you scared me," she said. "I was about to call the police."

"So very sorry," said Harley, understanding her fright. "I'll try to be more careful."

"I'm just glad you are okay. 3333 was awfully close to 33."

"You are right," said Harley. "Right to be concerned."

"Anyway, glad you are safe."

"Thanks so much."

"I'll let you go," said Leah, ending the call. Harley made sure that his phone was not on the texting screen, and then he put it back in his pocket.

"Sorry about that," he said, as he turned back to Tim and Nanette.

"Everything okay?" asked Tim.

"Yeah, I just accidentally sent a text that scared a friend."

"Really?" said Nanette.

"Yes," said Harley, feeling embarrassed. "Accidentally sent a code number to a friend."

"What's the code?" she asked. "Or is it a secret?"

"No," said Harley. "Just the number thirty-three, which is police code for an emergency."

"Okay," said Nanette, thinking the arrangement sounded juvenile. "And who is the friend?"

"Leah Silverman," said Harley.

"They go back a long way," said Tim, trying to lighten the mood. "Back to college. Right, Harley?" Harley nodded. "A couple of Blue Devils. You two spend a lot of time in the Grindhouse, don't you?" There was not much that missed Tim's eye.

"Is that right?" asked Nanette, recalling the woman she saw holding hands with Harley.

"Yes," said Harley, innocently. "That's right."

"Well, I'm going to need to be going," said Nanette, sounding bothered. "In fact, Harley, I'm going to be going away for a while. I need to return to Seattle to cover for a colleague who is taking some medical leave."

"Really?" said Harley, disappointed. "For how long?"

"A couple of weeks, probably. So, you won't see me around town. Leaving tomorrow."

"So sorry to hear that. Will you be back by Easter?"

"Maybe," said Nanette. "We'll see."

Harley's face fell. "I'll miss you," he said.

Turning to Tim, Nanette said, "Thanks for the personal history of the town." Tim nodded. Then, looking at Harley, she said, "Take care of yourself." The wind kicked up, and Harley felt the cold air sting his cheeks. Without a handshake or hug, Nanette turned and walked toward her apartment.

Monday morning, Harley locked the front door of his Victorian townhouse and walked down the wrought-iron stairs to Mill Street. The pear trees along the street had lost their blooms, only to be followed by the delicate blossoms of the cherry and crabapple trees. The season of spring was offering a nonstop flower show, free of charge, to all the residents of Occoquan. But Harley was feeling too unsettled by Nanette's departure to notice the ever-changing palettes of color all around him.

Walking past the post office on his way to church, he turned right to cut through the parking lot. There, he ran into Mary Ranger, postmistress and member of Riverside Methodist Church. Flashing a bright smile, she called out, "Harley!"

"Morning, Mary."

"Busy time of year for you, right?"

"Absolutely. Easter is almost here."

"Well, you've had some good sermons."

"Appreciate that."

"You're on a roll!" she said, pushing her bleach-blond hair out of her face.

Mary had been a great supporter of Harley since he showed up in Occoquan. Although she knew everyone's business, and had bit of a reputation as a gossip, she had never bad-mouthed him—to his knowledge. Maybe his awareness of her husband's fondness for vintage erotica had kept her in check, or perhaps she was genuinely fond of him. Regardless, he considered her to be a friend. "You are kind to say that," said Harley.

"Did you hear about Andy?" she asked. "Got a visit from Terry Stone."

"Really?" said Harley. *Here comes the gossip.*

"Yeah, he was making a resident uncomfortable. Showed up at her house with a petition about a book. Was wearing a Confederate uniform and carrying a sword."

"I knew he was a Civil War buff . . ."

"But *really*," said Mary. She was a large woman, strong in her opinions. "Bad judgment."

Harley hated to criticize one church member to another, but he gave her a slight nod. Then, remembering Tim's comment from the night before, he said, "Occoquan has always been a house divided."

"You are right," said Mary. "This place was divided in the 1860s, and it is divided today. You won't believe what I see at the post office."

"Like what?"

"Got a minute?" she asked. "I have a few before I open up."

"No early appointments for me," said Harley.

Pointing to a bench, she asked him to sit down. "I'm in a unique spot," she said, "since everyone in town comes to the post office to get their mail. I see it all: Black Lives Matter buttons, anti-abortion pins, 'Bring Back Hillary' t-shirts, MAGA hats, jackets with the Gadsden flag . . ."

"The what?" asked Harley.

"The Gadsden flag. You know, the yellow flag with the coiled rattlesnake. The words, 'Don't Tread on Me.'"

"Oh yeah," said Harley. "From the American Revolution."

"That's right," said Mary. "But it is used now to signal libertarianism. Or a far-right agenda. It has been flown next to the Confederate battle flag."

"Does that make you nervous?" asked Harley.

"Only if the person wearing it is strongly anti-government," she said. "After all, I *am* the face of the federal government. They see me every day. And you know that not everyone is in favor of voting by mail."

Harley felt empathy as he imagined her standing at her counter, encountering a cross-section of the population every single day. What if someone took out their frustrations on her, yelling at her or even attacking her? To his knowledge, postal workers were armed with nothing but their postmark stamps. "Do you ever feel scared?" he asked.

"Not really," she said, trying to sound cheerful. "Most people are very courteous. But you would be amazed by the number of people who subscribe to 'Guns & Ammo' magazine. On the left and on the right."

Harley had a sense that there were gun owners all around him, but he assumed that they bought firearms for hunting or sport shooting or self-defense. Now he wondered if the political tensions in the county would erupt in violence. "Are we heading toward another Civil War?" he asked.

"Hard to say," said Mary. "I hope not."

"There is certainly a lot of upset," said Harley. "In elections, extremists are knocking off moderates—from the left and from the right. FBI agents are being threatened, right along with school board members. We're seeing protests and counter-protests around social justice issues. Training camps for radicals, with target practice. Anti-Semitic violence."

"Seems so far away from little Occoquan," said Mary. "But I know it's not."

"No, the Civil War came here, and it can come again."

Mary knew he was right, but did not want to admit it. "I better open the post office," she said, "and you get yourself to church."

"I will," said Harley. "Thanks for the talk."

As he walked across Washington Street to his office, Harley found himself imagining the little Quaker village that stood in what is now River Mill Park: The simple homes, the gristmill, the cotton factory. He was feeling drawn to their complete commitment to pacifism, envious of the deep confidence and serenity that must have radiated from that conviction. *They knew where they stood. They did not struggle with division. Polarization did not pull them apart. They had purity of heart!*

As he opened his office door, a question appeared out of nowhere.
*Or did they?*

# 17

## End of Third Month 1862

A STEADY, SOAKING RAIN had fallen throughout First Day, the thirtieth day of Third Month, 1862. In the stillness of the meeting for worship that morning, Samuel had wondered if the clouds would remain in place, through the day and through the night. He knew that he was supposed to be using the silence to make connections with the people around him, with his own soul, and perhaps with God. He was aware that Quaker silence was a time for growth, and an opportunity to see the world and its people in a new way. In previous meetings for worship, he had certainly felt himself being transported beyond himself, beyond his own thoughts and ideas, to a place where he gained new insights into how he could respond to the challenges of life in a new way.

But on that particular First Day, all he could think about was the weather.

After the meeting, he and his mother walked carefully through the mud, making their way from the meetinghouse to their home. On sunny days, there would be chatter among Friends in the streets after the meeting for worship, but on dreary days people would head straight home and dry themselves beside a fire. Samuel and Ann took off their boots at the door, hung their wool coats on pegs inside the house, and moved quickly to the fireplace. The fire had died down during their time of worship, but Samuel quickly brought it back to life by throwing a few logs into the fireplace. In a minute, the flames were leaping and radiating warmth into the room.

"That feels good, does it not?" asked Samuel, holding his hands in front of the fire.

"Indeed," said his mother. "The day is raw."

"I expected it to be warm by this time in Third Month, but the season of spring is slow to arrive."

"All time is holy," said Ann. "No one day or season is better than another."

"True," said Samuel. "But I do worry about William, camped out in this cold."

"As do I," said Ann, nodding. "What dost thou hear about the movements on the Peninsula?"

"Not very much," said Samuel. "But in this case, the lack of news is good news. Bushrod told me that General McClellan and his troops have not yet begun their march to Richmond."

"The General is cautious, is he not?"

Samuel nodded. "Thou heard what President Lincoln said, didst thou not?" Ann shook her head. Samuel quoted the president, *"If General Mc-Clellan does not want to use the army, I would like to borrow it."*

Ann smiled, showing Samuel an expression of delight that he had not seen for several months. The firelight sparkled in her eyes, transporting him back to days when the family was together, laughing around the table after a meeting for worship. His father had been there, telling stories about his childhood and mimicking the voices of eccentric relatives. William had sat with elbows on the table, acting contrary and disputing everything that Samuel said. Through it all, his mother had sat at the table, quietly beaming, justifiably proud of the big dinner she had put before them. She loved her three men more than anything else, and delighted in making them happy. But then, the spell was suddenly broken when Ann turned toward the fire and said, "I admit that my heart is rent. I want the Union to take Richmond and end this war. But I do not want William to come to harm. I fear the violence that is to come."

"As do I," said Samuel. "As do I."

Turning from the fire toward Samuel, Ann said, "Dost thou think that the campaign delayed his leave?"

"That is entirely likely. His letter said he would be home by the middle of this month."

"The war bug," said Ann, sighing.

"So powerful," said Samuel.

The skies were still cloudy at midnight, making the night as dark as India ink and giving Samuel excellent cover as he walked to the Janney cotton warehouse by the wharf. He was dressed in black, with a dark felt hat and a black scarf around his face. Looking up and down Mill Street, he saw no one in either direction. Then he tapped lightly on the wooden door. Three taps. A pause. And then one tap. He hoped he remembered the code.

The door opened slowly, and its hinges gave an ominous groan. Inside was Josiah Farlow, the miller, also dressed in black but with charcoal covering his face. He pulled Samuel into a dark storage room, lit by a single candle. He whispered, "The scarf will have to go. Use this coal to blacken thy face."

Samuel's eyes adjusted to the darkness as he rubbed the coal over his face. In a few seconds, he saw that they were not alone. A group of blacks sat on barrels on the wharf side of the warehouse, dressed in dark clothes: Two men, a woman, and two children. They were silent and invisible, except for the whites of their eyes.

Keeping his voice down, Josiah gave Samuel the plan. "We will use two canoes," he said. "Thou and I will be in the stern, since we know the river best." Pointing to the first man across the room, he said, "Obadiah will be in the bow of thy canoe with a paddle. His wife Ruth will be in the middle with their youngest child, Naomi." Then, pointing to the second man, he said, "Jonah is Ruth's brother. He will paddle with me in the second canoe. In the middle will be Ruth and Obadiah's son David." Samuel was not sure he was registering all the names and relations, but he had a sense of who would be in his boat. He said, "I understand."

Walking across the storage room, Josiah asked the family if they were ready. The adults nodded. Then he slowly opened a door on the river side of the warehouse, and they stepped into the night. Samuel looked up and was relieved to see that the cloud cover had remained thick, with no light from moon or stars.

"Obadiah?" he said, as he walked next to the first of the men. "Yes, sir," whispered the man. Samuel was embarrassed that he had not grasped the names of the woman and her child, so he simply pointed them toward the wharf. When they got to the dock where the canoes were tied up, he climbed into the stern and steadied the vessel. Obadiah said, "Ruth, let me help you," as he lowered her into the canoe. Samuel noted the name. Then the man handed his daughter to his wife and whispered, "Naomi, you sit with your mother." *Obadiah, Ruth, Naomi. Noted.* Obadiah was the last to board, and Samuel handed him a paddle.

Josiah pushed off first, in the canoe with Jonah and David, and gave Samuel a hand signal to follow. Josiah's arms and shoulders were powerful, so his canoe moved quickly toward the center of the river. Samuel tried to keep up, working hard but not wanting to paddle so hard that he would make a splashing noise. Josiah had told him previously that the most dangerous leg of the journey was from the wharf to the edge of town, and that they needed to cross that distance quickly and silently.

Fortunately, Obadiah was a strong paddler in the front of the canoe, so their vessel stayed close to the boat being propelled by Josiah and Jonah. Samuel was breathing heavily at the start of the trip, but his body soon adjusted to the exertion. Little Naomi gave a squeal of delight as their canoe slid smoothly across the water, but her mother immediately shushed her. Samuel glanced back toward the town to see if anyone heard her, but the wharf remained still and empty. He paddled on the right side of the canoe and Obadiah paddled on the left, and they quickly got in sync. Samuel had to make only minor adjustments to his paddle to keep in line with Josiah's canoe. The only sounds on the river were the dipping of their paddles and the slap of waves against the sides of the boats.

Then, suddenly, a shout from the shoreline on the Occoquan side, "Who goes there?" Josiah pushed David down to the bottom of the boat, so Samuel did the same with Ruth and Naomi. Josiah gave a hand signal to paddle toward the opposite side of the river, which they all began to do with vigor. "Announce yourself!" said the voice from the shore. Samuel's heart was pounding, both from the exertion and from the fear of what might happen. Josiah had told him that sentries might spot them, but they would probably not shoot unless they had good reason to do so. Samuel prayed that the person would hold fire.

Within a few minutes, the two canoes passed the eastern edge of the Town of Occoquan, and the voice went silent. Obadiah turned and smiled at Samuel, relieved that they had escaped. Samuel gave him a nod, followed by a deep sigh. For a few beats, they stopped paddling and let the canoes drift. But then, knowing that they had a long journey ahead of them, Samuel plunged his paddle back in the water and they resumed their rhythm. Obadiah matched his strokes perfectly, and they continued to cut through the water on their eastward course. Under Josiah's direction, the two boats moved toward the center of the river, where the current was the strongest, flowing toward the Potomac River.

Although Josiah and Jonah were powerful paddlers, Samuel and Oba-diah were able to keep up with them by working so efficiently together. Samuel realized that he had never worked so closely beside a black man, and he was impressed by how quickly the two developed a pattern of silent coordination and communication. By watching Obadiah, Samuel made subtle adjustments to his strokes, and by listening to Samuel, Obadiah was able to do the same. Within a mile of paddling, they were synchronized perfectly. Their strokes were strong and propulsive, but as silent as spoons stirring tea.

*How can Virginians see blacks as less than human?* Samuel had heard stories of beatings, rapes, and families torn apart. *Even Thomas Jefferson believed that blacks were inferior to whites in both body and mind.* Looking forward in the canoe, Samuel saw Ruth comforting Naomi with the strength and compassion of a loving mother. He watched as Obadiah propelled the boat with power and precision. He knew that the family was taking an enormous risk to secure their freedom, to claim what the Declaration of Independence called life, liberty, and the pursuit of happiness. *How could anyone see these people as inferior?*

As they reached the spot where the Occoquan River flowed into the Potomac, a shot rang out from the point of land on the southern side. *What is going on?* Samuel felt a rising panic, and his paddling fell out of harmony with Obadiah. He looked across the river and saw the glow of torches: One, two, three, four. Looking to Josiah for guidance, he saw the miller motion the boats to move again toward the northern bank of the river. Another shot rang out, and this time a bullet made a splash in the water next to Josiah. "Keep paddling," said the miller. "We are too far away for them to hit us." Samuel desperately hoped that he was correct.

Several men gave shouts from the point of land, followed by three more rifle shots. One sliced through a branch on a tree hanging over the river. Another clipped the bow of Samuel's canoe, a few short feet from Obadiah, causing Naomi to cry out. "Paddle!" shouted Josiah, not caring if the men on the shore heard him. Obadiah told his wife and daughter to get down, as he pulled on his paddle with superhuman strength. Samuel tried his best to keep pace with him, and within a few moments the canoe was cutting through the water like a schooner under full sail. *Where did those men come from?* Samuel wondered as he worked. *Did the Occoquan sentry alert them? How could he have moved down the shoreline so fast? Did he have a horse?* Samuel did not really expect to find answers, but his rapid series of questions matched his paddle strokes.

Then, as quickly as the shooting had started, it stopped. The two canoes were now out of rifle range, and the torches on the shoreline became distant points of light. The four men continued to paddle across the Potomac River, a wide but shallow body of water that was as smooth as glass on that March night. They stroked silently, reflecting on the danger they had just escaped, feeling thankful to be alive. Then, after an hour of progress, they saw a single torch on the Maryland side. Ruth began to sing, softly, "*When Israel was in Egypt's land / Let my people go / Oppress'd so hard they could not stand / Let my people go . . .*"

Obadiah joined in for the chorus, which Samuel could hear Jonah and David singing in the other boat as well: "*Go down, Moses / Way down in Egypt's land / Tell old Pharaoh / Let my people go . . .*"

The torch was the signal for the Underground Railroad. The light of freedom.

Samuel slept late on Monday morning, having returned to Occoquan with Josiah just an hour before daybreak. Their return to town had been uneventful, but slower than their trip to Maryland since they no longer had strong paddlers in the bows of their canoes. The men propelled their boats from the stern, with fishing poles propped up in the bows to give the impression that they were on a nighttime fishing expedition. Samuel wondered if they would actually have to catch some fish to be credible, but Josiah assured him that any sentry or soldier would understand the lament, "Nothing biting tonight." The two returned along the southern bank of the Occoquan River, paddling slowly and preparing to reveal themselves to any Rebels who might confront them. But they saw no one. The party that had shot at them earlier had disappeared.

The sun was high in the sky when Samuel jerked awake, panicked that he was late for work. But then he remembered that Josiah had told him to take the day off. "Thou deservest a day of recovery," said the miller at the end of the journey, promising to tell Bushrod that Samuel was feeling ill. Ann knew of their adventure, so she let Samuel stay in bed for as long as he wanted. When she heard him stirring, she brought him some hot coffee in a tin cup.

"Didst thou sleep well?" she asked him.

"Well, but not long enough," he said, rubbing his eyes.

"Thou wast doing the Lord's work."

Sitting up in bed, he took the cup and said, "I thank thee." Then he sipped it, enjoying its warmth and rich, earthy taste. His mother had made it strong and black, as he liked it.

"I bought thee a newspaper," Ann said, placing the paper on his lap. "I am so concerned about the war, and about William."

"What is happening?" asked Samuel.

"General McClellan has still not begun his march," said Ann. "This does not bother me, since I suspect that William is in the army that will encounter him."

"Dost thou not want the Union to take Richmond?"

"Not at the expense of thy brother."

Samuel nodded, and took another sip. He felt the same ambivalence about the Peninsula Campaign.

"Thou will see," Ann continued, pointing to the paper, "that the Union has begun a siege of Fort Macon."

"Where is that?"

"North Carolina. The Union wants to close off Beaufort, one of the last ports open to the Rebels."

"May they have success," said Samuel.

"Indeed."

"My hope is that this war will end without more loss of life," said Samuel. "Since the Confederacy needs trade, the closing of ports may force their surrender."

Ann smiled, grateful that Samuel was committed to a peaceful resolution to the conflict, in line with their Quaker principles. She loved her son William no less than his older brother, but she had remained deeply distressed and perplexed by his decision to join the army. She wanted so badly to see him, to hold him, and to discover what was going on in his heart and mind. *Perhaps he will return to the light.*

At that moment, a rap came on the door. Samuel stiffened, fearful that someone was coming to confront him about his nighttime journey. Ann put a hand on his shoulder and said, "Fear not. I will get it." She stepped out of the bedroom, and crossed the main room to the front door. She opened the door to see the town letter carrier.

"Good morning, Mrs. Bagley," he said with a respectful nod.

"How dost thou do, Edward Smith?" she replied.

"Very well, thank you. You have a letter from the army. I hope it is good news."

Ann felt a shock run through her, head to toe. "It will be news," she replied, taking the letter from the carrier.

"A good day to you," said Edward.

Since Ann would never say "good day" or "good-bye," she simply said "farewell" and returned to the inside of her house. After closing the door, she called to Samuel, "We have a letter." Then she tore it open.

> Saturday, Mar. 15th, 1862
> Mrs. Ann Bagley
> Occoquan, Virginia
>
> With feelings of deepest sorrow, I announce to you the death of your son, Private William Bagley. He was killed in training in Williamsburg. A caisson carriage, carrying black powder, exploded. While nothing can atone to you and your family for his loss, it will be a consolation to know that he died nobly at his post. He expired without a struggle. None excelled him in devotion to his family, fidelity to his country, and gallantry as a champion in our glorious struggle. As his commander, I mourn with you his loss. His remains have been embalmed with arsenic, and will be returned to you by military transport.
>
> Very truly, your Obedient Servant,
> H.P. Sampson
> Colonel, Botetourt Artillery, C.S.A.

Samuel stood at the doorway of his bedroom, watching his mother's face as it quickly lost all color. She shook her head twice, unable to believe what she was reading. Then she looked straight at her son and let out a scream that sounded like the howl of a wild red fox at night.

# 18

## Beginning of Holy Week 2022

UNDER A BRILLIANT BLUE sky, Harley stood on a lawn overlooking the Potomac River. About fifty mourners sat in folding chairs in front of him, and he offered prayers from a portable podium. There was not a cloud in the sky, so sunlight sparkled on the water and illuminated the camouflage colors of the trees that covered the Maryland shoreline. Harley was standing in front of George Washington's Mount Vernon, aware of the fact that he was being treated to the same view that the first president enjoyed every morning. He tried to imagine barges carrying grain from Occoquan to Alexandria, or canoes transporting pelts from Maryland hunting grounds to Washington markets. Plus, enslaved people working the land along the shoreline. Lots of enslaved people.

In summertime, Harley often anchored his boat in front of Mount Vernon and had picnics with friends while taking in the view of the mansion. But this was the first time he had been on the Mount Vernon grounds, enabling him to see the opposite vista. He had been called on to offer a funeral for a member of the Mount Vernon Ladies' Association, a woman who was part of a group that owned the mansion and had been taking care of it since 1860. Mount Vernon had been glorious in the time of George and Martha Washington, but by the 1850s it was falling apart, which inspired the pioneers of this women's group to raise money to buy the home and its two hundred acres. The Civil War interrupted the association's efforts to restore the mansion, but the women found a way to keep the property protected and open to the public throughout the conflict. Since then, they had done a marvelous job with the mansion and grounds, and Harley appreciated their recent efforts to research and reveal the lives of the people enslaved at Mount Vernon.

But he was not standing in front of the mansion to present a history lesson that day. Instead, he was offering remembrances of a Methodist woman who had donated countless hours to the work of the association. Harley did not know her personally, but he had been called upon to officiate at the service because he was a local Methodist pastor. Although she had not been active in church in recent years, Harley had visited with her family, learned about her life, and crafted a message that would give thanks for her contributions while also expressing gratitude to God for the gift of everlasting life. Part of him hated these services, because they revealed the size of the recent American exodus from organized religion. Only a minority of people in the Washington area were active in any church or congregation in a meaningful way. But he also felt obligated to officiate, because he knew that grieving families needed compassionate ministry at their time of loss.

So, there Harley stood, looking out over a small crowd of people he did not know, giving thanks for the life of a woman he did not know. He wore a black robe and a white stole, the color of resurrection, but he really wished he was in a wool coat, since the temperatures were in the fifties and a stiff wind was blowing. *April is the cruelest month,* he thought to himself, remembering the words of T.S. Eliot, *breeding / Lilacs out of the dead land, mixing / Memory and desire.* At least the redbuds around the mansion were beginning to bloom, sending out their distinctive purple flowers in a fiery burst of color. *You can always see a sign of life,* he thought to himself, *even on a cold, cruel day.*

"Give rest, O Christ, to thy servant with all thy saints," Harley said to the congregation, "where sorrow and pain are no more, but only life everlasting." He believed these words as much as he believed anything in the Christian faith. It was incomprehensible to him that God would create people in the divine image, place them in the world, and then abandon them at death. Harley truly was a believer in resurrection, and he counted on it to be a reality for him and for the people he loved. But as he stood on the windswept lawn in front of Mount Vernon, he did not experience the joy of the resurrection. No, he was feeling "lilacs" and "the dead land," and was remembering the loss of his wife Karen and his daughter Jessica. Looking at the garden area to the right of the podium, he pictured the memorial garden where their ashes had been interred after they died in 2016. The last time he had been there, on Thanksgiving Day, fallen leaves had covered the ground, along with debris from flowers that had died at the end of the season. The cloudy sky had been the color of lead, and the day had been bitter cold. He had fixated on the Latin phrase *memento mori*, "remember that you have to die." *Yes, the resurrection is true. But so is death. Lilacs and the dead land. Memory and desire.*

"All we go down to the dust," Harley said at the end of the service, "and, weeping over the grave we make our song; Alleluia, alleluia, alleluia." *That's right: Even at the grave, we say alleluia. Even at the moment of death, we praise God.* And then, Harley lifted his right hand in blessing and concluded by saying, "The grace of our Lord Jesus Christ, the love of God, and the fellowship of the Holy Spirit be with you all. Amen."

A few people in the congregation said "amen," but most remained silent. They did not know what to say. Then, a representative of Mount Vernon stepped to the podium and invited everyone to come inside for a reception. The congregation stood and began to move toward the mansion. The son of the deceased woman stepped forward, said, "Thank you, pastor," and pressed three hundred dollars into Harley's hand.

His job was done.

*Alleluia, alleluia, alleluia.*

That same morning, Nanette walked into a brightly lit room at Swedish Hospital in Seattle. She was grateful for the strong artificial light, since the sun that day was obscured by a thick blanket of clouds. *Typical Seattle*, she thought. *Don't miss that part of it.*

"How are you doing, girlfriend?" she asked her colleague Janet, who was lying in bed, recovering from a hysterectomy. The two had worked together for years.

"Painkillers are great," Janet said, smiling. She had a round face, short brown hair, and bright blue eyes.

"Looks like you don't need any flowers," said Nanette, looking around the room and seeing a dozen vases on various shelves and tabletops.

"When you work in HR," said Janet, wincing slightly as she shifted in bed, "everyone wants to be your friend."

"Don't I know it," said Nanette. "But please, take these." She held up a vase with a dozen long-stemmed roses. "I don't expect any favors."

"Flowers from a true friend," said Janet. "Always appreciated."

"I'll put them here, under the TV. That way, you can think of me when you watch your trashy reality shows."

"You know me too well."

After putting the vase in place, Nanette pulled a chair close to the bed and sat down. "Everything okay with the surgery?" she asked. Janet looked pale, but Nanette could not tell if that was from loss of blood or lack of make-up.

"Doc says it went well," said Janet. "No complications. Just the regular recovery, which takes longer as we age."

"Take your time," said Nanette. "I can stay another week. There are no crises brewing at the office." She knew that Janet would not want to return to work until she could project an image of strength and vitality. Appearances mattered to Janet, and Nanette was not going to rush her.

"Good to hear," said Janet, reaching for the water bottle on her meal tray. Nanette shifted the rolling tray closer to her.

"You left everything in great shape," said Nanette. "I don't really feel that I need to be here."

"I disagree," said Janet, shaking her head. "The fact that you are sitting at my desk is enough to keep the chaos at bay."

"Well, I'm happy to help," said Nanette. "And it is good to see you, even under the circumstances."

"And you," said Janet. "So, how is life at HQ2?"

"So far, so good," said Nanette. "Same HR system as here. But the building is nice: Brand new, in Arlington, near the airport."

"And how is Occoquan?" Janet asked. "I love the name."

"Cute town. Very historic, and right on the Occoquan River."

"I saw the picture you sent, the one from your apartment window. What a view!"

"Yes, I love my place," said Nanette. "A penthouse apartment on the water would cost a fortune here in Seattle. Or in Arlington. But in Occoquan: Quite affordable."

"I'm jealous," said Janet. "But happy for you."

Nanette knew that she was not truly jealous. The two had supported each other through numerous losses and setbacks, so each of them was thrilled when the other found joy. Smiling, Nanette said, "When do you think you'll get out of here?"

"Doctor said by Monday, if all goes well."

"Need a ride home?" asked Nanette.

"No, but thanks. Rick will pick me up." Janet had lost her husband to cancer a few years earlier, but her son Rick was in the area.

"That's good news," said Nanette. "You are making a great recovery."

"Seem to be," said Janet. Then, shifting the topic, she asked, "Are you seeing anyone these days?"

Nanette took a deep breath. "I was," she said, speaking slowly. "Had a date with a man that I really liked."

"From the office?"

"No, from church."

"You *are* a church lover," said Janet. "I know that about you."

"He seemed great. Kind. Intelligent. Easy on the eyes." Then, after pausing for a second, she added, "He is the pastor."

"Wow," said Janet, genuinely surprised. "You go right to the top."

"Stop it," said Nanette. "It's probably not going to work."

"Because he's a pastor?"

"No," said Nanette. "Because he is involved with someone else."

"How do you know?"

"Saw him holding hands with her in a coffee shop."

"Okay."

"Then he got some secret message from her while we were taking a walk together."

"I'm sorry," said Janet. She could tell how crushed Nanette was.

"I cannot go through that again," Nanette said. "You know what happened in my marriage. The lies. The cheating. The disrespect."

"I know, honey," said Janet, taking her hand. "You deserve honesty and respect. You have every right to happiness."

Tearing up, Nanette said, "Look at you, comforting me. I came here to comfort you."

"That's what friends are for."

Back in Occoquan, Harley changed out of his funeral clothes and put on a track suit and running shoes. He was determined to get some exercise on such a clear, cool, spring day. After stepping out of his front door and walking down the cast iron steps, he took a left on Mill Street and headed toward the American Legion. A crowd was gathered there, standing beside two long tables under a red canopy.

"What's going on?" he asked waitress Jessica Simpson, who was standing outside for a smoke break.

Pushing her black hair to one side, she said, "CPR training." Then, after tossing her cigarette butt on the ground and crushing it, she asked, "Want to get certified?"

"No," said Harley. "Just curious."

"So, how you been?" she asked.

"Not bad. Had a funeral this morning."

"Sorry to hear it."

"No tragedy," said Harley. "Eighty-nine years old."

"Like my customers," she said with sly smile.

"And what's up with you?" asked Harley. Although she looked nothing like his daughter Jessica, he felt a warmth toward her based on the shared name.

"Same old, same old," she said. "Serving the beer cold and the eggs hot."

"I never get used to your guys and their breakfast beers."

"That's a cry for help, for sure," she said. "But not everyone has the habit. Your friend Nanette has become a regular."

"Really?" said Harley. Just the mention of her name gave him a wave of melancholy.

"Yeah, she's good people," said Jessica. "No-Change Nanette."

"She is generous, for sure."

"People have heard about what she does," said Jessica, "and now they are tipping more. All around town."

"Interesting," said Harley.

"You've heard of downward spirals, right? Well, she has started an upward spiral. People are tipping more, servers are working harder, people are tipping even more . . . an upward spiral."

"I like it," said Harley, always on the lookout for good sermon material. But as inspiring as the story was, the focus on Nanette was not lifting him up. Ready to change the subject, he asked, "So, what's the deal with the CPR?"

"A joint venture between the town and the American Legion. You see deputy Sharon Madison by one of the tables?"

Harley nodded, spotting her curly red hair. Then he said, "I see Mary the postmistress as well."

"And there is the new guy, Don Abad," Jessica said. "Sharon put out the call for CPR instructors and he showed up."

"Yeah, I see him," said Harley. The man was unmistakable with his long scar and shoulder-length blond hair. "Do you know him?"

"No really," she said. "I see him on the street, but have never spoken to him."

"I talked with him briefly, a month or so ago."

"I think he lives in Nanette's apartment building," said Jessica.

"Yes, you're right." Again, the sadness. "I guess he is doing his public service."

"Apparently so," said Jessica. "You can see that it is mostly Boy Scouts who are getting the training. But it's open to anyone."

"Kind of cold for outdoor training."

"You're right," she said. "But Scouts are used to it."

"Well, I'll just take my walk," said Harley. "Strengthen my heart. Then I won't need CPR."

"Sounds like a plan," said Jessica. "Later, Harley."

Palm Sunday was April 10, almost three weeks after the start of spring, but winter weather was not letting go. Harley stepped out of his townhouse without an overcoat, which he immediately regretted. The temperature was in the forties, much too chilly for a sport jacket and tie. But since he was running late, he did not turn around. Instead, he hustled down the street, wondering if warm weather would ever come. His only consolation came from the fact that the redbuds were in furious bloom, as they had been at Mount Vernon, and their purple flowers seemed to be a sign that nature was in harmony with the color of the Lenten season.

Harley's second shock was received when he entered the Sanctuary and discovered that the furnace had malfunctioned during the night. The room was as cold as a barn, and the thermostat registered fifty degrees. "This church is going to *kill* me," he mumbled to Andy Stackhouse, who arrived minutes later to serve as an usher.

"Guess we'll have to keep our coats on," said Andy.

"I suppose so," said Harley.

Fortunately, the start of Holy Week drew a good crowd, and the number of people in the Sanctuary warmed the room by a few degrees. Spirits were lifted by the sight of smiling children waving palm branches and processing around the Sanctuary, as the congregation sang a triumphant hymn.

"Welcome back, all of you," said Harley after the singing stopped. "So good to see a Palm Sunday procession, for the first time since 2019!" Despite the cold, the congregation was excited to be experiencing their first post-pandemic Holy Week. Then the choir offered a Sermon in Music, a moving choral piece that focused on the sacrificial death of Jesus. "Today is not just Palm Sunday," Harley said by way of introduction, "but also Passion Sunday—the day each year that we focus on the suffering of Jesus." *A bipolar day*, thought Harley, *one that celebrates the glorious entry of Jesus into Jerusalem, while also grieving the death of Christ on the cross.* "The word passion means 'suffering,' and we are grateful for what Jesus suffered to bring us forgiveness and new life." *Now, if we can just get some new life in our heating system.*

Coffee hour after worship was a festive time in the social hall downstairs, with pink and green streamers hanging from the ceiling in anticipation of Easter. Children chased each other around the hall, dodging the legs of adults who were sipping coffee and chatting, while a handful of youths stood in a corner looking at their phones. Since the public-school spring break aligned with Holy Week, Harley was sure that they were anxious to get out of church and into their vacation activities.

"Harley," said Andy, walking up behind him with a cup of coffee in hand. "I found something that might interest you."

"Really? What's that?"

"I've been doing some research at the Library of Congress," said the retired Navy man. "They have an amazing collection of Civil War letters."

"Is that right?" Harley was interested, but reluctant to get pulled down a rabbit hole.

"I've been focusing on letters connected to Occoquan," said Andy. "And one this past week really grabbed me. You know about the Liberty Pole at Rockledge, right?"

"Sure."

"Well," said Andy. "This letter was written by an abolitionist, and it indicates that his group had nothing to do with the Liberty Pole."

"Really?" said Harley, suddenly interested. "But the pole was very pro-Lincoln."

"Exactly. The author suggests that it was a Southern group that put up the pole and then tore it down. It was what you would call a 'false flag' operation."

"A false *what*?"

"False flag," said Andy. "An act committed to disguise a responsible party, and to put blame on another party. The term has Navy roots, when a ship would fly the flag of another country in order to hide its identity."

"So why would a Southern group erect a Liberty Pole?" asked Harley.

"Hard to say, exactly," said Andy. "The writer of letter was speculating. He says that the pole was on Joseph Janney's property, but he did not erect it. The writer thinks that Southerners wanted to demonize the abolitionists and polarize the community. By erecting the pole and then chopping it down, the Southerners sent a message to the community that loyalty to Lincoln would not be tolerated."

"Kind of brilliant," said Harley, "when you think about it. A pro-Lincoln pole is erected, which draws attention to Quakers and abolitionists, the minority group in town. Then the pole is publicly chopped down, which lets the minority know what will happen if they get out of line."

"Very scary for the Lincoln supporters," said Andy. "No doubt about it."

"Your discovery could change history."

"Well, I wouldn't go that far," said Andy. "As I said, it is speculation. But things are not always what they appear to be."

"You are right about that," said Harley.

At that point, Mary Ranger tapped Harley on the shoulder. She flashed him a big smile and asked, "When you going to get your boat out, pastor?"

"Soon, I hope."

"I thought it was in the shop," said Andy, taking another sip of coffee.

"That's right," said Harley. "But it's just a balky power steering mechanism. Marina repair shop says it could be ready by Wednesday."

"That would be perfect," said Mary. "I hear the temps are finally going to rise. Maybe hit eighty by mid-week."

"If that happens, the river will be packed," said Andy. "I always love the return of boating season." Then, seeing his wife waving to him across the room, Andy said goodbye and slipped off.

"I saw you outside the American Legion," said Harley.

"That's right. CPR training."

"How did it go?"

"Very well," said Mary. "Got a number of people certified. Mostly Boy Scouts."

"Well, it was a cold day to be outside."

"True," said Mary. "Those Scouts camp year-round, so they don't care."

"You were working with Don Abad, right?"

"Yes," she said. "New resident. Had seen him picking up his mail, but hadn't really talked with him before the training day."

"What did you learn?"

Mary turned her head and gave him a quizzical look. "What do you want to know? Looking to recruit him for Riverside?"

Harley smiled and said, "Not really. I met him once and thought I knew him from somewhere. Cannot figure him out."

"Well, we talked after the training," said Mary. "Went into the American Legion to warm up, get a cup of coffee. He said he worked in IT and did most his work from home. Said he really loved his new apartment."

"That building is nice, no doubt about it."

"I asked about where he was from, but he was very cryptic," said Mary. "Said something weird, like 'everywhere . . . and nowhere.' I asked about family, and he said, 'Nobody.' But then I pushed him a bit, saying that he must have *some* family. You know how I can be! Finally, he said that he had a younger brother who got mixed up in drugs. Lost him to an overdose."

"That's terrible," said Harley. "A tragedy."

"And a conversation stopper," said Mary. "And that point, the small talk came to an end."

"Yeah, it's hard to know where to go from there," said Harley. "But we are going to keep dealing with it. Crack cocaine, crystal meth, and now fentanyl. The carnage is mind-blowing."

"Hard to know what to do."

"Juan Erazo is really concerned about the rise in gang activity around here."

"I bet he is," said Mary.

"He really loves the kids," said Harley.

"I know he wants to keep them safe from gangs and drugs."

"Do you think he would ever . . . take matters into his own hands?"

"Juan?" asked Mary. "No, I don't think so. He's a peaceful man. *San Juan.*"

Harley knew the history of the name, but did not feel it was his place to tell Juan's story. "So," said Harley, "anything else about Don?"

"No, that's it," said Mary. "Like I said, he told me about his brother, and that brought the conversation to an end. I thanked him for helping with the CPR and the Boy Scouts, and we went our separate ways."

"He is quite the mystery man," said Harley. "But now I am feeling sympathetic."

"I am, too," said Mary.

When Harley returned to his office, he found a photocopy of the old Occoquan letter that Andy had discovered. At the top, written in Andy's hand,
were the words, "Things are not always what they appear to be."

# 19

## Fourth Month 1862

A WOMAN IN A long black dress appeared at the door of the Bagley house. She had a thick belt around her waist and a scarf over her head, covering most of her face. Emerging from her back were two large wings, which swept downward into a resting position. In her left hand was a bouquet of poppies.

The woman knocked on the door three times, slowly and forcefully. Ann Bagley answered, surprised and confused. Then she grasped the identity of the woman. "Why?" she asked, to which the visitor said nothing. Ann began to retreat into the house. The visitor entered, crouching slightly to allow her wings to pass through the door.

"Why didst thou take him?" Ann asked. Her anger was beginning to rise. "What did he do to deserve it? He was my boy!"

The woman removed her scarf, revealing an expression that was both calm and determined. With her right hand, she reached out to touch Ann on the shoulder. Then she said, gently and clearly, "He had to die, so that others could live."

Ann awoke with a start.

"You have my deepest sympathy," said Thomas Washington to the young man standing on the other side of the counter. Samuel Bagley had come to the dry goods store to buy sugar and coffee for his mother. Standing tall and thinner than ever, he looked like a grieving scarecrow.

"I thank thee," said Samuel, bowing his head to the older man. "Our loss is profound."

"I believe you," said Thomas. "Your brother was a fine young man." The news of William's death had stunned the older man, given that the young man was so close in age to his own son, and it had strengthened his resolve to keep Bushrod out of the war. "I know that Bushrod admired him," he continued. "And Abigail is . . . devastated."

"Yes," said Samuel, feeling an unwanted jolt of jealousy toward his dead brother. "She was very fond of him, I know."

"He died for a good cause," said Thomas, trying to move the conversation away from uncomfortable emotional terrain. But as he did, his round face flushed and he dropped his eyes to the floor. He was overcome by an unexpected wave of shame, one that was generated by his decision to withhold his own son from battle.

Samuel was unsure of how to respond. *Surely he knows that I do not consider it a good cause.* But since Quakers are comfortable with silence, he let Thomas's words hang in the air for a moment. Then he asked, "What dost thou hear about the progress of the war?"

Thomas looked up and said, "McClellan is marching up the peninsula." He was relieved to have the conversation shift to current events. "Magruder confronted him at Yorktown, and convinced him that the Confederate forces were strong. As of one week ago, McClellan began a siege."

"Is that wise?" asked Samuel, not knowing very much about military strategy.

"Hard to say," said Thomas, giving a shrug. "A siege will be hard on Magruder and his forces. But it will give time for Johnston to move his army down the Peninsula to support him."

"And that will make it more difficult for McClellan to attack Richmond," asked Samuel, "will it not?"

"I would think so," said Thomas.

"My brother died on the Peninsula," said Samuel. "In Williamsburg."

Thomas nodded. He wanted to offer the young man consolation, but he could not find the right words. Instead, he returned to talk of military movements. "There has been much action out west as well."

"Do tell," said Samuel.

"About the time that McClellan started his siege," said Thomas, warming to the topic, "our army attacked the Union forces under Ulysses S.

Grant. This was at Shiloh, Tennessee. At the end of the first day of fighting, the federal troops were close to defeat."

"That would have been significant," said Samuel.

"Indeed," said Thomas. "We have struggled mightily in that region. But during the night, Union reinforcements arrived, and on the second day the Union dominated the field. Our forces retreated. The federal forces did not follow. Casualties were heavy—over ten thousand on each side."

"Horrible," said Samuel. He tried to imagine his own grief being multiplied by the thousands. "The war bug is spreading."

Thomas was perplexed. "War bug?"

"A term we use in the Society of Friends," said Samuel. "A way to talk about violence and destruction and death."

"That fits the scene at Shiloh," Thomas said. "Terrible carnage. Soldiers from both sides, on the ground, dead and dying."

"The angel of death was at work."

"No doubt," said Thomas. "But there were other angels as well."

Samuel tilted his head, confused. "Other angels?"

"Yes," said Thomas, reaching under his counter. "I just read a story." Putting a newspaper on the counter, he opened it and scanned several pages. Then, placing his fat index finger on a column, he read aloud, "When fighting ceased at Shiloh, troops lay wounded in forests and fields. They cried out for water, for help, for God, for their families. Robert Murray, the attending Union Medical Director, reported that there were 'very inadequate arrangements' for the wounded. But then, as the soldiers waited for medics, the wounds of many men began to give off a blue glow. Witnesses reported small orbs of blue light, thousands of them, across the battlefield. With so many dying or close to death, they called it 'the Angel's Glow.' Some thought the glow was the souls of dying men, while others thought it was a sign of angels visiting men in an effort to save them."

"A sign of angels?" asked Samuel.

"That is what they were saying," said Thomas. "But note this: The soldiers who had the Angel's Glow lived longer than those who did not."

Samuel nodded and said, "I only wish my brother had such a visit."

"As do I," said Thomas, feeling the young man's pain. "As do I."

Later that morning, Occoquan's Society of Friends came together in a gathering called a clearness committee. Ann had requested that William be buried in the Quaker cemetery, next to his father, despite his removal from the community following his enlistment in the army. Since this was an extraordinary request, a group of leaders had to gather and gain clarity about God's will.

As Ann and Samuel walked to the meetinghouse on that clear spring morning, birds were singing loudly in the trees, joyfully announcing the return of life and light. Their songs did not match the mood of the Bagley family. After a few minutes of silent walking, Ann said to Samuel, "Last night, I was visited by an angel."

"An angel?" he said.

"Yes, the angel of death."

"How dost thou know?" Samuel asked. He was surprised, but at the same time curious. *The Angel's Glow?*

"She had a long black dress," said Ann. "Large wings." Clearly, this was not the orbs of blue light seen at Shiloh.

"She said," Ann continued, "that his death would bring life to others."

"I do not understand," said Samuel.

At that point, Josiah Farlow called to them from the door of the meetinghouse. He beckoned them to enter, and gave Samuel an affectionate squeeze on the shoulder. Sunlight was pouring into the large room through the clear glass windows that lined the walls, and a handful of Quaker leaders were taking seats on the austere wooden pews that ringed the room. Unlike the pews in most churches, which were placed in rows to face the pulpit, the pews of this meetinghouse were positioned to face the center of the room. There was no pulpit and no altar. Friends gathered for worship by facing each other, and waiting for the Spirit to speak to them.

The clearness committee was made up of five leaders of the community: Josiah Farlow, Patience Cadwallader, Joseph Janney, George Trueblood, and Elizabeth Milhous. The Bagleys knew them all very well. Samuel saw Josiah every day, as they worked together at the mill. Patience was close to Ann in age, and the two of them sewed together along with Elizabeth, a single woman in her forties. Joseph was the town's business leader and most eligible bachelor, while George was a teller at the Bank of Occoquan, married to Ann's friend Emily. There could be no group more sympathetic to Ann's request, and yet their work as a committee was to discern Christ's will, not her will.

The committee was small, so they sat in one corner of the room. Ann and Samuel sat down on chairs facing the corner, while the five leaders sat in the first and second pews in front of them. Josiah began the meeting by saying, "Friends, let us worship together." They entered into a period of silence, seeking to quiet their minds. Their worship did not include any singing or preaching or spoken prayers. Bibles were available in the pews, for those who wanted to meditate on Scripture, but no lessons were read aloud. Throughout this period, the worshippers tried to open their hearts and minds to the light of Jesus, the one they believed to be the light of the world.

After about ten minutes, Josiah broke the silence by saying, "Ann Bagley, thou hast a request for us today."

Ann nodded and said, "I request that my son William Bagley be interred in our burial ground, next to his father."

The group sat in respectful silence, considering this request. Although no immediate response was given, the members of the clearness committee thought long and hard about what she was asking. After several minutes, Elizabeth spoke gently and carefully. "Tell us, Ann Bagley, why this location is so important to thee."

"William is a child of this community," she said. "For most of his life, he followed our way. I want him to be laid to rest beside his father, so that our family unity, and the unity of this community, can be preserved."

More silence followed. Then George, the bank teller, asked, "Dost thou not think that William chose to leave this community through his enlistment?"

"Perhaps," said Ann, clearly grieved. "We will never know. Since he left so suddenly, I was never able to discern what was in his heart."

The committee knew that Ann was speaking the truth. They had all been mystified by William's departure and his joining of the Confederate Army. But then Josiah said, in words that surprised Samuel, "Still, a man's actions reveal his heart. By his enlistment, William chose to separate himself from us." Samuel had hoped that Josiah would be an advocate for his brother, but clearly he was not being led to do so.

"I had great affection for William," said Joseph, "but Jesus is clear: 'Blessed are the peacemakers.'"

"Put your sword back in its place," added George, quoting Jesus, "for all who live by the sword will die by the sword."

"Friends," said Patience, "thou art right to quote the Prince of Peace." Then, picking up a Bible, she searched for a page and said, "Jesus also proclaimed, 'I did not come to bring peace, but a sword.'"

"Respectfully, that is not to be taken literally," said George.

"Perhaps it is," she said, "perhaps it is not." Her own son Amos had just left Occoquan—and the Quaker meeting—to join the Union Army. While she did not agree with his choice, she understood his desire to fight for a just cause.

Then quiet Elizabeth spoke again. "Ann Bagley, my heart breaks for thee and for Samuel. Thy loss is profound. But our challenge today is to discern the will of our Savior. I cannot deny that he wanted us to live in peace with everybody. Our faith requires that we never try to overcome evil by evil, but instead overcome evil with good."

Elizabeth's words were profound, revealing the very heart of the Quaker commitment to pacifism. Josiah stretched out his massive arms toward Ann, trying to signal openness to her, and said, "May I reflect what thou hast said to us?" Ann nodded. "Thou desirest interment for William as a child of this community. Thou knowest he has departed from our way, for reasons thou cannot discern. Thou askest for burial beside his father, for the sake of family unity, and community unity."

"Thou hast heard me, Josiah Farlow," Ann said. "I thank thee."

"Committee, we have a decision to make," said the miller. "Ann Bagley has shared her request with us. We need to find clearness as a committee. Does the request reflect Christ's will?"

Stout Patience shifted in her pew, pushed a strand of blond hair out of her face and said, "I need more time." Handsome Joseph nodded in agreement. "Let us take a few minutes," said Josiah. The committee sat back in their pews, closed their eyes, and waited for the inner light to become clear.

Samuel found the wait to be excruciating. Yes, he respected the practice of his community, but he questioned whether the silence could actually shape consensus. His mother Ann was clearly agitated, but she sat quietly in her chair, her eyes closed.

Finally, gentle Elizabeth broke the silence. "I believe I am clear," she said. "As much as a I love thee, Ann Bagley, I do not believe we can support thy request." Ann's face fell. "William made a free choice to leave our community, leave our faith. I cannot support interment in our burial ground."

"It is clear," said George, nodding. "William made his choice."

"Agreed," said Joseph, followed by Josiah. All eyes shifted to Patience, since clearness had to be unanimous. "Agreed, with deep sorrow," she said. "My own son has made his choice as well. If he loses his life, he will have to be buried elsewhere. Our Lord commands peace."

Samuel looked at his mother, wondering if she would respond. He watched the muscles of her strong forearms ripple. She was upset, and he knew how contrary she could be. But all she said was, "Committee, I thank thee for thy consideration." Then she stood up and motioned for Samuel to do the same. Ever the peacemaker, he dared not defy her or the committee.

Ann moved quickly toward the door, not wanting to have any further conversation. Samuel moved ahead of her and opened the large wooden door of the meetinghouse. But then, as she reached the portal, she turned around and spoke to the group. "Scripture tells us that Jesus had compassion for the people around him. He chose to suffer with them. Because thou hast refused to suffer with me, I will no longer be a Friend. I join my son William in leaving the faith." Then she spun on her heels and left the building.

Samuel stood in stunned silence, holding the door.

Dinner at the Bagley house was rushed that night, since Ann was determined to resolve the matter of William's burial. She picked up Samuel's plate before he had finished his meat and potatoes, and he had to stab a final morsel with a fork as the plate was being spirited away. "Mother," he said, "there is nothing we can do tonight."

"Is that true?" she said.

Samuel chewed his last bite, wondering what she was thinking about. "Perhaps I can talk with Thomas Washington tomorrow," he said. "His church has a graveyard, and he so admires what William did."

"Too far," said Ann. "I want him close to us."

"But he does not have to be buried near us," said Samuel. "Remember what thou said? 'This is the comfort of the good, that the grave cannot hold them.'"

"Those are the words of William Penn. I am no longer guided by Quaker sentiments."

Samuel sat back, pondering this change of heart. His mother had been so devout. And now she was following William out of the faith. "So, what dost thou suggest?"

"Bury him here," she said. "In our house." Samuel had never heard such a thing. It struck him as barbaric.

Then, moving quickly across the room, Ann threw open the back door, stepped into the evening light and grabbed the shovel leaning against the back of the house. Returning inside, she gave Samuel the tool and pointed to a spot inside the door. "Remove the floorboards and dig," she said. "If anyone questions thee, tell them thou art digging a root cellar."

# 20

## Good Friday 2022

CLOUDS ROLLED ACROSS THE sky on the morning of Good Friday, making the water of the river a deep green one minute and then dappled with sunlight the next. Looking out his office window, Harley wondered if darkness would come over the whole land until three in the afternoon, as it had when Jesus was hanging on the cross. *Appropriately grey,* he mused, *given that it is both Good Friday and Tax Day.* The gloom fit the mood of most of the people in town, whether they were going to church or simply filing their returns. Harley spent the morning in his office, answering emails about Easter and preparing for the Good Friday service that was scheduled for that evening. His plan was to offer a service called Tenebrae, which means "shadows," one that included Scripture readings about the betrayal, trial, and crucifixion of Jesus, interspersed with dirge-like hymns. As the service progressed and the readings became darker, Harley would snuff out candles until the entire Sanctuary was pitch black. Then he would ring a large bell thirty-three times, one time for each year in the life of Jesus. It was a dramatic service, one that he had offered before, and he knew that people were moved by it.

The air temperature was not aligning with feelings of doom, however. The thermometer had climbed steadily through the week, giving the day a springlike feel, and the trees across town were defying the death of Jesus with their gorgeous blossoms. As he walked from his house to the church at the start of the day, he had stopped to admire several dogwood trees, blooming with white and pink flowers in the shape of a cross. Looking closely, he saw that the center of each flower looked like a crown of thorns.

The tip of each petal was indented, as though it bore the mark of a nail, and the reddish color of the indentations looked like drops of blood. *That could be a good sermon illustration,* he thought. *But not this year. No room for a sermon in the Tenebrae service.*

A knock came at his office door at twelve noon, and he stood and stretched his arms over his head before answering it. *Must be Abdul.* The big man was scheduled to get keys to the social hall for the first of the Muslim prayer services. Sure enough, when Harley opened his door, he saw Abdul dressed in a long white gown, which was the standard attire for Friday prayers. Since the gown was loosely fitting, he looked less intimidating than normal. Harley could not see his enormous arms beneath the folds.

"Welcome," he said, as he opened the door.

"*As-salamu alaikum,*" said Abdul, bowing slightly.

"And peace to you as well," said Harley, motioning for him to enter.

"This is an exciting day for me," said Abdul, flashing a smile that surprised Harley. The man was usually quite stoic. "Our very first service." Harley knew that a smile could be a sign of dominance, and he wondered if Abdul was sending a message of contempt. But then he thought, *No, don't be paranoid.* Abdul was not sneering, and he had shown nothing but good intent about his use of the church.

"Hope it goes well," says Harley.

"I need to do a little setup downstairs," said Abdul, "so I stopped by for the keys."

"Right here," said Harley, walking to his old oak desk and opening the center drawer. "The keys to the kingdom." He tossed them to Abdul, who caught them with his beefy left hand. "Hope the Easter decorations will not bother you."

"It is your space, pastor. We are your guests."

"Thank you, Abdul."

"No, I thank you," said Abdul, putting the keys in a pocket beneath his gown. "By the way, I wanted to let you know that I just finished the *el Castillo* deal."

"The visitor's center, right?"

"Yes. Fairfax County will put a museum on the suffragists in the basement. Complete with an actual cell from the Lorton Workhouse, where they were tortured."

"The Night of Terror," said Harley.

"Indeed," said Abdul. "History that should not be forgotten."

"You've got some history with the place as well."

Abdul looked at Harley quizzically, wondering where he was going. After a few seconds, he said, "Yes, I have a sense of what those women went through."

"Kind of ironic," said Harley, "don't you think?"

"How so?"

"You paid your debt in Lorton, and now Lorton is going to pay you."

"I guess so," said Abdul, nodding. "The sale of *el Castillo* is going to be quite profitable. Allah can turn bad into good."

"No doubt," said Harley.

"You will remember that tonight, right?"

Now Harley was puzzled. "Tonight?"

"At your Good Friday service?"

"Of course," said Harley. "That is what today is all about."

Abdul smiled again. "I may be Muslim," he said, "but I grew up going to church on Good Friday."

"Glad it stayed with you," said Harley.

Looking at his watch, Abdul said, "I better head downstairs. But first, let me ask you: Would you be willing to welcome our community on this first day? Maybe say a few words?"

"I'd be honored," said Harley. "What time?"

"One o'clock," said Abdul.

"I'll be there."

"And here is our check for the first month," said Abdul, reaching into his pocket. Harley knew that this payment would give the finance committee of Riverside Methodist an even more joyful Easter.

After offering some words of welcome to the Muslims and eating his lunch at home, Harley took a long walk through Occoquan Regional Park, which ran along the northern bank of the Occoquan River. He needed the break. Workdays were long through Holy Week, especially with the addition of evening services, so he tried to escape for a few hours every afternoon to get some exercise. Friday was the third day in a row that he had walked after lunch, and he planned to stay in the park until he met Leah for a mid-afternoon coffee at the Grindhouse. The morning clouds had blown away, leaving behind a sky that was as blue as a robin's egg.

Having parked his car in a lot next to a suffragist statue, Harley walked along the gravel service road that ran along the northern perimeter of the park. The road had trees on both sides, and as he looked around he remembered the words of Robert Frost, "*Nature's first green is gold, her hardest hue to hold.*" Although the new leaves on the trees were gold, Harley knew they would be green within a week. A breeze blew in from the south, rippling the delicate foliage and bringing cool air from the river. Harley shivered, unexpectedly, and looked toward the grassy mound of the landfill to his north. "*So Eden sank to grief,*" he recalled Frost saying. "*So dawn goes down to day. Nothing gold can stay.*" Harley was reminded of his thoughts from the start of the year, the day he ran past the sleeping giant. *What secrets does it contain? Will my church end up here? When the doors finally close, will its pieces be carted off and buried?*

*Dark thoughts. Good Friday thoughts.*

Rounding a bend in the road, Harley encountered Don Abad, rail-thin and standing tall. *What was he doing here?* Don's shoulder-length blond hair flowed over the collar of a long black trench coat. The dress was odd, especially for April, but so was the coil of rope he had in his right hand.

"Don!" said Harley, trying not to sound surprised.

"Harley. I've been waiting for you."

Don's words stopped Harley cold. His pulse quickened. "Oh . . . really?"

"You are predictable," Don said. "You have walked here every day."

Harley knew he was right, but said nothing.

"This is a tragic day for you," said Don.

Harley nodded and said, "Good Friday."

"A day of death," said Don. "Appropriate for you and for your church."

Harley felt a jolt of panic. *What does he mean?*

"Your church is dying, pastor."

Looking left and right, Harley could see no escape through the thickly wooded area around him. He began to backpedal, but Don walked slowly toward him. If he turned and ran, he knew that the younger man would be able to overtake him.

"There is no future for your church," said Don. "Admit it, pastor. No future for you."

There was some truth in Don's words, but Harley was not going to confess it. Yes, he knew that the Methodist denomination was struggling, but he did not expect a quick death for his church. He stopped walking backwards, knowing that he could not escape on his own. Looking beyond

Don's shoulder, he hoped that a group of hikers would appear on the path and interrupt them.

"I am the angel of death," said Don, lifting his coil of rope. "Enforcer of the survival of the fittest. Sent to restore balance to the world." Harley's breathing was shallow, and he felt himself becoming lightheaded. *This guy is not just dangerous. He is insane.*

"Why am I here?" asked Don. "To eliminate those who are a burden on the community. A drain on its resources. I am here to thin the herd."

*Why is no one coming?* Harley wondered. He could not believe that he was alone with this madman.

"I am nature," said Don. "In its purest form."

Looking into the man's dark eyes, Harley had a sudden realization. "You are John Jonas. The witch."

Don stopped his forward progress and smiled. "I am . . . and I am not."

"You were a big guy with a brown beard," said Harley.

"Yes, I did have a beard," said Don. "Back in 2018." Harley had always sensed that John was a violent man, but he could never prove it. "I made some changes," Don continued. "Dyed my hair, lost forty pounds, shaved my beard, and carved this scar into my face. Removed some tats as well. A little pain, but a lot of gain."

Harley stared at the man for a moment, and then asked, "Why?"

"Whether you call me John Jonas or Don Abad, it doesn't really matter. Your God calls himself 'I am who I am.' I prefer to think of myself as 'I am *not* who I am.'"

"So, who are you?" asked Harley. *What are you?*

"Abaddon, the Destroyer, the angel of the Abyss."

Harley thought "Abaddon" sounded vaguely familiar, but he could not place it. "Abaddon?" he asked.

"Yes," said Don. "Your Book of Revelation speaks of me. Abaddon, a destroying angel. King of an army of locusts. My name means destruction and doom."

Out of nowhere, an unexpected calm came over Harley. *Maybe this happens when you are about to die.* "So, you are really Abaddon?" he asked, his voice strangely confident. "Not John Jonas?"

"I took that identity for a while, but then I destroyed it. In the Civil War, I was General Hill. In the Second World War, Doctor Mengele. Now I call myself Don Abad. But I have always been Abaddon."

"Abaddon," said Harley. "Don Abad. Makes sense."

"Whatever you call me," said Don, "I am the angel of death." Another stiff breezed passed through the trees. "Ever since the world came into being."

Harley's adrenaline suddenly kicked in, and he wanted to put it to use. Figuring that he would benefit from time, he asked, "Did you kill the man in the flood? Back in 2018?

"Absolutely," said Don. "He was a member of a drug-dealing gang. Caused my brother's death. Deserved to die."

"And were you the shooter at PW Outlets?"

"They called me a Good Samaritan," said Don with a smirk.

"And how about the young men in the woods?" asked Harley. "Survivors said the shooter had black hair."

"Ever heard of a wig?" asked Don. "Getting away with murder is really not hard at all."

"They said he called himself *San Juan*."

"Cool name," said Don. "Heard it around town. Nice twist on John Jonas."

"What about the attack on Father Black?"

"Not me," said Don. "But I approve. Catholics are as worthless as you Methodists."

"You've got the war bug."

"What's that?" asked Don.

"A parasite," said Harley. "Lives for violence."

"Violence works," said Don. "At least in the natural world."

Harley flashed back to something John Jonas had said to him before the pandemic. *Hawks use their talons to pluck fish out of the river, snakeheads eat frogs, coyotes attack chickens. Nature is a fierce and violent system.* Harley could not argue with him about nature, but he knew that there was more to life than survival of the fittest. "You call yourself the angel of death," he said, "but I saw you teaching CPR in front of the American Legion."

Don smiled again. "What better way to decide who lives . . . and who dies?"

Harley realized that he had a point.

"You can find me everywhere," said Don. "I am the spirit of the age. The *zeitgeist*. The invisible force that dominates our world. Win at all costs. No compromise. Destroy the opposition."

Harley knew he was speaking the truth, but did not want to agree with him. "You are what is *wrong* with our age," he said.

"No, I am right," said Don. "Always have been." Shifting the coil of rope from his right hand to his left, he said, "Now, Harley, give me your cell phone."

"My phone?"

"Yes, your phone. There will be no conversation, except between the two of us."

Pulling out his phone, Harley noticed that it was after three o'clock. He was scheduled to meet Leah in ten minutes. "All right," he said, "I'll give it to you. But first, I need to send a message."

"Why?" asked Don, not expecting resistance.

"I am meeting a friend in ten minutes. If I do not show up, she will come looking for me." Don looked skeptical. "She knows where I am," said Harley.

"So, let me text her," said Don. "We'll tell her you will be delayed."

"Okay," said Harley. "I'll write. You send."

"Let me watch," said Don, reaching out and putting the coil of rope on Harley's shoulder.

Harley let Don observe him as he wrote, "CU @ 53, not 33."

"What does that mean?" asked Don, his breath hot in Harley's face.

"See you at five-thirty, not three-thirty."

"All right," said Don, taking the phone and pressing the send button. Then he dropped the phone in his coat pocket. Once again, Harley looked around, hoping that someone would appear on the road. The mound of the landfill seemed to be growing taller beside him. *So Eden sank to grief,* said Frost. *So dawn goes down to day. Nothing gold can stay.*

"Now," said Don, beginning to uncoil the rope, "it is time for you to enter the Abyss." Striking as quickly as a snake, Don grabbed Harley, spun him around, and threw him down on the road. As he hit the gravel, Harley was surprised by the force of the attack, although he knew that he should have seen it coming. Pinning him down, Don tied Harley's hands with the end of the rope, like a calf being roped. He could feel Don's long hair tickling the back of his neck, an oddly gentle contrast to the gravel that was stinging his face. Then Don stood up and told Harley to get to his feet. Giving him a push, he told Harley to walk into the woods. Don followed, using the remainder of the rope as a long leash. "Keep walking," said Don. "We're going toward the landfill."

*Of course.*

"You are depressed," Don said, pushing him forward, "like so many of your colleagues. You have no hope."

"I disagree," said Harley. *May as well say it. What do I have to lose?*

"Pastors are leaving the ministry," said Don. "Membership is shrinking. The pandemic has simply accelerated a completely natural process."

"So you say," said Harley, stumbling over a root. "But the church has survived worse than this."

"But you will not," said Don.

They walked in silence, for what seemed like an eternity. Finally, arriving at the edge of the landfill, they came across a hulking tree that was growing out of the hillside. "This is the place," said Don.

"What place?" asked Harley, knowing the answer but wanting to prolong the conversation.

"The place you will die," said Don. "Where you will hang yourself." He pushed Harley toward the trunk of the tree and told him to stand on a flat root that was holding the tree into the hillside. The tree had large branches that cantilevered over the gulley that ran along the edge of the landfill. Harley tried to resist, but Don pushed him against the tree and told him to stay there. "You are full of despair," he added. "You *want* to die." When Harley tried to move, Don pulled a handgun out of his pocket. "Stand there," said Don. "I'm serious."

"Okay," said Harley. He was shocked by the sight of the gun, but he realized that he should not have been surprised, given Don's history. *Death by rope; death by gun. What difference does it make?* His father had died in his forties and his mother in her late fifties, so Harley knew he had been living on borrowed time. *Remember that you are dust, and to dust you shall return.* At this point, the two of them were so far into the woods that Harley knew there would be no hikers to save him.

Putting his gun back in his pocket, Don made a big knot at the end of the rope. Then he threw it over a large branch that extended twenty feet above the gulley floor. He pulled the rope tight so that Harley felt a tug against his hands. Don secured the end of the rope against a neighboring tree, so that the tension would remain strong.

"At one point, Kelly loved you," said Harley, again trying to buy some time. *Even borrowed time is precious.*

Don seemed to be thrown a little off balance by the comment. Kelly Westbrook had been a fellow Wiccan in Occoquan, and the two of them had lived together. After a pause, he said, "She didn't really know me."

"But she cared for you, John." Harley hoped that the use of his old name would draw him back to a better time.

"Perhaps she did," said Don. "But caring is not my nature. Does an osprey care for the fish it grabs with its talons?" Don waited a second for an answer, pulled on the rope, and then said, "Of course not. Survival is all that matters." Then, walking toward Harley, he said, "Here is how this will go. I am going to release your hands, and then you are going to tie a noose around your neck. As I release your hands, you will have no freedom to escape. I have my gun, and you know that I will use it."

Don untied Harley and quickly pulled his gun out of his pocket. Harley felt relieved to be free, but knew that he could not get away. Don kept the gun trained on him and told him to make a noose.

Harley followed his order, slowly and carefully. At first, he fumbled with the rope, but after several tries made a knot that he had learned when he first bought his boat. Although he had been required to master several knots at a Coast Guard class, he never dreamed he would tie one around his neck. Don stepped forward and pulled on the noose to make sure it was secure. His breath was acrid in Harley's face.

"Now," said Don, stepping back, "stand against the tree." He pointed his gun at Harley's chest, to emphasize how serious he was. "The tree will hold the rope tight, while you let yourself fall into the gulley."

"Why would I do that?" asked Harley, again trying to buy time.

"Suicide," said Don. "Quick and easy."

Harley put his hands on the noose, hoping that he would be able to hold himself up if he was forced to swing. Holding tightly, he had no idea how long he would be able to keep the pressure off his neck.

"That won't work," said Don. "You will die, and then your church will die." Lowering his gun, he walked to the end of the rope that was tied to the neighboring tree, and began to put tension on it. Harley felt the rope tug against his neck, burning his skin as it moved. "Let yourself go," said Don, "into the Abyss." *Is this the end?*

At that moment, the sound of a distant siren came through the trees. Don was surprised, which caused him to ease up on the rope for a second, but then he gave it a second tug and said, "Jump!" Harley resisted, hoping that the siren would get louder, which it did. Don pointed his gun at Harley but did not pull the trigger, fearing that he would divulge their location. "Now!" he shouted, as the first siren was joined by a second. Harley hoped that the wailing would only grow louder and louder and louder, until he was rescued.

Unfortunately, the two sirens abruptly went silent. Harley felt his heart sink, but then realized that the vehicles had simply stopped moving. *Were the occupants now approaching on foot?* Don scanned the trees to see if anyone was coming toward them, and then gave the rope a violent tug. Despite having his hands on the noose, the rope choked Harley. A shout came through the woods, a male voice calling out, "Harley Camden!" Harley tried to respond, but Don yanked the rope even harder, pulling Harley off the flat root and into a pendulum swing across the gulley. He felt like he was riding a rope swing from childhood, although in this case he was suspended by his neck, with only his hands on the noose to prevent asphyxiation. As he sailed across the gulley, he heard a woman echoing the man, and then another female called out his name. Harley knew that he had only a few seconds to get the rope off before he lost consciousness, so as he sailed back towards the landfill he yanked the end of the rope and fell to the earth.

Harley hit the ground at an angle and tumbled to one side, twisting an ankle and falling face first into the thick leaves of the gulley floor. The dirt was wet and aromatic, like the earth of a freshly dug grave, and he simply breathed it in, wanting the earth to protect him from the danger above. For a second, he lay there, lightheaded. Then, realizing that he had to protect himself, he climbed awkwardly into a crouch and looked up at the tree where Don had been standing. The man was gone, vanished. Then he turned his head in the direction of the voices, and saw two sheriffs and his friend Leah running toward him. "Harley!" she shouted. "You're alive!" He tried to stand up, but pain shot up his leg, causing him to sit down hard in the leaves.

Sheriff Terry Stone was the first to reach him. "How are you?" he asked. "We saw you fall from the rope."

"Thank God for the mooring hitch," said Harley, rubbing his neck. The blood was returning to his head.

"Mooring hitch?" asked Terry.

"An excellent quick-release knot."

The sheriff did not appreciate Harley's attempt at gallows humor. "Why were you on the rope?"

"Don Abad was trying to kill me," Harley said. "Wanted me to hang myself."

"Really?" said the sheriff.

"No kidding. If you catch him, you'll find that he has a gun. I think it has been used before."

"Where is he?" asked Deputy Sharon Madison, the second to arrive.

"Not sure," said Harley. "But you can track him. He is carrying my phone."

"I've still got the signal," said the sheriff. "Sharon, let's go. Leah, make sure Harley is okay. Call an ambulance if he needs one." The two officers ran into the woods on the landfill side of the gulley.

Leah sat down next to her friend and reached out to caress his neck. "I am so glad you're not hurt."

"Well, I'm a bit banged up. Twisted my ankle. But I'm okay."

"Thanks for the text message," she said.

"Thanks for responding."

"Could have been a little clearer," she said, poking him gently in the chest. "CU @ 53, not 33?"

"Hey," said Harley, "I included 33."

"You said '*not* 33.'"

"Picky, picky," he said, smiling. "You got the message."

"Thank God I did," she said. "But what is going on with Don Abad?"

"Says he's the angel of death."

"What?" said Leah.

"No joke," said Harley. "And he's playing the part pretty well."

# 21

## Good Friday 1862

ABIGAIL WASHINGTON WALKED SLOWLY toward the Bagley house with a bouquet of white lilies. She was surprised by the roar of the Occoquan River pouring over the rocks at the Quaker end of town. This was the power that drove the gears of the gristmill, day in and day out, but the sound of the water was largely muted by the time it reached the center of town. She realized that she had been shielded from this energy throughout her childhood, growing up as the daughter of the dry goods merchant. The sound was thrilling to her, but also frightening.

Her parents walked behind her, feeling a bit awkward as they passed through the no-nonsense timber homes of the Quaker community. The dwellings were simple compared to their elegant Gothic Revival House with pointed windows, a house so lovely that visitors to the town would stop and stare. Bushrod brought up the rear, feeling resentful that he had to visit a family that did not support the Confederacy, in order to express condolences for a son who died for the Confederacy, at the very same time that his father forbade him from joining the army of the Confederacy. The contradictions made any kind of simple sentiment quite impossible for him to communicate.

"We must express our sympathy," said Martha, the petite, blond mother of Abigail, as they walked through town. "Today is Good Friday, when our Lord gave his life for us. We cannot ignore the sacrifice of Ann Bagley's son." Since no one was working on Good Friday, the day was a good one to call on people at home.

"You are right," said her husband Thomas. "William gave his all. We stand in his debt."

"Something you would not let *me* do," said Bushrod, bringing up the rear.

"You also serve, son," said his father, "by serving your family."

"But I am needed!" said Bushrod, holding up his hands in exasperation. "On the Peninsula!"

"Not now," said Thomas. "The lines are holding."

On April 4, General McClellan had begun his march toward Richmond, but he had quickly been slowed by heavy spring rains. Then, his army ran into Confederate forces that were entrenched along a twelve-mile front near the Warwick River. The Rebels were heavily outnumbered, but they created the illusion of a powerful army. The Union army was stopped in its tracks, unable to move along its intended path through Yorktown. No one "but McClellan could have hesitated to attack," said Confederate General Joseph Johnston, McClellan's nemesis. *But hesitate he did.* Seeing that the delay in Union progress gave him an opportunity to reinforce the defense of Richmond, Johnston moved his entire army to the lower Peninsula. In this case, he was not "Retreatin' Joe."

"Yes, they may be holding for now," said Bushrod. "But they may not be able to do so forever."

"This is not the day to talk warfare," said Martha, scolding her husband and son. "This is the day to talk peace."

Reaching the Bagley house, Abigail knocked on the heavy wooden door. Samuel answered, both surprised and delighted to see her. "Abigail!" he said, wiping his mouth with a cloth napkin. "How pleasant to see thee."

"We are here to express our condolences," said Abigail, motioning toward her parents and brother. "Is your mother home?"

"She is not," said Samuel. "She is walking. On the river path, I believe."

"I am sorry to hear that," said Abigail. "My family very much wanted to see her." Then, after a moment's hesitation, she added, "And you."

"Thou art very kind," said Samuel to the Washington family. "Our hearts are very heavy."

"We share your grief," said Martha, looking pained.

"Your brother was a hero," added Thomas. Bushrod nodded, but remained silent.

"My mother would like to see thee," said Samuel, stretching the truth a bit. In fact, it was he who was very happy to see Abigail. "Would thou likest to walk up the river, on the chance that we will encounter her?"

Thomas looked at Martha, trying to gauge if she wanted to continue to walk. She gave a nod, and said, "If it is not too far."

"My mother enjoys sitting at a spot near the falls," said Samuel. "It is not far at all." Folding his napkin, he said, "I have finished my noon meal. Let me take a minute to clean up, and then I will join thee."

Abigail turned to her parents and Bushrod. "I am glad we are here. Such a condolence call is the right thing to do."

"Indeed, it is," said Martha, proud that she had raised her daughter well.

"Will you be comfortable on the river path?" Thomas asked the two women.

"I believe so," said his wife. "Abigail, let me bustle your dress so that it does not get dirty."

"I'll do the same for you, mother," said Abigail.

While the women were adjusting their dresses, Samuel returned to the doorway. Bushrod stepped forward, met him on the threshold, and said, "Have you heard that McClellen is bogged down?"

"Yes," said Samuel, knowing that Bushrod was not able to offer words of sympathy. "The Peninsula Campaign seems to be stalled."

"Young Napoleon has lost his magic touch," said Bushrod, mocking McClellan by using one of his nicknames.

"But the Union is succeeding elsewhere," said Samuel, somewhat warily. He did not want to get in an argument with Bushrod or Thomas. "Down in Savannah, General Gillmore has battered Fort Pulaski into submission."

"You are correct, I am sorry to say," said Thomas, joining the conversation. "The victory took less than two days."

"I worry about our defeats along the coast," said Bushrod.

"As do I," said his father.

"Gentlemen, we are ready," said Abigail. "Please stop talking about the war."

"You are right to say so," said Thomas. "I will oblige."

"Samuel, will you lead us?" asked Abigail, still carrying her lilies.

"It would be my pleasure," said Samuel.

A small black cloud hovered in the air, west of the Town of Occoquan. The sight was curious, since the skies were blue except for a few fluffy clouds, as white as cotton balls in the field. "What could that be?" Abigail asked Samuel, as she walked behind him on the river path. The path was smooth but narrow, winding in a snakelike pattern along the river, moving steadily upward toward the falls. Since the group had to walk single file, conversation was difficult.

Stopping at the crossing where the three Union men had been taken prisoner by the Night Riders, Samuel turned and said to Abigail, "A kettle of vultures."

"A what?" said Abigail.

"A kettle of vultures." The rest of the Washingtons gathered around to listen to him. "It's not a cloud at all. When vultures spiral upward to gain altitude, they look like water boiling in a pot," said Samuel. "Dost thou not see it?" he asked, pointing to the west. "The appearance of a kettle."

"You are right," said Thomas. "Now that we are closer, I can see the birds."

"Why are they gathered?" asked Bushrod.

"There is something dead," said Samuel. "Some carrion."

Abigail felt a wave of dread, but she did not want to turn around. "Let us continue," she said. "We want to see your mother."

"Very well," said Samuel. "We are not far from where she likes to sit."

The path become steeper and rockier as they moved westward, and Martha was beginning to wonder if the journey was a mistake. The roar of water on rocks became louder, and Thomas wondered if they would put themselves in danger by continuing toward the falls. But then, suddenly, the path turned a corner and revealed a wide and sparkling pool of deep blue water at the base of the falls. None of the Washingtons had ever ventured this far along the river path. "This is beautiful," said Abigail, her eyes wide with amazement.

"Except for the vultures," said Bushrod, pointing to a spot on the northern side of the pool. A dead deer lay on the bank, and was being devoured by vultures.

"Let us ignore that unpleasant sight," said Martha, turning toward the falls.

"There she is," said Samuel, pointing to a rocky outcropping on the southern side of the pool. "Mother likes to read on that ledge near the waterfall." He waved to her and then said to the Washingtons, "Wouldst thou care to visit with her?"

Martha looked at the path to the ledge, assessed her ability to navigate it, and then said, "Yes." Samuel held out his hand to assist her. Thomas did the same for Abigail, and the group moved slowly toward Ann Bagley. She stood as they approached, and motioned for them to join her.

"This is a surprise," she said as they stepped onto the ledge. Martha was glad to see that it was dry and level, with several flat-topped slabs of stone sitting against the hillside. "Please, join me," said Ann.

"We are here to express our condolences," said Martha, speaking loudly to be heard over the roar of the falls. "We are so very sorry about your loss."

"Thou art kind," said Ann.

"Please accept these lilies," said Abigail, handing the bouquet to Ann.

"The resurrection flower," said Ann. "I thank thee." Then, pointing to the large stones on the ledge, she said, "Have a seat."

"Your son has made the supreme sacrifice," said Thomas, bowing his head toward Ann. "Our country is grateful."

"I appreciate thy sincerity," said Ann. "But I have my own feelings about the significance of his death."

"Where is William buried?" asked Bushrod.

His mother was mortified, and quickly said, "Bushrod, that it a rude question."

"I apologize," said Bushrod, realizing that he had overstepped.

"The interment was private," said Ann, cutting off any further inquiries. Bushrod looked back across the pool toward the deer being picked clean. The vultures were flapping their wings and fighting over the most desirable parts.

"This is a lovely spot," said Thomas, anxious to change the subject. "Do you come here often?"

"I do," said Ann. "It calms my spirit." Abigail found the roar of the falls to be more thrilling than calming, but she was curious about Ann's experience in the place. Ann said, "I find it to be a good place to read the psalms."

"What have you read today?" asked Martha.

"The forty-sixth psalm," said Ann. "Do you know it?"

"Not by heart," said Martha.

Opening her psalter, Ann read, "*God is our refuge and strength, a very present help in trouble. Therefore will not we fear, though the earth be removed, and though the mountains be carried into the midst of the sea; Though the waters thereof roar and be troubled, though the mountains shake with the swelling thereof."*

"That is beautiful," said Abigail. "And it fits this place so well."

"Indeed," said Ann. "When waters roar and mountains shake, I feel that God is with me."

"I feel the same when I hear the psalms," said Abigail. "They are a part of our church services."

"Yes, we share the psalms," said Thomas. "Whether one is Quaker or Episcopalian, the psalms are the same."

"But hear this," said Ann. "The psalm continues: *Come, behold the works of the LORD, what desolations he hath made in the earth. He maketh wars to cease unto the end of the earth; he breaketh the bow, and cutteth the spear in sunder; he burneth the chariot in the fire. Be still, and know that I am God."*

None of the Washingtons had an immediate response to these verses. They sat in silence until Ann said, "God maketh wars to cease."

"Indeed," said Thomas. "We all want this war to end. We want the Union to leave us alone."

"He breaketh the bow," said Ann. "He cutteth the spear in sunder. God despises war."

Once again, her words were followed by an awkward silence. Then Thomas said, "Our struggle is virtuous, I believe. We are protecting our homes and our way of life."

"He burnest the chariot in the fire," said Ann, loud enough to be heard over the falls.

Feeling the tension rising, Martha stepped in to mediate. "We know that you Quakers are pacifists," she said. "But we Episcopalians feel that a war can be just."

"I do not speak for the Society of Friends," said Ann. "I speak only for myself. I have left that fellowship."

Abigail was surprised, and looked at Samuel. She had not heard this news. Samuel nodded and said, "I remain in fellowship, but my mother no longer attends meetings."

"I am sorry to hear this," said Martha.

"I follow the counsel of Scripture," said Ann: "*Be still, and know that I am God.* I respect Quaker stillness, but cannot abide by the Society's judgments."

Bushrod realized that his family's condolence visit had turned into something else. What it was, he did not know. But he was fascinated. Stroking the scar on his face, he sat back and listened.

"There is no congregation that I can abide at this time," said Ann, warming to the subject. "All contain the hypocrites that our Lord Jesus condemned. 'Thou tithest mint, dill, and cummin,' he said, 'and have neglected the weightier matters of the law: justice and mercy and faith.'"

"None of us is perfect," said Thomas, nodding. "All are sinners."

"Indeed," said Ann. "But how can thou goest to church and pay thy tithes, while neglecting justice for the slaves all around thee. The slaves who sit in the balcony of thy church!"

"You are right," said Abigail. "Slavery is not just." Her parents looked at her with surprise. Perhaps the power of the water coming over the falls was giving her courage, along with the words of Ann Bagley. "The institution of slavery will end," said Abigail, no longer a mouselike young woman. "It *must* end."

"Abigail!" said her mother. "Your words are disrespectful."

"Her words are true," said Ann, continuing her reflection on Scripture. "But Jesus does not reserve his condemnation for those who neglect justice. He also condemns those who neglect mercy. This is the reason I have left the Society of Friends."

Samuel looked at the Washingtons and said, "My mother requested that William be interred at the Quaker burial ground, and her request was denied. They feel he lost that right when he enlisted. My mother believed they should have shown us mercy."

"I believe in mercy," said Abigail. "And in justice."

"Jesus requires both," said Ann.

"So, what will you do," said Thomas, "if you have left the Society of Friends?"

"I will continue to live in my house," said Ann. "I have many close relationships in the Quaker community. But I know that I must venture beyond my community as well. No one has all the truth. No one has all the virtue."

"You are welcome in our house," said Martha, feeling compassion for Ann. She could not imagine losing a husband, a son, and a community of faith.

"Thou art very kind," said Ann. "I will find a path. And I will welcome thy friendship on that path."

Bushrod had always felt as though his community was made of building blocks as solid and unbreakable as the rocks along the Occoquan River. People in town were either abolitionist or slaveowner. Slave or free. Quaker or Presbyterian or Baptist or Episcopalian. But now he saw that there were fissures and cracks and shifts and realignments. *Would it be possible for Ann Bagley to be welcomed into our home? As a friend?*

"We are grateful to have this time with you," said Martha. "You have our support in this time of loss."

"I do appreciate it," said Ann. "I thank thee."

"And now we must take our leave," said Martha. "The hour is getting late."

"May I stay with Samuel?" asked Abigail. For a second time that day, she surprised her parents.

"If your brother acts as chaperone," said Martha. Bushrod rolled his eyes.

"Yes, if Bushrod is with you, you may do so," said Thomas.

Abigail and Samuel stood by his father's grave, after a long and strenuous walk up the hill to the Quaker burial ground. Dark clouds had moved in and covered the sky, a fitting sight for a Good Friday afternoon. Bushrod stood at a distance, leaning on the iron fence that surrounded the cemetery. The afternoon had given him much to think about.

"I am so very sad about William," said Abigail, taking Samuel's hand in hers. "I wish he could be buried here."

"As do I," said Samuel. "The decision of the Society has been devastating for my mother."

"And for you?" she asked.

"I would like it to have happened," said Samuel. "But I understand the logic. I do not expect that others will always do as I desire."

"You are very understanding," said Abigail.

"To a fault," said Samuel. "I sometimes feel that I am too much of a peacemaker."

Abigail smiled. "I did not think that such a thing would be possible for a Quaker."

Bushrod interrupted them. "I'm bored," he said. "I am going to see a friend and then go home. Abigail, do not be long. If we meet at the mill in fifteen minutes, we can arrive home together."

"I will not be long," she promised. Bushrod gave Samuel a punch on the shoulder and then headed down the hill.

Samuel squeezed her hand. "I know how much thou cared for William."

"Yes, I did."

"Thou art grieving as well."

"I am."

"Know that I am with thee in thy grief. We can share it."

Abigail looked deeply into Samuel's eyes. There, and in the shape of his face, she could see William. They were clearly brothers. The two had much in common. But as she looked at Samuel, she felt that William was fading. Her connection to him was shifting, transforming, turning into something new. *How well did I really know William?* she wondered. *Not as well as I know Samuel.* She was beginning to feel an attraction to a very different Bagley, one who was more thoughtful than funny, more caring than contrary. *So what if he is brown-haired instead of blond; wiry instead of muscular?* She did not want to be disloyal to her first love, but she had to accept that her feelings were changing. Her passion was taking a new form.

"Thou art a good man," Abigail said to Samuel, using the Quaker thee and thou.

"I thank you," said Samuel, smiling. "You are a fine young woman." And then, despite the fact that they were in a graveyard, they kissed.

*Death cannot kill what never dies.*

Then they walked down the hill, hand in hand.

# 22

## Holy Saturday 2022

"YOU'VE GOT THE ANGEL'S GLOW," said Leah to Harley. The two were having coffee at the Grindhouse, early on Holy Saturday. The place was deserted except for the tattooed clerk behind the counter, grinding beans in anticipation of the morning rush.

"Angel's . . . what?" asked Harley. The smell of the beans reminded him of the forest floor.

"Glow. A mysterious glow that saved a lot of men."

"That's odd," he said, rubbing the back of his neck. "Never heard of it. But if I'm glowing, great."

"You've got the glow," she said. "For sure."

"Guess that's what a brush with death can do," said Harley. "Makes the sky bluer and the grass greener." Looking out the window, he saw a cloudless sky though the tender young leaves of a sycamore tree. It hit him that the morning was a pure gift, completely undeserved, like every morning. He knew that he did not deserve to die, but at the very same time he did not deserve to live. Then he shifted his legs and felt pain shoot up from his ankle. *Nothing gold can stay.*

"A doc at the clinic told me about the Angel's Glow," said Leah. "He's a Civil War buff."

"And what is it?"

"A lot of men were wounded at the Battle of Shiloh," she said. "One of the bloodiest battles of the war, out in Tennessee. More than twenty thousand casualties."

"My God," said Harley.

"It was a nightmare," said Leah. "The wounded lay in the fields for days until they could be treated. A lot were in the forest as well."

"I can relate," said Harley, sipping his black coffee.

"Late at night, the men began to notice glowing orbs of bluish light, all around them. The soldiers thought they were angels from heaven. The blue light was illuminating their wounds. Giving them hope."

"Really?"

"No kidding," said Leah. "Strange but true. The soldiers who had the Angel's Glow ended up surviving longer than those without the glow. They somehow avoided infection."

Harley sat quietly, processing the strange story. Then he asked, "What was going on?"

"No one knew for a long time," said Leah, taking a drink of her latte. "Angel's Glow was the stuff of legend. But then, about twenty years ago, a discovery was made. By a seventeen-year-old!"

"What did he find?"

"He visited Shiloh with his mother, a microbiologist who studied soil bacteria. These bacteria are bioluminescent, which means that they give off their own light. In this case, a blue light. These bacteria live inside tiny parasitic worms."

"Disgusting," said Harley. He had been thinking about getting a scone, but the story was killing his appetite. *Parasitic worms.*

"Sure, but it gave him an idea. He and a friend did an experiment, and found that these worms tend to vomit up the glowing bacteria. The glowing bacteria then kill other microorganisms."

"So that was the Angel's Glow?" asked Harley. "Bacteria vomited up by parasitic worms?"

"Seems to be," said Leah. "The doc told me that the conditions at Shiloh were perfect for these bacteria to thrive. They die at normal human body temperature, but these soldiers were lying on the cold, wet ground for days. Their body temperatures went down, and the bacteria went wild. They released chemicals that cleaned the wounds of the men, helping them to live much longer than those who did not have the glow."

Harley smiled. "Nature can be cruel, but it can also be kind."

"Even angelic," said Leah.

The string of bells on the Grindhouse door tinkled wildly, causing Harley and Leah to turn their heads. In came the sheriff and the deputy, clearly pleased with themselves.

"We got him," said Terry Stone, smiling behind his close-cropped beard.

"Right outside Fredericksburg," added Sharon Madison. She had a gap-toothed grin, surrounded by freckles and red hair. The two plopped down in chairs next to Leah and Harley, putting their hats on the table.

"Not that we did it alone," said Terry, leavening his pride with some modesty. "Sharon and I chased him through the woods, but he got away. We found deep tire tracks near the landfill, evidence of a quick getaway."

"Fortunately, he was carrying your phone," said Sharon.

"I think he forgot he had it," added Terry with a sly smile. "The State Troopers tracked him and pulled him over north of Fredericksburg. They tell me he was acting innocent, wondering what the problem was."

"So, he was heading south?" asked Harley.

"In a stolen car," said Sharon.

"That's odd," said Harley. "He owns a car. I've seen him driving."

"Sounds like he was trying to disappear," said Leah. "Again."

"Probably right," said Terry. "His car was parked in the garage of his building. Nothing was amiss in his apartment. Looks like he just walked away."

"We'll be going through it very carefully," added Sharon. "But he probably didn't leave anything of value to us."

"Fortunately, he had his gun with him, in the car," said Terry. "Ballistics will have some fun with it."

"A very strange man," said Harley. "Although . . . he didn't think he *was* a man."

Sharon tilted her head, causing her red curls to shake. "What do you mean by that?"

"He thought he was supernatural," said Harley. "The angel of death."

"What?" said Terry. His brown eyes had lost their warm glow.

"That's what he said," recounted Harley. "He called himself the Destroyer, the angel of the Abyss, Abaddon."

"That's insane," said Terry. "You don't believe him, do you?" Part of him wondered if Harley, as a pastor, would fall for this supernatural talk.

"No, I don't think he is supernatural," said Harley. "But he is convinced, in his own mind, that he has existed forever. His mission is to kill. To destroy. To balance the scales. To thin the herd."

"That is crazy," said the deputy.

"I agree," said Harley.

"I would call it mental illness," interjected Leah, ever the health care professional.

"I hope he doesn't make an insanity plea," said Terry, shaking his head. "I hate it when that happens."

"He does not think he is insane," said Harley. "He is very clear on his mission. Very calculating."

"Give an example," said the sheriff.

"You remember John Jonas, don't you?" asked Harley.

"Sure," said Terry. "Lived here until a few years ago. IT guy. Softball player. Part of that Wiccan group." Terry was proud of knowing everyone in town.

"Exactly," Harley nodded. "Well, guess what? Don Abad is John Jonas."

"No way!" said Terry.

"Changed his appearance," said Harley. "Part of his mission."

"I never would have made the connection," said Terry.

"Neither would I," said Sharon. "I remember Jonas well. His team played ours. He was so much bigger back then."

"He says he is Abaddon," Harley said. "That is his true identity. He just appears for a while as John Jonas or Don Abad. Does his work and moves on."

"Until now," said Terry.

"Thank God we got him," added Sharon.

"Absolutely," added Leah. "We need a person like that off the street."

"We'll want a statement from you, Harley," said Terry, picking up his hat and beginning to rise. Sharon followed his lead.

"No problem," said Harley to the officers, "If you dig a little deeper, I think you'll be able close your case on the young man who was found dead in the flood debris."

Harley and Leah intended to leave the Grindhouse after their coffee, but a steady stream of townspeople kept them in their seats until lunchtime. The story of Don's capture had spread quickly through Occoquan, and there was widespread relief that Harley had escaped injury. Everyone who spotted him through the window of the coffeeshop immediately pushed through the door to see him and express their concern and gratitude. Many brought scones and pastries to the table, and soon a small crowd was feasting and talking.

"Harley, thank God you are okay," said Andy Stackhouse, his head freshly buzzed, as he marched across the shop. "I don't know what we would do without you."

The pastor was touched by this sentiment, since he always counted Andy among his critics. "Thanks, Andy."

"He has the Angel's Glow," said Leah, trying to support her old friend.

"I've heard of that," said Jim Dotson, the professor of archaeology at the next table. "Something about glowing bacteria?"

"Yes, that's right," said Andy, pulling up a chair next to Harley. "I read about that."

"Well, Harley's got it," said Leah. "Saved him from the angel of death."

"Not exactly," said Harley. "That bacteria helped soldiers to avoid infections. I've got a sore neck and a twisted ankle."

"Still," said Leah, "you've got angels looking over you."

"No doubt," said Harley, smiling.

"From what I remember," said Andy, wanting to share his knowledge, "that Angel's Glow bacteria was discovered by a local kid. From Bowie, Maryland, I think. He and a buddy won themselves a major science fair!"

"You're right," added Jim. "It took a long time for someone to discover that the blue light was not really angelic. But you know what? If it cleaned their wounds and saved their lives, I would call it an angel!"

"Amen to that," said round-faced Gretchen Bennett, a church member sitting next to Jim.

"What's more," said Leah, "the men who were the coldest were the ones who did best. The bacteria would have died if they were warm."

"So, something that was bad," said Harley, "turned out to be very good."

"Hypothermia was a life-saving factor," said Leah.

"Bad can turn to good," said Gretchen, taking a sip of coffee. "Life is like that, more often than not."

The bells on the door tinkled again, and in walked Nanette Glebesman, back from her trip to Seattle. Her blond hair was tied back in a pony tail, and her slender face was lined with concern. But when she reached the table and saw Leah at Harley's side, she pulled up short. "Harley," she said, "I just heard. Are you okay?"

"Alive and well," he said, truly happy to see her.

"I cannot believe that my neighbor tried to hurt you."

"Yeah," said Harley, looking around at the faces of people around him. "Don could have been a more neighborly neighbor."

"Just terrible," Nanette said, shaking her head.

"I'll be okay," said Harley. "My neck and ankle will need some time to heal. But no permanent damage."

Nanette stood awkwardly for a moment, not knowing whether she should join the group. Then Leah said, "Andy, don't be rude. Get the woman a chair." He immediately complied.

"What was Don trying to do?" asked Nanette, once seated.

"Kill me," said Harley. "And then kill the church."

"But why?"

"Who knows?" said Harley. "He believed that it was his job to enforce the rules of nature. Survival of the fittest."

"Bizarre," said Nanette.

"Guess he doesn't have much respect for Methodists," said Harley.

"Wish we could have been with you," said Gretchen, putting an arm around Andy. "We would have been Methodist Strong!"

"I appreciate it," said Harley. "Churches like ours are tough to kill."

"Well, I am relieved," said Nanette. Then, after a pause, she said, "But I had better go."

"Why?" asked Harley. "You just got here."

"You are with friends," she said. Then, looking at Leah, she said, "Special friends."

Harley was confused. "You are as special as anyone," he said, looking around the room. He could not understand her discomfort. Then, taking a chance, he said, "Maybe even *more* special."

Leah immediately sensed what was going on. Offering a hand to Nanette, she said, "Harley and I have been friends for a long time." Nanette nodded. "But Nanette, we are just friends. I am a lesbian."

"Really?" said Nanette. Leah squeezed her hand and let it go. Nanette put her hands in her lap and looked from Leah to Harley. "I had no idea."

"Yes," said Leah. "Harley had a crush on me when we worked on an archaeological site, back when we were in school." Harley blushed. "But I was still figuring myself out. It never went anywhere. We met up here in Occoquan years later, and we've been good for each other. He has taken care of me, and I have taken care of him."

"Friends are good," said Nanette, as her fear and frustration began to vanish like the morning mist. All around her, church members and town residents were watching the drama in awkward silence.

"We really are very close," said Harley. "But friends. Platonic friends."

"He is all yours," said Leah. "Please, enjoy him."

# 23

## Holy Saturday 1862

THE WASHINGTON HOUSE WAS full of activity on the day before Easter, 1862. Martha was busy in the kitchen, putting the finishing touches on the apple and cherry pies that she would be serving at dinner the next day. Bushrod swept the front steps and cleaned the panes of glass in the front door, noticing how much brighter the spring sunlight streamed into the foyer after he completed his chore. Then he joined his father for the task of moving chairs into the dining room and setting the table for relatives who would be joining them for the holiday. And then, late in the morning, when brother James Washington and his family arrived with two of their slaves, the energy level in the house surged.

Milicent, the heavyset wife of James, carried several loaves of freshly baked bread into the kitchen and gave Martha a big hug. James shook hands with Thomas and presented him with a pouch of tobacco. Bushrod helped his twin cousins Emily and Ellen to take their bags to the guest room upstairs, and then returned to transport the bags of his aunt and uncle to another spare room. The male slave carried a large smoked ham into the kitchen, while the female slave delivered a bag of potatoes. Martha showed the two slaves where her vegetables were stored, and joined Milicent in giving them instructions in the preparation of the Easter dinner. Then the Washingtons repaired to the parlor for refreshments.

"We are so happy that you are here for Easter," said Martha to Milicent and James. "The holiday will be so festive with you and the girls with us."

"Thank you for the invitation," said Milicent. "We always enjoy visiting Occoquan."

"Would you like some tea?" asked Martha.

"Yes, please," said Milicent.

"A tea cake, James?" offered Martha.

"Why, yes," said James, who had taken a seat next to Thomas. James had the same red hair as Thomas, but was tall and thin instead of rotund. "They look delicious," he said. Martha poured tea for the four adults, and served them each a piece of tea cake on her best china plates.

"How was your trip?" asked Thomas.

"Quite good," answered James. "The road was dry and the horses were in good spirits. My boy Caleb always drives the carriage well, so we enjoyed the trip."

"I remember how we got stuck in the mud last year," said Milicent. "Such a dreadful experience."

"Thank God you avoided that," said Thomas.

"Is that a new girl you brought with you?" asked Martha.

"Yes," said Milicent. "Her name is Harriet and she is quite skilled in the kitchen. She and Caleb will put together a feast for us."

"I do appreciate it," said Martha. "I will enjoy the break from cooking, and the chance to spend time with you."

"We are glad to bring them," said James. "It is the least we can do, after you have opened your beautiful home to us."

"How is the plantation?" asked Thomas, always curious about life outside the Town of Occoquan.

"We are in the middle of spring planting," said James, "and look forward to expanding our tobacco acreage. Last year was a good crop, and we hope the same for this year. But the movement of troops has us worried. Johnston's army passed by us on their journey south, but fortunately they did not cross our land."

"We want to be supportive," Milicent added. "But we all know what damage they can do."

"With any luck," said James, "future action will stay south of us, on the Peninsula or near Richmond."

"May it be so," said Thomas, taking a sip of tea. "We have had quite a bit of military activity here in Occoquan. Hampton's Legion was encamped here, and more recently of group of Union troops passed through."

"Really?" said James. "That must have been disconcerting."

"They caused no trouble, fortunately. Just a group of released prisoners heading north."

"But we did experience some shelling and shooting over the winter," added Martha.

"How dreadful!" said Milicent.

"Indeed," said Martha. "I was so afraid our store or house would be hit. Some neighbors had windows shattered by bullets."

"We do hope you continue to escape any damage," said James, putting his fork into a tea cake. "None of this would be happening if the Union simply left us alone."

"The year has been eventful," said Thomas. "Can you believe that it was one year ago, almost to the day, that our delegates voted to secede?"

"How can that be?" said Milicent. "It seems like an eternity."

"So much has happened," said James, stroking a long sideburn. "So much upheaval. So much fighting."

"We all hope it ends soon," Thomas said. "With a Southern victory, of course."

"Indeed," said James.

Then Martha, wanting to change the subject, asked, "So, how are Emily and Ellen?"

"Doing very well," said Milicent. "They are both good students, and so helpful around the house." At that moment, a shriek came from upstairs, followed by laughter.

"Sounds like Bushrod is entertaining them," said Thomas. The pounding of footsteps crossed over their heads.

"Bushrod is teasing us!" shouted Emily, from the top of the stairs.

"Bushrod," said Martha, calling upstairs, "be a gentleman." Then, turning back to the adults, she said, "He is twenty-three years old, but can be such a rascal."

"He has always been a jokester," said James. "Full of vim and vigor."

"His cousins adore him," added Milicent.

At that moment, the three young people came down the stairs, smiling broadly. "These two are troublemakers," said Bushrod. Emily punched him on the shoulder and Ellen gave him a tickle.

"You are responsible," said Martha to Bushrod. "After all, you are the oldest by far."

"All right," said Bushrod, "but there is only so much I can do."

"I know what you are talking about," said James. "My girls are a handful!"

"Let's go outside," said Bushrod to his cousins. "I'll show you the garden."

"Sounds like a good idea," said Martha.

After the cousins left the house, Milicent asked, "So where is Abigail?"

Martha realized that she had no idea. In the swirl of morning activity, she had lost track of her. "I am embarrassed to say that I do not know. Thomas?"

"I have not seen her since breakfast."

"Didst thou hear what happened in Congress this week?" Samuel asked his mother the question as they sat down for their noon meal.

"No, I did not," said Ann, slicing a loaf of bread at the table. "I have not seen a newspaper for several days."

"Congress abolished slavery in the District of Columbia."

"Truly?" said Ann, quite surprised. "That is a bold step."

"The government is paying owners for their slaves," said Samuel. "About three hundred dollars per person. And the freed men and women are being given money to move, if they so choose."

"The Confederacy will not be pleased," said Ann.

"You are right. The move is quite provocative."

"How many slaves were freed?" asked Ann.

"Over three thousand, I hear," said Samuel, eating a piece of bread with butter. "Quite a significant number."

"Were the slaveowners upset?"

"I am sure they were," said Samuel. "But they could see the writing on the wall. The city has been a center of slavery and the slave trade for years, but also an anti-slavery hotbed. The two factions could not co-exist much longer, especially with Lincoln in the White House. My guess is that some slaveowners have moved south, while others have remained in the District and simply accepted the money."

"May this decision be a harbinger of things to come!" said Ann.

Samuel nodded, and took a bite of the sausage on his plate. After chewing and swallowing, he said, "There is talk of Congress banning slavery in the territories."

"That would be good as well."

"Slowly, slowly, we will see the end of this terrible institution."

"It cannot be God's will," said Ann. "Of that I am certain."

After taking a drink of water, Samuel said, "I am pleased that Abigail Washington feels the same way."

Ann swallowed what she was eating, smiled, and said, "I was delighted that she spoke up at the falls."

"As was I," said Samuel. "She is a person of conviction."

"I can only imagine what her parents said to her last night."

"Not very much," said Samuel.

Ann paused and looked at him quizzically. She asked, "How dost thou know?"

"I saw her this morning."

"Thou didst?"

"Indeed. We had a conversation by the mill."

"Unchaperoned?"

"Yes, mother. But in public. We sat under a tree. The morning was so lovely."

Ann sat still for a moment, wondering if her life were going to change again. Then she said, "Abigail is how old? Nineteen? And thou art twenty-two. Thy lives will be thine own, apart from parents, before too long."

"I do want to talk with thee about this," said Samuel. "But not here. Wouldst thou be willing to join me in making a call upon the Washingtons this afternoon?"

"I suppose so," said Ann. "They were kind to visit me yesterday."

"Let us go before too long," said Samuel, sounding somewhat anxious.

"I will clean the dishes, put on a nicer dress, and join thee."

"Thank you, mother." After taking his plate to the wash basin, Samuel walked to the corner of the room in which William was buried beneath the floorboards. He sat in the rocking chair that Ann had placed over the spot, and began to rock. Looking out the window, his mind went back to the cold winter day on which William disappeared. He closed his eyes and tried to discern what his brother would have him do. Then, out of nowhere, the quotation that his mother had shared came into his mind: *Death is but crossing the world, as friends do the seas; they live in one another still.*

*So, has William simply crossed to another world?*

*And is he living in me?*

Abigail arrived home in time for lunch, and she was pleased that the enthusiastic welcome of her twin cousins prevented any interrogation by her parents. The three girls dominated conversation at the table, catching up on their activities and sharing their impressions of people in their social circles. The chatter of the girls was constant, giving the older members of the family no opportunity to speak. Then, as the extended Washington family was finishing its meal, Abigail heard a knock at the front door and ran to answer it. Through the glass panes of the door, she could see Samuel and his mother, standing on the porch.

"Come in, please," she said.

"How art thou?" said Ann. "Samuel encouraged me to make a call this afternoon."

"You are most welcome," said Abigail. And then, calling out to the dining room, she said, "Mother and father, Ann and Samuel Bagley are here."

Thomas and Martha were surprised by the visit, but not upset. Thomas lifted his large torso out of his chair and moved toward the doorway, wanting to greet his guests. Martha followed him, wiping her face with a napkin to make sure that she was presentable.

"Please, come in, Mrs. Bagley," said Thomas, pointing towards the parlor.

"I prefer Ann," she said. "No title."

"Welcome, Ann," said Martha. "And you, Samuel, as well."

Ann entered the parlor, looking out of place in her Quaker colors. "Thy home is lovely," she said to Martha.

"Thank you so much," said her hostess. Then, turning to her son, Martha said, "Bushrod, bring some extra chairs into the parlor so that we can all sit."

James and Milicent entered the parlor along with Emily and Ellen. Thomas introduced his brother, sister-in-law, and nieces to the Bagleys, and encouraged them all to take a seat. Bushrod brought in chairs until there were enough for everyone, eight Washingtons and two Bagleys. The room was quite packed.

"Ann and Samuel are our neighbors," said Thomas to his relatives. James gave him a skeptical look, doubting that Quakers could be true neighbors of Episcopalians. *Are they not abolitionists?* he wondered.

"Ann lost a son in the war," said Thomas, sensing his brother's discomfort. "He died on the Peninsula, fighting for our cause."

"You have my sympathy," said James. His wife nodded in agreement. "You have made a great sacrifice."

"I thank thee for thy condolences," said Ann.

"Samuel and Bushrod work together at the mill," said Martha. Emily whispered to Ellen, and they both giggled. They thought Samuel was quite handsome.

"That is hard work," said James. "I respect it."

"And what dost thou do?" asked Ann. She always spoke plainly.

"I operate a plantation," said James, "in the southern part of the county. Various crops, but mostly tobacco."

"And thou ownest slaves?" Ann asked, seeing the black man and woman standing at the door to the kitchen.

"I do," said James, who was beginning to feel interrogated. His face was becoming as red as his hair. "The plantation could not be run without them." The temperature of the room seemed to increase by several degrees.

"This war is being fought for the benefit of slaveowners," Ann said. She always spoke the truth as she perceived it. "It does nothing for Southerners like ourselves. Except kill our sons." Samuel was very uncomfortable with the conversation, and tried to catch his mother's eye. He was unsuccessful.

James opened his mouth to speak, but petite Martha jumped in, anxious to change the subject. "We are so happy you have come calling," she said. "You were so kind to receive us yesterday." Samuel breathed a sigh of relief.

"We are neighbors, indeed," said Ann, without adding anything more. Quakers were comfortable with silence, even awkward silence.

"Would you like tea?" asked Martha.

"No, thank thee," said Ann. More silence.

Finally, Samuel spoke up. "This call was my idea." Then, looking at Abigail, who was sitting next to him, he said, "Actually, *our* idea." She nodded.

"We need to talk with all of you, both families, about something," she said.

"The past months have been difficult," said Samuel. "The death of my brother has been devasting to us all." His mother looked at him, agreeing with every word. "Abigail and I have grieved together. We have shared much sorrow, talked often, and become very close."

Martha's eyes became wide. She was getting a sense of where this conversation was going. Her husband was listening, but he seemed to be unaware of the trajectory.

"We have discovered that life is precious and fragile," said Samuel. "We do not want to be victims of war or accident or illness. We need to find happiness and companionship while we can. Fortunately, we have found each other. Thomas Washington and Martha Washington, may I have thy daughter's hand in marriage?"

A look of shock crossed Thomas's face. Martha reacted differently, smiling broadly and clapping her hands. She jumped up from her seat to hug her daughter, and then she embraced Samuel. Ann was less demonstrative, simply reaching over and giving her son's hand a squeeze.

"You are asking permission to be married?" said Thomas, regaining his composure.

"Yes, we are," said Samuel. "We are at a good age and I have a good job." Then, looking at Abigail, he said, "And we love each other."

"But you are a Quaker!" said James, inserting himself in the conversation. "You are not loyal to the Confederacy."

Thomas turned on his brother with ferocity. "How dare you question the loyalty of this young man! His brother has made a sacrifice for our cause that you will never make!" Ellen and Emily cowered, never having seen their uncle explode like this. Caleb and Harriet were delighted by the verbal assault, but covered their faces to hide their glee. "Yes," Thomas continued, "they are Quakers. And some are abolitionists. But we are neighbors in Occoquan. We bear each other's burdens. We share each other's joys." Then he turned back to Samuel and Abigail, effectively putting his brother out of the picture.

"Ann, what do you think?" asked Martha. "Will the Quaker community accept this marriage?"

"I am supportive," said Ann. "Thy daughter is a fine young woman. I have had my eye on her for years." Martha smiled. "As for the Society of Friends, you know that I am no longer in fellowship. But I would guess that they would approve, as long as Samuel is free to practice his faith."

"He will be, of course," said Abigail, looking at Samuel. "That is part of what I love about him."

"How about our priest?" said Bushrod, not afraid of stirring up controversy. "Would he perform the wedding?"

"Do not worry about him," said Thomas. "I give enough money to the church. He will do it, if I ask him."

"As for me, I am for it," said Bushrod. This came as a surprise to Samuel, since the two had so often been at odds. "Samuel, you are a good man. I enjoy working with you. You will make a good husband for my sister."

"Thank thee," said Samuel. "I enjoy thy friendship as well. Even though I know thou would rather be on the front lines instead of with me."

"Indeed," said Bushrod, "if only my father would allow it." Then, turning toward his relatives, he said, "Uncle James, give Samuel a chance. You

193

will learn to love him, as I have." James nodded, but was still stewing from Thomas's rebuke.

Attempting to get the proposal back on course, Abigail said, "So, father, do we have your blessing?"

"Daughter, I love you," Thomas said. "And I admire this young man. He is from a fine family. We may not agree on all things, but that would be true even if he were an Episcopalian. Our world is being torn apart by people who want everything to be a certain way, the way they want it."

Samuel was moved by Thomas's words. He was right. Society was being torn apart by people who want the world to be structured according to their own desires. This was true in the North and in the South, in the town and on the plantation. Total agreement was never going to be possible.

"I agree with thee, Thomas," said Ann. "Let us allow this union to take place." She smiled at Samuel and Abigail.

"Are you in agreement, Martha?" Thomas asked. His wife nodded, her eyes full of tears. "Then, yes, Samuel and Abigail, you have our blessing."

"Thank you, father," said Abigail, jumping up to hug him. "And thank you, mother!" She gave her mother a kiss. Samuel stood up and shook hands with Thomas and Martha, offering them his thanks. Emily and Ellen started clapping their hands, but stopped suddenly when their father glared at them. Milicent motioned for the girls to stand up, and she led them out of the room. James followed.

"Do not worry about him," said Thomas to the couple. "He is my brother. We have fought before. We will make peace."

"We are excited," said Abigail, her blond hair bouncing.

"One request," said Thomas. "Allow me to build you a house here in town. I could not allow my daughter to live too far from her mother."

Abigail looked at Samuel, and he agreed. "Yes, thank you," she said. "That would be very generous of you." While they were both happy to accept the offer, the truth was that Samuel was ready to exit the house that contained his brother's secret grave. He wanted some distance from the angel of death.

# 24

## Easter Sunday 2022

"THE RESURRECTION WAS GOD'S greatest act of generosity," said Harley as he began his Easter sermon. He was thrilled to see the Sanctuary packed with people in their Sunday best—lots of pastel ties and flowery dresses—for the first time since before the pandemic. "It appeared as though the life of Jesus was over, after a week of conflict, trial, torture, and crucifixion. His followers grieved his death, deeply, but they knew that the tomb was the end. Even the greatest of people are destined to die. The disciples were beginning the long struggle of adjusting to life without Jesus, remembering the many amazing things he did as a teacher, a healer, a miracle worker, and a friend. But then God said, 'There's more. You thought that you had been given everything, but there's more. In a world of limits, I am going beyond. In a world of scarcity, I am offering abundance. In a world of death, I am providing new life.' Two of God's messengers said to the followers of Jesus, 'He is not here, but has risen.'"

Looking out over the congregation, he could see the many people who had been so generous to him. Bill Stanford of the finance committee had made sure that Harley always got paid, even when the church was running a deficit. Mary Ranger was a constant source of support and encouragement, quick to compliment him for his sermons. Andy Stackhouse had been a critic at times, but he was a loyal parishioner who really cared for his pastor and his church. Juan Erazo had been a true *San Juan* to Harley, showing compassion towards him and towards members of the Latino Students Association. And smiling Nanette Glebesman was, of course, "No-Change Nanette," famous throughout the town for her generous tipping.

"I have experienced the power of generosity this week," he continued, shifting his weight away from the leg that was still hurting from the fall. "It has saved my life. As most of you know, my life was threatened on Friday by a resident of Occoquan, a man who was determined to kill me, and to kill this church. He was an embodiment of the spirit of our age—what theologians call the *zeitgeist*—a spirit of winning at all costs, accepting no compromises, crushing the opposition. I want you to know that he tried to destroy me, and destroy this congregation. He believed that we deserve to die because we are not growing, in terms of membership or budget or influence. He saw us as a burden on the community and a drain on its resources. For him, nothing mattered except for survival of the fittest. And so, he tried to get me to kill myself, and in so doing cripple this church."

The congregation was riveted. Never before had they heard such testimony from the pulpit. Harley paused for a moment, looked back at the black Jesus, and them forward to the people in the very last rows of the well-worn oak pews. "Well, guess what?" he continued. "God does not care about the survival of the fittest. God is concerned only with the survival of *the faithful*." A loud "amen" came from a man in the choir behind him, followed by "amens" from a handful of people throughout the congregation. Everyone smiled, including Harley, since an "amen chorus" had never been heard in the worship of Riverside Methodist Church. When he was about to continue, Andy shouted "Preach it!"—another response that had never been offered in the church. This caused the entire congregation to break out in laughter, followed by applause. The Spirit was alive and well in that Sunday morning service.

"Yes, God is concerned only with the survival of the faithful," Harley continued. "Consider the facts leading up to that first Easter morning: Jesus had died; Judas had betrayed; Peter had denied; the rest of the disciples had lost their nerve; the supportive Palm Sunday crowd had ended up calling for crucifixion. No reasonable person would have said that the Jesus movement was winning the battle for survival. Am I right?" Harley saw nods throughout the congregation. "But in the eyes of God, faithfulness is fitness. Because Jesus was faithful, God raised him from the dead. Because the witnesses to the resurrection were faithful, God gave birth to the church. Because Riverside Methodist is faithful in the face of so many challenges today, God will give us new life as well." Juan offered a raised fist from his place in the second row, and several members did the same in response. Harley shook his head and smiled. This was all so new to him.

"The man who threatened me on Friday called himself Abaddon. Said he was the destroying angel from the Book of Revelation. King of an army of locusts. The angel of death." Harley paused, knowing that people would need a moment to process his words. Then he said, "Honestly, I don't know what he was. But I will tell you this: When he introduced himself to me, I felt an unexpected calm. I should have been terrified—and on one level, I *was*—but deep down I felt a sense of peace. I knew that God was with me. In that moment, God was incredibly generous to me. I felt like the apostle Paul, who says to the Romans, 'I am convinced that neither death, nor life, nor angels, nor rulers, nor things present, nor things to come, nor powers, nor height, nor depth, nor anything else in all creation will be able to separate us from the love of God in Christ Jesus our Lord.' I believe that. I really do. I knew that I would be all right, in this life or the next. *Survival of the faithful.*" Once again, a loud "amen" was shouted, followed by several others.

"The world of nature is based on the survival of the fittest, and I get that," Harley continued. "Animals compete for food. Trees compete for sunlight. Businesses compete for customers. Politicians compete for votes. But as human beings, we need to remember that we are more than animals. We don't have to kill or be killed. We are made in the image and likeness of God, which means that we have the ability to sacrifice for one another and be generous to one another. When did we lose that awareness? When I look around today, I see everyone trying to knock each other out: Red States and Blue States, gays and straights, Muslims and Christians, vaxxers and antivaxxers, pro-gun and anti-gun. Everything is framed as 'win-lose' instead of 'win-win.' Everyone assumes malice instead of good intent. Everyone condemns the things they do not like, seeing nothing of value in them. 'Burn it down!' seems to be the rallying cry of the day." Harley paused to let these points sink in. The faces in the congregation were solemn, but he saw a few nods.

"We can do better than this," he continued. "We do not have to be driven by survival of the fittest. That was Abaddon's approach, and I can tell you that it only leads to death." Harley's voice became raspy, so he paused to take a sip of water. "It almost led to my death. It could have led to this church's death."

Then he returned to his focal point. "I said before that I have experienced the power of generosity this week. Not only in the generosity shown by God in the resurrection of Jesus. Not only in the generosity of God in bringing life to the first followers of Jesus. Not only in the generosity of

God to me, in a terrifying moment. Also in the generosity of a friend who rushed to my aid. In the generosity of our sheriffs, who dropped everything to respond. But I am also grateful for the generosity shown by the Muslims who are renting our social hall for prayer. For the generosity of our church council, which gave permission for this to happen. For the generosity of all of you who support the mission of this church, feeding the hungry and housing the homeless, not just during Holy Week but throughout the year. For the generosity of individuals who have increased their tips"—at this point he looked straight at Nanette—"spreading joy throughout our town. For the generosity of so many neighbors who surrounded me after my ordeal, letting them know just how much they cared for me and for the ministry of this church."

Then, knowing it was time to bring his message home, he said, "The good news of Easter is that God gave Jesus the gift of new life. In a world of limits, God went beyond. In a world of scarcity, God offered abundance. In a world of death, God created life. We can give in the very same way. Since God loves a generous giver, we can show our faith by living with generous hearts and generous minds. It is going to be the secret to our survival."

*Amen.*

The congregation gathered after worship in a small triangular park near the church. The air was cooler than expected, with temperatures in the sixties, but the sky was a brilliant blue and the park was surrounded by azaleas beginning to bloom in a riot of colors. Cups of lemonade had been placed on several long tables, alongside plates of cookies covered in pink and pale blue icing. Children ran through the grass with baskets, looking for the Easter eggs that had been hidden for them.

"It's odd, isn't it?" said Harley to Mary, as they stood surveying the scene, "We spend three-hundred-and-sixty-four days telling children not to eat what they find on the ground. Then, on Easter, we give them baskets and say, 'Grab as much as you can!'"

"A mixed message, for sure," said Mary. "If my grandchildren told me next week that they found chocolate in the grass and the bushes, I'd say, 'Throw it in the trash.'"

"Pastor Harley," said Abdul, "Happy Easter!" He was dressed in form-fitting exercise clothes, and had spotted the pastor as he walked by the park.

"Abdul, good morning," said Harley. Mary greeted him as well.

"You have quite a crowd here," said Abdul.

"I'm so happy to see it," said Harley.

"Feels like we are coming out of the pandemic," said Mary. "Finally."

"I heard about what happened Friday," said Abdul to Harley. "Right after you welcomed my group to prayer. I am so sorry."

"It was traumatic," said Harley, rubbing his neck. "I'm still processing it. Did a little unloading on my congregation this morning."

"Oh, that was great," said Mary. "You were speaking from the heart."

"I wish I could have done something," said Abdul. "Don Abad was a tenant of mine. I had no idea."

"None of us did," said Harley. "He was not what he seemed to be."

A little girl ran up to Harley to show him how many eggs she had in her basket. He crouched down to inspect her haul, then gave her a pat on the back. Standing up, he felt the pain in his leg again, and he gave it a shake.

"You are busy, I know," said Abdul. "I'll be on my way. But I'm here for you, pastor. Trauma has been part of my story, as you know." Harley gave a nod. "I'm glad to talk any time."

"Very generous of you, Abdul," said Harley. *Good to have the big man on my side.*

As Abdul was walking away, Andy approached Harley with a sheet of paper in his hand. "I am so excited to show you this," he said. "Jean told me that I had to wait until after Easter worship."

"What have you got?" asked Harley.

Handing him the paper, Andy said, "It is a copy of a letter I found in the Library of Congress. Written to Ann Bagley of Occoquan, by General George McClellan."

"Really?" said Harley.

"That's quite a find," said Mary.

"The original that went to her is long gone," said Andy. "This was in a collection of his correspondence, both letters he received and copies of letters he sent out. All written after the war."

"You have done some digging," said Harley.

"I'm excited," said Andy, "because it sheds light on the identity of the body in the Quaker house." At that point, Nanette walked up and joined them.

Glancing at her and the others, Harley said, "Let me read it aloud."

*Monday, Nov. 13th, 1865*
*Mrs. Ann Bagley*
*Occoquan, Virginia*

*I have waited until the cessation of hostilities to write this letter, not wanting to endanger you or your family in any way. Having left military service, I write as a private citizen, one with family members in the Society of Friends. I feel obligated to inform you that your son William Bagley was an invaluable asset to the cause of the Union. He performed espionage behind enemy lines, and communicated information to the army that was essential to the success of our cause. Although his untimely death may have slowed our march to Richmond, he gathered intelligence about Confederate military organization and strategy that was useful to the Union for the duration of the war, and he no doubt saved many lives. I met him in late 1861, and was impressed by his intelligence and courage. I gave him my personal challenge coin, so that he could present it as a token of loyalty, in the event of capture by Union forces. Although I cannot assuage your grief, I want you to know that your son helped to achieve victory in the cause of free institutions and self-government, and helped to preserve the Constitution and the Union, at the cost of his time, effort, and blood. I thank you for the supreme sacrifice that he has made to our noble cause, and I offer my gratitude for the sacrifice that you and your family have made as well.*

*Very truly,*
*Geo. B. McClellan*
*Major General, U.S.A.*
*(Retired)*

"So, he was a spy?" asked Harley.

"Looks like it," said Andy. "Served in the Confederate Army, which accounts for the buttons on his uniform. But he was doing espionage for the Union, and carrying McClellan's challenge coin in case he was captured."

"Let me get this straight," said Mary. "The man buried in the Quaker house . . . what was his name, William?"

"William Bagley," said Harley.

"He was a Quaker," she continued, "so he was a pacifist. He joined the Confederate Army, which must have caused conflict in his community. But he was spying for the Union, which would have been agreeable to some."

"That's right," said Andy. "Many Occoquan Quakers were abolitionists, so they secretly supported the Union. But they would not have known that he was doing this until the war was over."

"The Civil War was full of tension, full of contradictions," said Harley.

"Right about that," said Andy. "You know Jubal Early, the Confederate General? He strongly opposed the secession of Virginia from the Union. But then, by the end of the war, he was a Confederate hero who came close to invading Washington, D.C. Talk about contradictions!"

"I wonder if William's mother got the letter," asked Nanette, more interested in the people of Occoquan. "I cannot imagine her anguish, thinking that he had broken with the Quakers to fight for the South."

"We'll never know," said Harley. "The house burned down and everything was lost."

"But I do hope she received it," said Nanette. "I think it would have brought her some comfort. William was trying to save the Union. Trying to free the slaves."

"Things are not always what they appear to be," said Andy. "Right, Harley?"

"You know it," said the pastor. Handing the letter back to Andy, he said, "I really appreciate this, and I know the archaeological team will consider it a major find."

"Wanted you to see it first," said Andy. "I'll take it to the site in the morning."

"I love to see a good letter," said Mary. "Makes my work in the post office seem truly important."

"It is," said Harley. "Letters can change the world. You heard me this morning: Paul's letter to the Romans!"

"Wonder what Paul paid for postage?" joked Mary. "We'll never know!" At that point she said she was going to run home and get Easter dinner on the table. Andy bowed out as well, leaving only Harley and Nanette.

"You've got people to talk to," said Nanette. "I'm going to go home and change. Meet you at two o'clock?"

"Looking forward to it," said Harley.

Boating season had begun, so Harley's twenty-three-foot powerboat was back in the dock near his house, with the power-steering problem fixed. Nanette met him at his house, and the two of them walked to the dock, with Harley carrying a cooler and Nanette transporting his bag of snacks.

"So nice of you to invite me out," said Nanette, smiling.

"First cruise of the season," said Harley. "You're special!"

"I feel it," she said. "Feel a little chilly as well." The temperature had climbed, but only into the seventies.

"It can be cool in April," said Harley. "That's why I recommended a fleece."

"I'm glad you did," she said. "But no worries; I spent years in Seattle."

"It's a very different story in the summer," said Harley. "Go out in August, and you'll be so hot you have to jump in the water."

Arriving at the boat, Harley took the cooler aboard and then helped Nanette to step from the dock to the swim platform at the stern of the boat. He stowed the snacks and showed her to the first mate's chair on the port side of the boat. "Make yourself comfortable," he said. "We'll be under way soon." He ran the bilge and blower, turned the ignition, and then released the lines that held the boat to the floating dock. "Ready to go?" he asked, after sitting down in the captain's chair. She nodded yes, and they pulled slowly out of the dock.

Nanette loved the way that the boat glided smoothly across the water, making its way effortlessly toward the concrete bridge that connected Fairfax County to Prince William County. "There's *el Castillo*," said Harley, "the place that was once the ferryman's house. It will soon be a museum of the imprisoned suffragists." Nanette was just beginning to learn the history of the area, and found it to be both fascinating and disturbing. The sunlight sparkled on the water, and as they passed under the bridge they were treated to a light show on the bottom of the roadway, one created by the reflected light. Moving eastward, Harley pointed to the rocks along the river that dated to the time of the creation of modern continents, three hundred million years ago. And then he showed her the dock of the Occoquan Regional Park, which was once the landing site for boats bringing prisoners to the Lorton Reformatory. Harley wondered if Abdul had once taken that ride. "See that hillside?" said Harley, pointing north, beyond the dock. "That's the landfill. The forest at the bottom is where I had my not-so-Good Friday."

"Glad you can joke about it," said Nanette.

"What else can you do?" he said. "It was a brush with death. Glad I got through it."

Over the next few minutes, they passed under Interstate 95, then under Route One, then under the train tracks that ran north and south along the east coast. The breeze began to pick up, but they were both comfortable in blue jeans and fleeces. Two bald eagles flew out of the trees on the northern bank and crossed the river, one chasing the other. "Spectacular!" said Nanette, watching their flight.

"Never gets old," said Harley, enjoying the sight as well. *Not one but two eagles. Guess they should not be alone. Just like humans.*

Near the mouth of the Occoquan River, Harley pulled north into a small bay and dropped anchor. Unknown to him, the spot was where Samuel Bagley had the bow of his canoe clipped by a Confederate bullet in 1862. But all was peaceful on that Easter afternoon.

"Care for a glass of white wine?" he asked, pulling a bottle out of the cooler. He thought her blond hair looked lovely, pulled back in a sporty ponytail.

"Don't mind if I do," said Nanette.

Harley guided her to the bench seats in the stern, which gave them access to a table attached to the deck. He poured two glasses of wine and put out the snacks that he had stowed.

"You are quite the host," said Nanette, looking at a plate of cheese and crackers, a bowl of nuts, and a bowl of grapes.

"This is my social life," said Harley. "My house is small, so I do most of my entertaining on the boat."

"Could not be more lovely," said Nanette. "Cheers to you," she said, holding up her glass. They touched rims and sipped.

"I want to thank you for what you have been doing in Occoquan," said Harley.

"What's that?"

"Your generosity," he said. "You've developed a reputation. 'No-Change Nanette.'"

"Oh that," she said. "That's the least I can do."

"But it makes a difference," said Harley. "It really does. Jessica at the Legion says that you have created an upward spiral. People are tipping more, servers are doing more, people are giving more . . . on it goes."

"That's really nice to hear."

"It's a culture change," said Harley, eating a grape. "Our country is full of such selfishness, everyone looking out for their own interests and agendas. But you are practicing *selflessness*, and it has an impact."

"I can afford it," she said. "It's really not a big deal."

"But I think it is. That kind of generosity spreads."

"You were right to say what you did in your sermon this morning," she said. "There is real generosity in our church, with contributions to feed the hungry and house the homeless. There was a spirit of generosity in the council's decision to open the social hall to the Muslims. There was generosity from the Muslims, offering to make contributions for the privilege of praying there."

"Think of the generosity of that young man William Bagley," said Harley. "He gave his life in service to the Union, even though he got no credit for it."

Nanette nodded and said, "He was probably shunned by his community for going off with the Confederate Army."

"The Quakers talk about the war bug," said Harley. "It is an infection that spreads. Maybe we can replace it."

"With a generosity bug?"

"That would be great," said Harley. "We can start it right here."

"A new kind of pandemic," said Nanette. "A positive pandemic."

"Like a bug that infects a computer system," said Harley, "changing the way the whole system functions. Except in a good way."

"I'm glad you talked about generosity this morning," said Nanette. "I had never seen it connected to God's action on Easter." She put a piece of cheese in her mouth, swallowed, and then said, "Generosity has the power to change the future. A new future. New life."

"William Bagley's sacrifice brought life to others," said Harley, "especially the enslaved."

"And generosity can change the future of Occoquan," said Nanette.

"I believe it," said Harley. "The upward spiral."

Nanette smiled, and Harley thought she was the most beautiful woman he had ever seen. She looked at him and saw a man who was attractive, yes—so attractive that she feared she had lost him to another woman. But more important than his good looks was his good heart. His faithful heart.

Harley pointed to the trees on the bank and said, "I thought on Good Friday that I might be seeing these tender leaves for the last time."

"*Nature's first green is gold*," said Nanette, quoting Robert Frost.

"*Her hardest hue to hold*," answered Harley.

The two sat in silence, looking at the shoreline as the boat gently rocked and the sunshine sparkled on the water. Harley turned back to her, smiled, and broke the silence by saying, "This day is gold. Let's hold on to it." They remained anchored in place, while the river beneath them continued to flow.

# Acknowledgments

HISTORY IS ALIVE IN the Town of Occoquan, Virginia, which my wife Nancy and I have called home since 2016. I am grateful to Occoquan's mayor Earnie Porta, author of *Images of America: Occoquan* (Charleston: Arcadia Publishing, 2010), for reviewing this novel for historical accuracy. Neighbors Noelle van der Eijk and Kay Hill read drafts and offered feedback. Another help was Dolores Elder's booklet *The Flow of Occoquan: The River and Its History*, published by the Occoquan Historical Society in 2018. I have attempted to reflect Occoquan's history accurately, with the only intentional embellishments being the creation of a stop in the Underground Railroad, the invention of a revolutionary war prison in the basement of *El Castillo*, and the inclusion of a letter that raises questions about the Liberty Pole incident of 1860. Many of the Occoquan characters from the Civil War period are based on historical figures, with the main exceptions being the members of the Bagley family.

Since letters were important during the Civil War, and were so elegantly written, I enjoyed creating a number of them for this book. Most are based on historical letters. William Bagley's letter to his mother and brother was grounded in an anonymous account of a winter in Richmond, contained in Richard B. Harwell's *The Civil War Reader* (New York: Mallard Press, 1957). This book also provided the satirical poem "Tardy George," about the slow-to-act Union General George B. McClellan, as well as McClellan's statement to his troops from March of 1862. A line from a letter that McClellan wrote to President Abraham Lincoln appears in my fictional letter attributed to the general. The original letter was written on July 7, 1862, when McClellan evacuated from the Peninsula Campaign, and it can be found on the website "American History: From Revolution to Reconstruction and beyond."

McClellan is an important historical figure in this book, not only because he was General-in-Chief of the Union forces in early 1862. He embodied so many of the tensions in the book, as a leader who had great success as the defender of Washington, DC, but who failed repeatedly in offensive efforts to defeat Confederate forces and capture Richmond. He loved his troops, and was revered by many of them, while having contempt for his commander-in-chief, Abraham Lincoln. McClellan is also part of my family, since his mother Elizabeth was a Brinton. He was part of the seventh generation of Brintons in the United States, while I am a member of the eleventh generation. None of us can choose our ancestors!

Among the Civil War material I found on the internet were a number of letters posted on historical websites. The Julius Alexander Robbins letter, written by a Confederate soldier to his family in March of 1862, came from the website of the "Louis Round Wilson Special Collections Library of the University of North Carolina at Chapel Hill." The letter to Ann Bagley from Confederate Colonel H.P. Sampson is based on a similar letter from Colonel H.P. Mabry to the wife of Major Robb. C. McCay, found on the website of "Mississippi History Now." The humorous story about Elizabeth McClellan and the oysters came from an old newspaper clipping posted on the website "Civil War Talk," under the heading, "Generals Have Mothers, Too."

Poetry was important to the people of Occoquan in 1862, and it speaks to current residents as well. "Requiem for 1861," attributed only to H.C.B. and quoted by Sarah Farlow, comes from Esther Parker Ellinger's book *The Southern War Poetry of the Civil War* (Hershey, Pa.: Hershey Press, 1918). Farlow also quotes John H. Hewett's *War: A Poem with Copious Notes, Founded on the Revolution of 1861–62* (Richmond: West and Johnston, 1862). Samuel Bagley talks about the "Quaker colors" mentioned in Henry David Thoreau's journal entry of November 20, 1858, found on the "American Literature" website. The spiritual "Go Down Moses" is sung by the family of African Americans being transported to Maryland, since it was a powerful poetic retelling of the biblical story of Moses leading his people to freedom, one that may have included coded references to the Underground Railroad. In Occoquan 2022, Harley Camden quotes Robert Frost's poem "Nothing Gold Can Stay," found in *Selected Poems of Robert Frost* (New York: Holt, Rinehart and Winston, Inc., 1963). He also references T.S. Eliot's poem "The Waste Land," from *The Waste Land and Other Poems: A Norton Critical Edition* (New York: W.W. Norton & Company, 2016).

A note on language: African Americans in Virginia would have been referred to as "negro slaves" in 1862. Since the word "negro" is problematic for twenty-first-century readers, I have substituted "black." I have retained the term "slaves," however, since the preferred term "enslaved persons" was not typical in 1862, and "slaves" was still being used by Occoquan residents in 2022. Most Civil-War-era quotations from Scripture come from the King James Version of the Bible, the standard at that time, while modern references are taken from the New Revised Standard Version. The latter would be Harley Camden's translation of choice, as a pastor in the United Methodist Church. I was struck by the language of the King James Version used by the Episcopal priest in 1862, which included the apostle Paul's words, "Servants, be obedient to them that are your masters." The original Greek of the New Testament says "slaves" instead of "servants," and I wonder if the softer term "servants" in the King James Version made it easier for the enslavers of 1862 to use the Bible as a means of control. The New Revised Standard Version is closer to the original Greek, saying, "Slaves, obey your earthly masters," which raises the larger question of how slave language should be used by Christians today.

I love the story of the Angel's Glow, which is documented on several websites, including "Notes from the Frontier" and "Science ABC." The two high school students who made the discovery about its origin were from my hometown of Bowie, Maryland, just forty-four miles from Occoquan. I share their interest in what research into the Civil War can teach us, not just about glowing bacteria but about the "war bug" that continues to afflict us as Americans. The nineteenth-century account of the Bagleys and the Washingtons, along with the twenty-first-century story of Harley Camden and the residents of Occoquan, offers a path to peace in polarized times. By showing generosity toward our neighbors instead of demonizing them, and by taking the risk of entering into personal relationships with them, we can begin to repair the fractures that threaten to destroy us. I am grateful to my neighbors in Occoquan, who do this important work every day.

www.ingramcontent.com/pod-product-compliance
Lightning Source LLC
Chambersburg PA
CBHW051133020726
47501CB00005B/1489